Lavender Lane

Hey!.
If you decide to
stock "The Beans of
Lavender Lane,"
contact me @:
sayer.shelby@gmail.com

My website is:
www.shelbyevesayer.com
Much thanks,
Shelby Sayer ☺

SHELBY EVE SAYER

Rev. date: 03/02/2021

To order additional copies of this book, contact:
Xlibris
844-714-8691
vww.Xlibris.com
rders@Xlibris.com

To Mom, for always believing in my dreams

CONTENTS

AUTHOR'S NOTE

To the children who crave adventure as much as I do.
To the children whose dreams stretch beyond the oceans.
To the children who have a million questions.
To the children who have all the answers.
To the children who live in quiet.
To the children who dance in chaos.
To the children who feel lost.

You are heard even when you feel ignored. You are brave even when you feel afraid. You are colourful even when you feel messy. You are understood even when you feel insignificant. You are full of spirit and imagination. Don't abandon your soul, cleave to the magic, and live your story. Because our stories are the most familiar, and the things that we can count on the most.

Love,
Shelby Eve Sayer

01

ONCE UPON A TIME

"Stop in the name of the law!" Flynn the Fantastic roared, adjusting the heroic feather atop his tweed hat.

"You won't get away with this!" Flynn's feisty twin sister- and partner in crime 'Rose the Radical' yelled at the passerby thief.

"Ha-ha!" the villain cackled. "You'll never catch me!"

The villain was really Bea disguised as a sly fox named "'the Ferocious Mr Flobberworm,'" a malicious title indeed. And Bea, being the most animated of the Beans, was almost always cast in villain roles.

"Not my crown!" Eve cried from the treehouse window, which was more widely known as the "'Castle of Lavender Lane," and Eve, being the fairest maiden in the land, made a marvelous princess.

"Our duty is your command, princess!" Flynn saluted, practically tripping down the hillside after Mr Flobberworm.

In Flobberworm's left hand was a bedazzled paper crown, and in his right, a leash was attached to five-year-old Lucy, who was wearing a detailed lamb costume from last year's Christmas pageant.

"In the name of Sir Buttkiss of Knightville, I command you to halt at once!" Flynn the Fantastic demanded.

"Use your manners, that's potty talk!" Lucy scolded her older brother from behind her lamb snout.

"Cut!" Rose called, pretending to slice her neck, and the actors paused. Rose ran to little Lucy's side.

"Lucy, you are a LAMB. A LAMB. And lambs don't speak. They say, 'Bahhhh.'" Rose was growing impatient with her little sister.

"Can you say 'bahh'?" Bea asked Lucy in a kind voice that was completely uncharacteristic of "the Ferocious Mr Flobberworm."

"Baah," Lucy imitated.

"Perfect," the older children agreed.

"Ready, set, action." Flynn motioned to the actors.

"And begin," Rose added.

"You will never retrieve your precious diadem!" Flobberworm shrieked, hoisting the crown into the air. "Never! Never! Mwahahaha!"

"Baah," Lucy the Lamb bellowed.

"Next time it will be your pretty princess I snatch," Flobberworm sneered maliciously.

"No!" Princess Eve whined from her tower.

It was then that Flynn the Fantastic and his trusty sidekick Rose the Radical launched for Flobberworm.

"Not this time, you wimpy fox." Flynn tied Flobberworm's hands behind his back as Rose the Radical used her dance fighting skills to karate chop the crown from the thief's hand.

"Ha-yah!" She kicked.

"I was only trying to protect it," Flobberworm pathetically lied.

"When have you ever tried to protect anything?" Rose pointed out. "Your own pet is a captured slave."

"Baah," Lucy the Lamb agreed, and Flynn handcuffed the guilty predator with homemade handcuffs.

"Come on, little lamb." Rose tugged the leash. "I know a gentle princess who needs some company."

"And scene."

Bea unclipped the fox tail from her trousers and pulled the headband with fox ears sewn to it from her head.

"How'd we do?" she asked the woman in the audience.

"Wonderful, my loves," the woman smiled and faced her children. She pulled Bea into a side hug. "What magnificent writing, Bea. You've done it again." She motioned for the other children to join the embrace.

"And what about my directing, Mummy?" Flynn asked.

"And my codirecting?" Rose asked, also seeking compliments.

"Out of this world," the woman laughed. "I especially loved your dance fighting, Rose."

"And Eve's wailing and Lucy's baahing. You all have such talent." Their mum smiled warmly upon them, and for a time the five of them stood in the meadow thinking contently of their many accomplishments.

"Now," Mum let go of her children and eyed them with sternness, "Dad will be home in a moments' time . . ."

"Daddy!" the children exclaimed, their excitement was quite clear.

"And I'm quite sure he will expect you to be washed for dinner."

The children eyed each other with a "we'd better hurry" urgency and broke into a sprint, racing to the loo to wash up.

Mum chuckled at her spirited children for they always got so anxious when it came to Dad's arrival. She looked down at her stomach that was bulging with number six, and hopefully the last, of the Bean children.

"You are next, love," Mum whispered as she headed to the kitchen to catch her bread from burning.

She could hear her children making a ruckus in the adjacent room. Flynn was blabbering about how noble it would be to be a brave hero like Flynn the Fantastic.

Rose was fighting for her place at the sink while twelve-year-old Eve was smoothing her hair. Lucy, being five and obsessed with bubbles, lathered her hands in layers of suds until they couldn't be seen behind them, and Bea was wondering what story Dad might have for them tonight. Her wonders were interrupted by a firm but kind knock at the door.

"Dad!" The children ceased their noise making at once and ran for the door.

The door swung open and the younger children leapt into Dad's arms.

For a brief moment he was their father, but in a snap, his role changed, and he was dubbed the steed of 421 Lavender Lane. He galloped around the sitting room with his three youngest ones trying to stay on his back.

"Yee-ha!" Lucy pretended to reign over her father, the noble horse.

"Dad?" Bea chirped up from behind. "Do you have a story for us tonight?"

"Indeed I do, Goldilocks." Dad bucked Flynn, Rose, and Lucy off his back. "As I would be afraid to come home *without* a story to tell."

He then skipped off to the kitchen in his goofy manner to greet his wife. "How's my Marie?" Dad asked, dipping his finger into the boiling soup for a taste.

Over the years, Mum had grown so used to her husband sampling her meals before they were served that she didn't even correct him anymore.

"Never better," Mum said, and then they kissed, much to the younger children's annoyance.

"Eww," they moaned and guarded their eyes.

That is, except for Eve, who had tried to explain to her siblings many times, "Kissing isn't gross!" But despite the frequent reminders, they remained rooted in their ways.

The Bean family sat at the table and dove into their supper. They fought over who got to tell Dad about the day's adventures.

These sorts of fights usually resulted in five children talking over one another. One of the children would spill something or break something, which was inevitable at a crowded table.

Impatient, Dad would pester his wife by asking at least four times, "Is Poppy coming today?" Poppy was the name Dad insisted on calling the new baby, believing that it would be a girl. He explained to Mum that he was sure she'd have loads of personality and the name Poppy would fit perfectly. Mum rolled her eyes and shook her head, even though deep down she too loved the name.

At the end of supper, Mum cleared her plate and headed to the bath for her evening soak, while Dad made dishes and bedtime his duty.

Once the kitchen sparkled and the children were in their pyjamas, the long-awaited bedtime stories were ready to be told. The children gathered around Dad in his big leather chair. He told tall tales of knights in shining armour, kind bakers, willing peasants, boisterous children, and beautiful maidens.

Somehow, every one of Dad's stories spoke in a certain way to each of his children, but not as much as they spoke to Bea. It would be an understatement to say that Bea lived for Dad's stories. The other children would be snoozing and snoring by the falling action, but not Bea. She perked up at each new word as if fuelled by the plot. When Dad was done, he carried each child one by one to tuck them in, and Bea followed with question after question, hungry for more. When it was her turn to be tucked in, she avoided going to bed at all costs. "Daddy?"

"Spanky?" Dad was known for the nicknames he had for his children, but Bea, who had the most personality, responded to countless greetings that her father invented.

"Dad, I don't think you should limit yourself to just us. I think you should write children's books and share your stories with the world."

"Is that so?" Dad raised a curious eyebrow.

"Uh-huh. We could be authors together, you know," Bea added in sing-song. For it had been her dream to be a writer ever since she learned her ABCs.

"I'm not sure the rest of the world would appreciate my bedtime stories," Dad chuckled lightly.

"Oh yes, they would," Bea disagreed.

"You think?"

"Definitely," Bea knew what she knew and could not be coerced into denying it. "Dad, you are the most colourful man in all the world."

"I think you're biased," Dad laughed.

"I'm not," Bea stuck her tongue out.

"You know, McGee," Dad threw the covers over her face, "I think you were destined to be the next best storyteller. You're a natural."

"I hope so," Bea smiled, imagining it.

"You will be." Dad kissed her head. "Now go to bed before Mum sacks me from bedtime duty," Dad playfully demanded as he flicked out the light. "I hope your dreams are filled with magical stories." And Dad vanished into the night.

Bea shut her eyes as tight as she could and watched the brilliant colours fly by. How they zipped and soared as they raced through her mind. As she watched them, she dreamt of the time when her own story would begin.

02

THE BEANS

Time had flown speedily since the children chased Mr Flobberworm through the meadow to the adoring audience of their mum. Five years had passed.

Eve Marie, the eldest, is almost eighteen, and known for playing "Mum" in every way. She has the same soft eyes and the same chocolate hair that is made of silk, just like her mum. And anyone who sees Eve in her mother's apron will have to blink twice to ensure that it is really Eve and not Marie herself. On top of this, she can whip up delicate suppers just like her mum. She'd even mastered her rosemary roast and shepherd's pie, much to her family's amazement—especially Flynn's. She is striking not only in beauty but also in kindness, and perhaps her only weakness is the guilt she harboured for her few sins.

Bea, the second, at fifteen, is not much of a lady like her sister. She does have a refreshing smile and poetic hazel eyes, but beyond that, her cheeks are borderline tomato from all the sun she soaks up and her golden-brown hair is a soft kind of crazy. Her head is found stuck in the clouds most times or concealed behind a notebook where she feverishly writes, and stories and laughter are her most visited sanctuaries. Her imagination, shameless flatulence, freestyle dancing, and unusual remarks all adjuncts to her far-from-ordinary personality.

Rose, being thirteen and the oldest of the twins by thirty minutes, is just as boastful of her seniority over Flynn as she is her dancing. Rose is an eternal flame of unpredictability, fire, and wit. Her hair is silk like Eve's but almost always tied away to keep from slipping during a particularly thrilling pirouette. Her eyes resemble a dragon, brilliant green and feisty. And her mind is constantly being made up and held against her strong will like a death sentence.

Flynn, being the younger of the twins by a jealous thirty minutes, can never seem to eat enough to catch up with his spurting growth. It is an obvious gift that Flynn is the only brother to the Bean girls considering his competitiveness. Though competitive to a fault, Flynn's heart is colossal compared to most teenage boys. His foremost duty is to protect his sisters, which he does wonderfully. When Flynn is not eating, or teasing his sisters, he can be found tripping across the moors after squirrels or crafting booby traps for the pesky animals in the forest. His hair is like the sand that touches the sea and his eyes green except one-half of the right one, which is brown. He is the type of brother who makes others laugh without meaning to, is permanently impatient, and dim-witted yet brilliant.

Lucy, the fifth of the Beans, is perhaps the kindest. Barely ten and she possesses more goodness than most well into their adult years who have had much more practice. Like a bluebird, she is always climbing to new heights, living for others, and full of love and song. She plays by the rules most times but allows for mischief when she can't help it. Her hair is a bit more golden than Bea's and her eyes resemble the ocean. Dad says that the "Ocean in Lucy's eyes matches her love for the ocean," and whether it was true or not, Lucy loved to believe it.

The caboose of the Bean train is the spunky, animal-loving, mischief-making Poppy. She is five and a spark of spontaneity and magic. Her attention span is equivalent to that of a fruit fly and her strawberry hair is short and wild, making it a comfy home for the twigs and leaves she runs into on her quests. Her face is showered with freckles and half the time her blue eyes are lost in the distance, as if imagining some far-off place that exists only in her head.

It was the birth of autumn 1954 and adventures loomed on the horizon for the Beans of Lavender Lane.

03

DEAR MAX

Evening snuck up on the moors and the homes on Lavender Lane. All fell silent as the lights dimmed and the moon hung in the sky, putting the town under its quiet spell. At 421 Lavender Lane, the living room was bathed in warm lamplight. The Bean cottage was quiet as a mouse, and the only sound to be heard was Dad rocking back and forth in his ample rocking chair. His greying hair untidy and sprinkled in sawdust from a day of hard work at the wood shop, he leaned back in his chair sipping tea with a cautious air to save himself from a burnt tongue. Dad moaned in a weary tone and wondered if there was some way he could feel whole again.

He looked down at the old shoebox on his lap and lifted the lid, peering inside to enjoy its memories. The cardboard walls held several folded letters penned on various types of paper. Dad picked up the letter on top and held it right to his heart. He caressed the neat and loopy penmanship as if he could hold the hand that wrote it. His eyes met the first words and he began to read.

My Dear Max,

I look at the life we're building and I am filled with joy and love for you. I see you in Eve's smile, in Bea's imagination, in Rose's laugh, in Flynn's impatience, in

Lucy's eyes, and in Poppy's spunk. I'm surrounded by little Maxes and I couldn't be luckier.

Love,
Your Marie

A single tear streamed down his fatigued face and he let it fall onto the yellowing paper. The droplet of sadness hit the letter with a quiet proclamation of love, the ink from the pen revolving around the droplet as if recording a memory. Dad folded it neatly and slid it back to its home in the shoebox. He pulled out a second letter, which looked as if it had been folded and unfolded several times before. He opened the letter gently as if it was fragile, his eyes travelled slowly down the page and he read in a slow whisper, *"My Dear Max."*

Marie's handwriting now shaky, and the lined piece of paper covered in long past dried tears.

I have this reoccurring dream. In the dream, it's just us and our six lovelies. We live in a perfect cottage that is always perfectly tidy. It's always summer in the meadow, and the children are always in good spirits. There is no sadness, sorrow, or sickness. No work, and we can run and play without requiring rest. Our children value everything we say, and our love is seamless. We're rich and have countless brilliant mates and no enemies. Doesn't that sound nice?

For the last five months since my diagnosis, I've woken up every day with a raging headache and an imperfect life. And to add to all that distress, my imperfect life gets shorter every day. Today, I woke up and I had every reason to be sad. My children were chasing butterflies, climbing trees, and riding bicycles in my favourite weather, and I couldn't join them.

Dad whimpered under his breath as he wiped his falling tears with the back of his hand.

And I was so close to being angry, but then I remembered that it's okay. I spent a great deal of the last five months wishing things were different and wanting to move on from my sickness but seeing how improbable that is.

And that's okay, because as one thing ends the next begins. Max, as each long day passes, the hours get shorter, the clock ticks faster. And although I wish we could grow old, I'm learning that it won't be so. So I must honestly tell you, my love, that I will soon slip away, and it may feel to my family like time has stopped. But I tell you now that it won't ever stop. Whether I'm up in the sky or down below, time will never cease and I will always be with my children and you.

Love,
Your Marie

Dad missed his wife and grieved her absence in every way. He held to his heart the last love letter she'd written to him, of the hundreds she'd drafted, and let the tears swell within his eyes. It had been one hundred and eighty days since she uttered her last words and Dad still grieved her silence. His head in his hands, he trembled, and he let out his quiet sob.

After long, lonesome moments, Dad was interrupted by the light tiptoes that approached him. In panic, he attempted to eliminate every trace of his tears shed. He wiped off his sorrowful face and rapidly replaced it with his usual jolly one.

"Dad?" the warm voice questioned. "Is that you?"

"Yes, dear," Dad croaked, trying too hard to conceal his sadness. For he always put a brave face on for his children.

The young girl stepped into the lamp's path; her kind face illuminated in the light. She embodied a childlike light that smiled in the echo of the rain. It was Lucy.

"Are you sad?" Lucy inquired as she grabbed a glass from the kitchen cupboard.

"No . . .," Dad hesitated as he lied.

"Dad, you don't have to be brave all the time," Lucy told him as she filled up her glass.

"Couldn't sleep then, could ya?"

"Daddy!" She plopped onto his lap in exasperation.

"What is it, Lucy?" he asked with a hint of impatience.

"You're changing the subject again!"

Dad chuckled his hearty chuckle that made Lucy shake in his lap. "I do that a lot, don't I, Luce?"

"Yes, you do." She smiled. "Rose sure hates it too, doesn't she, Daddy?" Lucy scoffed, thinking of her sister and her sharp remarks.

"And she always likes to remind me when I do it," Dad added, laughing.

"Dad, do you miss Mum?"

Dad looked at his daughter with watery eyes. After a moment of silence Dad spoke up, "Yes, Lucy. Yes, I do miss your mum a whole lot. What do you suppose she's doing right now?"

After a short pause, Lucy began, "Well, you know the game I play with Bea and Poppy sometimes where we set up all the pillows and blankets around the house and jump from one pillow pile to the next?"

"Yes, I know the one."

"When we do it, we pretend like we're bouncing from cloud to cloud."

"Hmmm." Dad smiled.

"Well, I like to think Mum has found an old friend up in heaven who she does that with. I think right now they are bouncing from cloud to cloud, thinking of us while she does it."

"I think you are spot on." Dad nodded gratefully.

Lucy smiled back, feeling satisfied with the happy picture she'd painted.

"You know, Lucy, I think your mum may have a part in the angel choir up in heaven too." Dad inhaled dreamily. "I think she sings while she bounces from cloud to cloud every morning when the sun wakes up."

"Like our rooster!" she piped in. "But much, much more beautiful!"

"Yes. Indeed, much more beautiful," he chuckled.

For a quiet moment, Dad sat with Lucy on his lap. Each pondering and illustrating the perfect picture of Mum bouncing and singing in the clouds. Time stood still as they sat thinking, and when the moment ended, and time started again, Dad walked Lucy back to her room and tucked her in the top bunk where she slept.

04

DR JOHN APPLESEED

"Bea, is that you?" Lucy whispered through the morning light. "Are you awake?"

Bea stretched her long arms into the air and said through a loud yawn, "Wha— yu—drwee— bou—?"

"What?" Lucy laughed. Not even a true magician could understand Bea when she was talking through yawns.

"What'd you dream about?" Bea repeated, much more clearly this time.

"Mum," Lucy said in a much quieter and almost solemn voice.

"You did?" Bea asked softly. "Was it a good one?" she hesitated.

It was then that Lucy let go of all she kept inside, "Well, I woke up in the middle of my sleep thirsty. So I went to fetch a drink of water and caught Dad crying over all of Mum's old letters."

"Poor Dad," Bea muttered.

"And then it made me dream about her. I wish none of this had ever happened and that Mum never got s-sick," Lucy stuttered over the thought of her mother's slow death.

"I know," Bea nodded sympathetically and then jumped from her bed quite suddenly. She pulled on her trousers and announced with as much purpose in her voice as she had sadness, "I've got to go."

"Where are you going?" Lucy sat bolt upright.

"To visit Dr John Appleseed," Bea said as she strutted out the door, and Lucy didn't question her.

She moved across the lawn and up the grassy slope that climbed to the home of a massive apple tree. The tree ascended boldly into the sky, bearing shiny red apples that sprang from its woody branches. When she reached the tree, she sat down on the bed of grass below the tree's covering. She knocked on the trunk of the tree, and without another pause, she began to voice her cries.

"Doctor," Bea started softly, "you've always been a good friend, the best confidant of all, but we all miss her terribly." Bea didn't know how else to put it, "Why did she have to go? I know you had nothing to do with her death, but why did she have to go?" Bea's cries gradually heightened as she went. "How do you suppose we explain to Poppy that her mummy isn't coming home? How does one do that? I know it's been six months, but what are we supposed to do when our own dad is poring over old love letters that won't do him any good? Is it rocket science? Because it sure feels like it is!" Bea reached the top of her voice. "When will it end? All this lonesome despair and crying. We all feel so lost." She returned to her soft voice. "When will that end?"

Bea leaned against the trunk of the tree in a defeated sort of way that cried for an answer that wasn't expected or probable but hoped for. She closed her eyes and thought of a time when the idea of confiding in this tree was innocent as ever.

(11 months earlier)

"It isn't fair," complained Rosemary Bean as she stomped her foot. "Most mums can stay around forever with their children," Her braids that hung on each side of her face swung to the tempo of anger.

Lucy reached for a sandwich on the picnic blanket, listening intently to her big sister's loud feelings. Bea sipped her lemonade alongside her two sisters as the autumn breeze brushed her hair from her face.

"I hate Mum being sick!" shouted Rose.

Lucy, who didn't like the idea of Mum sick in her bed either, bit awkwardly into her sandwich.

"You know miracles happen all the time," hopeful Bea offered.

"Is Mum going to die?" Lucy asked.

"No," Bea shook the idea from her head. "Dad and Eve say she won't, and they're the smartest of us all."

"What do they know?" Rose shook her head.

"What do you know?" Lucy asked Bea, for she was the oldest of the three of them and likely the most intelligent.

"I don't know, Lucy." Bea shrugged. "I wish I did, but I don't," she admitted.

It was a breezy fall day, perfect for flying a kite. The Bean sisters sat under the cover of a massive apple tree atop the big hill, above the garden.

"What are we ever going to do?" Rose groaned in a childlike voice that she often slipped into when she felt lost.

Bea looked from her sorrowful sisters to the shady apple tree that they enjoyed the shelter of, and then to young Rose again.

She thought of the many times before that she'd sat with her family under this tree. The times she'd run around its woody trunk in her early years with Eve to escape the "bad guys" that chased them through the meadow. She thought of the times she'd climbed its heavy branches with her siblings and hugged them as if they would forever hold her in safety. The times like this one where they'd lie in the cool grass hunting for cartoons in the clouds, and the times they'd rant of their troubles. Through the ages this curious apple tree had held them from the dangers and sorrows of the world.

"This tree! This tree is the answer to our troubles!" exclaimed Bea quite suddenly as she leapt into the air, her golden-brown hair swinging in the breeze.

"Yeah!" joined Lucy, pretending to understand.

Rose stared blankly from sister to sister. "Wait, WHAT?" she blurted, perplexed.

Bea took one deep breath in, preparing to elaborate. "This beautiful apple tree has stood here strong and tall since the day we moved here. It has deep roots and has survived every single, solitary one of Grasmere's WILD storms, and has been the end of many of our WILD adventures we've embarked on. We've swung on its swing." She motioned toward the old plank of wood that hung from the apple tree by two frayed ropes. "We've climbed its branches a million times, and we've found its fruit in our lunch sacks."

Rose, who was straightforward and practical, rolled her eyes at Bea's poetic monologue.

"Bea! Get to the point already," she yelped, exasperated.

Bea looked impatiently at her sister. "This tree, Rose," she stated stubbornly, "is always here to provide us shelter and safety. It listens to us and makes us feel safe. It's a good friend, and maybe even more than that. Like a therapist."

"Therapist?" Rose choked on the thought of a tree being a "therapist." It sounded so ridiculous.

"Therapist?" Lucy asked, wondering what it meant.

"It's someone who helps you with your problems in a really annoying way," explained Rose, who'd never had one herself, but then again, neither had Bea.

"And how do you suppose we'll tell a tree our troubles?"

"Well, that part's easy, Rose!" declared Lucy as the wind swept across her face. "It's a tree! Not a rock!"

Rose and Bea looked at their sister, then at each other and laughed.

When their laughter died, Lucy asked in a serious tone, "What shall we call our tree friend?"

Rose piped up, *"Well therapists are referred to as doctors. We could call it doctor."*

"Doctor what?" questioned Lucy.

"Hmm . . .," Rose considered.

"Doctor . . . Apple . . . Doctor Apple . . . seed," muttered Bea, formulating her idea. *"Doctor APPLESEED!"*

"That's nice!" proclaimed Lucy, who was easily impressed.

"Dr Appleseed is a little too silly for my taste," Rose protested.

"What about a nice name, like John?" offered Lucy.

"Yes! That's it! Dr John Appleseed!" Bea exclaimed.

"That'll do," Rose agreed.

"Like Johnny Appleseed!" said Bea.

"But kinder," shouted Lucy.

"And wiser," smiled Rose.

And the three girls leaped from the earth, dancing and singing as they circled the trunk of Dr John Appleseed.

"HOORAH FOR DR JOHN APPLESEED," Bea proclaimed.

"Hoorah! Hoorah!" sang the younger two in unison.

21

(Present day)

Bea stood up and looked straight at Dr. Appleseed.

"Sir," she stated clearly, "I know you can't bring Mum back or make this all go away, but . . . how are we to overcome this and feel alive again? 'Cause I can't go on like this, watching my family suffer. It's getting old." And that's all Bea said. She ended her plea abruptly and walked away, straining to think of things that might set her world back into place.

ART BY SHELBY RYER

05

THE TREE SPEAKS

The cock crowed on its usual perch on the wooden fence that lined the garden, just like it did every morning at dawn. Three days had passed since Bea visited the tree, and she'd been ruminating on the event ever since. Dad sauntered off to the wood shop hours before, planting a kiss on every one of his sleeping children's foreheads, not thinking once about being late. Bea was the first after Dad to rise from her sleep, rousing with the first ray of sunlight to pour into her room. That morning, something told Bea that everything was as it should be.

September 10 was born just as ordinarily as any other day; however, September 10 proved to be everything but ordinary.

The children gathered around the dining table for a meal made by Eve—buttered toast and sunny-side-up eggs. By ten o'clock, the house chores were done and each child was ready for their daily lessons with Ms Snow, who came to the cottage promptly at ten-thirty.

A quarter before noon, Bea slipped on her yellow wellies that hit her mid-calf and pulled back her frizzy waves into a loose ponytail. She marched purposefully into the garden, ready to do her part for the family. She admired the bluebirds mingling on the clothesline that were debating the hot topics of Lavender Lane. The grass still clinging to the morning dew, she thought she caught the wildflowers laughing in the breeze. The world danced to the beat of its own drum, and for the first time in six months, the meadow that she once ran through with her mother looked beautiful again.

Bea began singing her favourite tune beneath her breath, as she subconsciously did when she felt a bit distraught. It seemed that a bit of jolliness always helped clear the cobwebs and set her at ease. She swung the garden hose over her right shoulder and pulled her gardening gloves from the pocket of her denim overalls. She filled her watering can full and sprinkled a fresh drink on the garden boxes full of various flowers and vegetables. She picked a bundle of daisies and displayed them artfully in the chest pocket of her overalls. She began barely swaying to her melody, but quickly worked up enough momentum to prance. All this done without deliberately trying. Movement had always been a way for Bea to cope.

Flynn came jolting down the lawn and past the cottage. His crony Tommy Dee leaping after the squirrel they were chasing. Bea waved in laughter as she moved through the garden. Though her heart still held on to sadness, it felt so effortless to dance, and proved to be a succour to her pain, so she persisted.

After several minutes of uninterrupted dance, Bea was stopped by an alarming rustle of branches. She looked all around to identify the source of the rustle. She looked left and right, up and down, but she could not source the origin. In trepidation she called, "Who's there?"

There was silence, and Bea called out again, "Hello?"

"Don't be frightened. I was enjoying the show."

The voice rang through the lofty treetops with a crisp allure that resembled the sound of a brook running through the trees. Bea searched for the source of the voice with her sharp eye only to find a tall and slender boy wrapped in the arms of Dr John Appleseed's woody branches.

"How odd," thought Bea.

The boy held a half-eaten apple, which he'd surely plucked from the tree itself. He bit into his apple aggressively and waited for Bea to approach him. She climbed the slope that ascended out of the garden, reaching for each step she took. The damp grass matted beneath her boots as she hollered to the boy, "Ahh . . . and how did you wind up in my tree?"

The boy laughed as he swung his legs in the breeze. Bea, having reached the trunk, looked upwards toward the boy. "Do tell me, for I long to know the story of the Apple Thief."

"I have a feeling that I will be known as the Apple Thief from now on," the boy laughed.

"Do you have a better name in mind?"

"Well, most call me Oliver." The boy jumped from the tree to greet Bea, landing firmly on his feet.

"I'm assuming *most* don't know about your knack for stealing apples." Bea raised an eyebrow.

"I've only just begun the practice of stealing apples," Oliver laughed. "They wouldn't know any different."

"And you'd be ashamed to tell them?" Bea inquired.

"Most assuredly." Oliver hung his head in a dramatic and obviously sarcastic sort of way. "You won't tell?"

"Your secret is safe with me, Apple Thief." Bea bowed.

"Well thank you . . . Garden . . . Goon?" Oliver tried, hoping the nickname wouldn't offend.

Bea tried hard to keep a straight face. She attempted to seem powerful, like Rose, with the intent to frighten Oliver in a friendly sort of way, but instead she broke free of the binding chains of seriousness and sadness alike, and ran to her most visited sanctuary—laughter. She laughed, simply because the nickname "Garden Goon" was irresistible and seemed to fit her just so. Oliver laughed along with her until she calmed down, and then observed, "You like that one, do you?"

"Yes," Bea began to laugh once more. She'd almost forgotten what it felt like to laugh.

"Well then, you'll call me the Apple Thief as a punishment for my crime, and I'll call you Garden Goon to amuse you," Oliver pronounced, "But, say perhaps, I had to call you by your real name. What would it be?"

"They call me Bea," Bea paused. "My real name is Beatrice, but I've never been proper and ladylike enough, so I go by Bea."

"Bea," Oliver smiled brightly. "It suits you."

Bea smiled back at him like he was an old friend. He appeared tall and worn thin, as if he hadn't been given enough to eat. His clothes were sodden with dirt and frayed around the edges. His hair dark and untidy, and his eyes a deep blue that breathed both passion, mystery, and a bit of misery. His smile was sly and charming but ultimately kind. It was then Bea decided that Oliver was more than just an apple thief. There must've been some greater reason that such a boy had fallen out of Dr John Appleseed's grasp. Bea thought it wholly plausible that Oliver's appearance was the work of Dr Appleseed responding to her previous plea. So without caution she acted on impulse. "Would you like to stay for supper?"

"Erm . . .," Oliver hesitated.

"I'm sorry," Bea stepped back, "maybe it's a bit sudden. But if you're stealing apples you must be hungry . . . and my family would be more than happy to feed you. You wouldn't even have to steal."

"No, I'd love to," Oliver smiled, feeling that he didn't deserve such good fortune.

Bea and Oliver were quick to make friends. Bea was proud to have found a friend in a tree, and Oliver felt safe. She gave him a tour of her home. She walked him through the meadow, through the wood, and through the garden. She showed him Dad's garden shed that doubled as a wood shop. The two dropped by the playhouse (where Poppy spent most of her days), and then at last, she invited him into the cottage, where he met the rest of the family.

06

A TABLE FOR EIGHT

The Bean cottage was alive with the bustle of evening shenanigans and the anticipation of supper. Eve, who played both mother and chef, rushed around the kitchen to get the tasks done in time. When she heard that she'd have to set the table with an extra plate for a boy named Oliver, she was pleased she'd already started on her mum's delicious shepherd's pie. Getting wrapped up in her artistic flair and her need to impress through culinary mastery, she tied mum's old apron around her for good luck and pulled out more ingredients.

With Mum's well-loved bread baking softly in the oven, its warm scent drifting through the corridors of the cottage, Eve bounced effortlessly from counter to counter whipping up jams and stirring bowls of goodness. Every pot and pan in the humble home was dirtied, and come supper time, Eve was in her element. The sweet aroma of her creations drifted through the noses of her siblings and seemed to make them more antsy and hungry by the minute.

Flynn, who loved Eve's meals most, found his way to the kitchen every five minutes begging his tireless sister to rush a few steps so they could eat sooner. Eve scowled at his insensitive behaviour and tried to explain that, "Artistry just can't afford to be rushed." Flynn assured her that, "Nobody is going to notice whether it is beautiful or not!" Eve simply didn't find this comforting.

Rose argued loudly from the back room with young Poppy, who had snuck into her room yet again without permission, even though it was Poppy's room too.

"Poppy, you are such a bug! Get out of my way, I'm trying to rehearse!" You could audibly hear Rose shout from across the house.

Poppy persisted in doing "whatever it was she was doing" without an ounce of regret, because being the youngest of six children had taught her to "hold strong" in any given situation. And to add to Eve's stress, Bea, who was most capable of giving aid in the chaos, had escaped with Lucy and her new friend Oliver on a ridiculously long bicycle ride.

Eve stirred her boiling jam hastily as she wiped the sweat pearls from her forehead and hollered across the house, "ROSE!"

"What?" shouted Rose, who felt too grown up to be bossed around.

"Come here, please!"

"Why?" Rose protested.

"Just come here," Eve gasped in frustration.

"Fine."

Rose stomped into the room, her nose in the air. She tossed her exquisite braids out of the way, approaching with the purpose and grace of a true ballerina and the pretentious expression of a teenager.

"And . . . ?" she asked Eve.

"I would really appreciate it if you would settle down and give me a hand," Eve asked in a passive-aggressive tone.

"I'm a little busy right now."

"Rose, please," Eve begged, "all I'm asking is for someone to do the dishes and set the table. Is that so hard?"

"You sound like Mu-m," Rose bit her retort.

"Rose, someone must do it. Besides, nobody can set the table as good as you do."

"That's true," Rose agreed, sticking her nose in the air, and shuffled quickly to the cupboard, where she retrieved the china.

She crossed the room to the dining table, where she set down eight plates and filled eight glasses with fresh lemonade. She scrubbed the dishes dirtied by Eve with her strong hands, making them shine. And as a finishing touch she filled an empty vase with the last of summer's blooms and marched silently back to her room to rehearse for her ballet lesson tomorrow.

Despite Rose's attitude, Eve was grateful for her sister's helping hand. She took a deep breath in, savouring the pleasant silence and the clean kitchen.

"Ahh," she whispered in song, "peace and quiet."

She swayed as she buttered her hot bread and watched the butter soak into the blanket-like dough. It soothed her, and it felt as if the stress of her life soaked into the surface with the butter. The sun sank into the moors out the kitchen window, as if lying down for a nap, and Eve was in her happy place. She watched the world slow down as she revelled in her love for the kitchen.

However, Eve's "peace and quiet" was broken moments later by the opening of the French doors and the booming laughter of Bea, Lucy, and Oliver.

"That was brilliant!" cheered Lucy.

"Did you see the look on the squirrel's face when I tossed him that nut?" Oliver laughed, remembering it.

"He couldn't get enough of it," Bea noted, snorting.

"He was basically attacking it," Oliver grinned, playing with his wild hair.

"I can't believe that was your first time riding a bicycle!" Lucy exclaimed.

"You've never ridden a bicycle?" questioned Eve from across the room.

Oliver crossed into the kitchen, where he sat down on a stool at the bar top. "No, Eve, they didn't have them for us where I came from."

"Oh," nodded understanding Eve. She was curious about where he came from but saw the solemn look in his eyes and didn't dare ask.

"Well," she changed the subject, "why don't you guys go wash up for dinner? Dad will be home in a jiff."

Within moments, all seven of the children were seated at the table, their food dished out on their plates. They kindled the fire of evening conversation as they waited for Dad. Lucy spoke of the things they'd seen on their adventure, and Poppy informed the family of the state of her animals, which she tended to in the back of the meadow. Poppy's story was interrupted by the opening of the front door and the booming call of Dad. "Hello!" he hollered from the entrance of the cottage.

"Dad!" squealed Poppy and Lucy in unison. Slipping out from the table they ran to greet him. They leapt into his embrace and made it abundantly clear that he was missed. He looked up, catching a glimpse of the stranger in his house who sat at the table in his wife's spot.

"And who might you be, friend?" Dad approached Oliver, letting go of his children.

"Oh," said Oliver adjusting his posture, "I'm . . . erm . . . Oliver. Oliver West . . . Bea invited me in for dinner tonight." He smiled kindly. "I hope that's okay."

"Oh, it's more than okay," beamed Dad. "I'm thrilled to meet you, Oliver, welcome to our home."

"Thank you, sir," Oliver half grinned.

"Please, call me Dad or Max. I'm not much of a sir." Dad winked and sat down.

"Daddy! Daddy, you'll never believe what happened today!" Poppy bounced.

"Is that so? Tell me at once!" Dad said, showing genuine interest.

"I taught Daisy how to climb a tree, Daddy! Soon she'll be jumping through rings of fire!" (Daisy is the family's goofy goat.)

"That's great, Pops! She's halfway to the circus." Dad laughed. "Have you got Petey Hula-Hooping yet?" (Petey is Poppy's rabbit and most favourite pet by far.)

"Not yet, but that's next."

The Beans were all sitting in their designated spots. Oliver sat at the end of the table where Mum used to sit. And although having him there was not like having Mum there, the family was relieved to have the seat filled. Each plate was filled with a colourful assortment of foods: bread spread with jam, shepherd's pie, steamed peas, and berries.

"So . . .," Dad began between bites, "tell me about yourself, Oliver."

"What is it that you want to hear?" Oliver questioned.

"Whatever you want to share . . ." Dad saw the lost look that cast a shadow on Oliver's face, and so he asked in his jolly tone, "Where are you from?"

"Well . . .," Oliver hesitated, pushing peas on his plate, "I don't talk about it all that much, but when I was a baby, my parents passed away in some sort of accident. I had no other family . . . so they sent me to Greystone, Greystone Orphanage. I lasted fifteen years there, but I didn't much like a life of taking orders and boring days, so I fled . . . I guess you could say."

The Beans listened to Oliver's tale in full sympathy, for they were never quick to judge.

"How'd you get past the guards?" blurted Poppy, who loved a proper fairy tale.

"Poppy!" corrected Lucy, who was the most sympathetic of them all.

"What?" asked Poppy, who clearly didn't see the problem.

Oliver smirked and assured the Beans, "It's alright. It's a pretty epic story really, so I don't blame you for asking, Poppy." He laughed and continued, "I snuck out the window when they were asleep, because guards don't hide on the roof. Then I climbed down the ivy. And by then I'd awoken the spookiest guard of them all. His name is Mr Marty Furry Face—that's what I like to call him." Oliver winked. "He was no looker. Short, half-bald, with a wicked unibrow, all thick and furry." Oliver paused as Poppy, and Bea for that matter, giggled at the imagery. Poppy's eyes wide, he began again. "Luckily, Mr Furry Face isn't much of a runner either. I outran him and scaled the fence. He wagged his walking stick at me, but I just kept running and didn't stop. And then I found myself here." He smiled.

"Wow!" beamed Poppy.

"You must've really hated that place," Flynn observed, his mouth agape, amazed at Oliver.

"Yes, I did."

"What a story," Bea grinned, wide-eyed.

"That's remarkable," noted Eve.

"That can't possibly be true," Rose bluntly stated, not intending to be rude but she couldn't help it.

Dad shot her the all familiar glare that meant, "*Watch yourself.*"

And Lucy shouted, "Rose!"

Oliver fumbled with his napkin under the table. "It's alright. It sounds like rubbish, I know. But . . . erm . . . it actually happened."

"Do you think they'll come looking for you?" Flynn asked, hooked on Oliver's tale.

"Not if I stay hidden," Oliver laughed, beginning to like Flynn already. "Others have run away and they seem to forget quickly."

The Beans stood in awe of Oliver's courage. Their eyes wide, Dad began, "Oliver." He cleared his throat, "Why don't you stay here at Lavender Lane for now? You have nowhere else to stay, and everyone deserves to have a proper home."

The children sat up straight in surprise, but at the same time it felt right.

Oliver looked from Dad to his children, their heads nodding in both agreement and excitement.

"How could I ever accept such a thing?" Oliver protested with a hint of hope.

After all these years of struggle, Oliver could feel the light of good fortune finally smiling upon him. As if a pleasant and carefree day spent with the Bean children wasn't enough, he now had an offer of a home, even if only a temporary one. It was a dream he never imagined would find him.

"Son, it's not a suggestion. It's a command."

"Well, that sounds serious," Oliver laughed, barely hesitating. "I accept."

The Beans cheered, ready for a new brother in their already tight home.

"Yes!" Bea exclaimed, Flynn joining her in unison.

"This is your new home," declared Dad, his voice echoing through the room.

"How can I ever begin to thank you?"

"Don't worry about that," he winked.

Oliver's vibrant smile spread from cheek to cheek.

After dinner, Dad told his evening stories and sent Lucy and Poppy off to bed. Poppy fell asleep in seconds, but not Lucy. She waited silently for her big sisters to return, for she did not fancy falling asleep in the dark before she felt safe. Bea made a bed for Oliver on the floor of Flynn's room with Mum's best quilts. The twins came bursting in just as Oliver was shoving away a leather briefcase that the twins assumed was his trunk, and all at once they began chattering and bombarding Oliver with questions. After what seemed to be five minutes, Dad popped his head into the doorway. "Still up?" He raised an eyebrow. "I'm off to Bedfordshire myself, so why don't you do the same?"

The children may have rolled their eyes a bit, but they obeyed nevertheless. And Bea and Rose started off to their room. Rose fell asleep the same second she climbed in bed, and Bea, who was still anxious from the day of excitement, lay there, restless. She started to realize and remember things she wouldn't have otherwise realized or remembered as she lay, against her will, in bed. She realized that she was still hungry and that a piece of toast sounded marvelous. She remembered that she hadn't seen the night's stars, and that she'd left her book outside on the porch. Thinking that all these reasons justified getting out of bed, Bea tiptoed through the door.

"Bea," Lucy whispered, seeing her sister sneak out the door, "where are you going?"

"To see the stars," she whispered back in the dark. "You can come if you're quiet."

Lucy quickly joined her sister.

They tiptoed through the quiet hallway, and Bea opened the outside door as discreetly as she could, motioning for Lucy to follow her to the porch.

"Wait, Bea," Lucy whispered.

"Come on, Luce!"

"No, wait . . . do you hear that?"

Bea shut the door and listened for what Lucy had heard. A quiet sob pierced the silence, and the two sisters turned back from the open door to search for the source of the sound. They found beloved Eve wrapped in her shawl, leaned against the piano that Mum used to play, with tears emerging from her big brown eyes.

"Eve!" They rushed to her side and Eve dropped her head in Bea's lap.

"I'm no good," she gushed, for she was never very good at bottling things up.

"What do you mean?" Lucy asked. "You're perfect."

"Mum was perfect." Eve looked at her toes. "I'm just a stupid girl who can't keep her mind focused on what's really important."

"But you are our hero," Lucy piped up, who didn't understand why Eve would say such things.

"I don't feel like a hero!" she shouted in indignation.

"But you are!"

"I wish that one day we could trade eyes," Bea thought aloud in her mystical sort of way.

"What?"

"I wish for that one day you could see yourself through my eyes. I believe you would never doubt again," Bea explained to her sister.

"Why?" Eve wondered what it would be like to visit Bea's head for a lot of reasons, but perhaps she wondered how her sister saw her the most.

"Eve," Bea looked her dead in the eyes, "you have so much to offer! If only you would realize it."

"You do!" Lucy agreed.

"But what I think you need is a nice, long sleep. And when you wake, you'll realize that we can't survive without you. That's what Mum would've said."

Eve obeyed her sisters because she knew they were right about one thing: sleep always did her justice. Whether she really was a hero or not, she was less convinced. Meanwhile, Bea couldn't stop thinking about Eve that night. Words could only do so much, and who knew how much they would do for Eve. Would it be enough? So instead of dreaming, her mind raced all through the night as she brainstormed a way, bigger than words, to give her sister hope.

07

A YIP FROM THE CITY

"Hello," inquired the sweet-sounding woman on the other end of the line, "may I ask who's calling?"

"May! It's Bea!"

With the snap of a finger, May leapt from her honey-like greeting voice that she reserved for strangers to her usual spark-like voice that was her norm.

"Bea!" she squealed. "Are you faring well, my friend? I'm so happy to hear your voice!"

"Ha-ha," Bea chuckled softly. "Life here at home, if you really want to know the truth, is jollier than a clam dipped in jam! And how's life in London, you dashing wife, you?"

May laughed helplessly. To her, every word Bea uttered was hilarious. And without skipping a beat she hopped back into place, updating Bea at a mile a minute.

"Blimey, Bea, a clam dipped in jam! That's terrific! And to say the least, life in London is exhilarating! I love it so much! Arli and my flat is a block or two from the finest park in all of London! We walk there every day at lunch break, and I can only imagine what it will look like when the leaves turn. I can hardly wait! The whole city is alive and as charming as Queen Elizabeth, so just the way I like it! We've been exploring every kilometre of the city looking for the things to do and places to be, and let me tell you, we haven't been disappointed. We've found some of our favourite things to do—London's nightlife is exciting. And I know the weather here is supposedly grey and dreary, but I don't think that at all." May caught her breath and giggled, for she always found charm in dull things.

She started once again, right where she left off, "We've been to the most dashing get-togethers I've ever been to. I'm especially fond of the evening dances they throw for the young people such as us. I simply adore riding the bus everywhere I go and watching all of the interesting people. If you can keep a secret, I much prefer it over country life. I know my father talked against city life, but I find it heaps more interesting than watering his chickens. You must never tell!"

"I wouldn't dare!" laughed Bea.

"Oh, and . . .," May yelped, "Arli surprised me with a fascinating evening at the theatre. We saw *My Fair Lady* of course, and it's a strange thing to think that the actors can sing that loudly and yet still sound like a lark." May remembered the scene with envy, for she had never been able to sing without sounding like a shrieking eel, and then snapped back to reality. "When will my cousins ever come visit?"

As May's life update concluded, Bea felt a bit unsteady but tried to jot down each word in her memory, May's words seemed to shoot out rapidly like frenzy fire, and you had to be quite the fisherman to catch them all.

"My cousin! That sounds extraordinary! I'm so pleased life is so jolly. You sound like a regular Londoner, Mrs Michaelson!"

"Thank you, Bea," May responded. "Any life updates from the beloved Lavender Lane?" she asked sincerely. "I've had so much excitement, I forgot to even ask about your life!"

"Oh yes, thank you. This is half my purpose in calling. Though it's not necessarily good news," Bea sighed.

"I'm all ears," she said, shifting gears.

"Well . . .," began Bea, her voice solemn and uncertain, "it's about Eve. She's acting so strangely!"

"How so?" asked May thoughtfully, who'd always been fascinated by the human heart. And though society wouldn't have agreed, she saw herself as a physician dealing in human emotions.

Bea tapped her foot, trying to format her explanation just right before she spoke up again.

"Well, it's odd. She's so tense lately, and always second-guessing herself. Which is not normal for her, considering her usual confidence!" Bea blurted, a tone of concern present in her voice.

"Do you have any examples, Bea? When do you see it happening?"

"Well for starters, Lucy and I were sneaking out the other night to look at the stars, and we found Eve on the floor crying and holding the legs of Mum's piano. She always does that when she's sad. At first we thought she just missed Mum, but she then told us how inadequate she felt. Her words, not mine."

"Uh-huh," mumbled May, who was taking a thorough set of notes in her head.

"She also said something about how she tries to be good like Mum but can't keep her mind focused on what really matters."

"Poor girl," May mumbled, "she doesn't deserve such hardship."

"I agree. It isn't fair, not when she works so tirelessly," Bea agreed. "The greatest agony of all is I don't know how to convince her that she is enough. Words can only do so much."

"I see," May muttered. "Well, we best think of something."

Silence stretched through the call as both May and Bea thought.

"Didn't she once think that living in London was equivalent to being a princess?" laughed May in remembrance of their happy times as young girls.

"Yes! She's always viewed city life as a romantic thing." Bea laughed. "And I think deep down she still longs for an extravagant life of sorts, full of interesting people and expensive things."

"Indeed," considered May, "I know how that feels."

"Exactly! That's why I called you! On top of that, I catch her looking longingly out the window at nothing. Do you suppose she knows what she's looking for?"

"Very much so, yes," May plainly said.

"What do you suppose it might be?" Bea begged impatiently.

"It is my humble opinion that she may be looking for someone . . ."

"Like a friend? Or someone of romantic interest . . . ?" Bea blurted, and then added softly, "Please say 'friend.'"

"Oh, Bea," May chuckled, "will you ever change?"

"I don't know, May. Why so soon? Childhood is more fun!"

Half laughing, half scolding, May spoke up boldly, "Beatrice Bean! Not everyone thinks like you, cousin! Eve is showing that she's ready to move on and be her own woman!"

"Her own woman? You sound like Grandmum!" Bea cringed.

"You asked my opinion, cousin!" shouted May, who hated when her patients disregarded her diagnosis.

Bea gulped back her retorts and gave May the floor. "Sorry, continue," she stated with a reaffirmed sense of respect.

"Okay, as I was saying, she's treading a fine line between being a young, foolish child and a sensible adult. So you can see why she would be harsh with herself. She wants her wishes to come true, yet she feels remorse for wanting them in the first place. She wants to do the best for her motherless family, yet she wants to be a young person who does young person things, including falling in love. She tries to be the best she can for her family, but her foolish desires sometimes trump her wishes to keep her family in line. And who could blame her? She carries way too heavy a load for a girl."

"So she's playing tug-a-war in her brain."

"Yes, that's exactly right!" yelped May, excited that Bea was catching on.

"I know what that is like," muttered Bea.

"That's splendid! So give her empathy! You need to show her that she is validated and that it's okay to want a different life. That's all she needs, validation. And she can't give that to herself because she is a committed figure in the home and needs her family's approval."

"Well, how should I do that?"

Silence grasped the conversation yet again, and each contemplated what to do and how to do it. Stumbling upon a brilliant idea, May yipped loudly, and jumping up and down in her flat, practically screaming, "I'VE GOT IT! BEA, I'VE GOT IT!"

"WHAT?" exclaimed Bea, matching her pitch of energy.

"Surprise her! Surprise her with an enchanting trip to London. Get all the lads on board and plan an epic occasion behind her back. Eve has always wanted to experience a life in the city! You could snatch some train tickets to London, and Arli and I will plan a perfect weekend! We can make a big bed on the floor, since sleeping is far less important than helping Eve. It would make a beautiful break for her. Not to mention, there is a dance this weekend. It's no royal ball, but Eve could still get dressed up and go, and she would love it!" May beamed, her voice smiling.

"QUEEN ELIZABETH! That's a brilliant, beyond brilliant, idea! May, that's just what she needs!"

"Oh, Bea, it would be perfect!"

"And you think Dad would let us? It sounds wonderful but expensive."

"It's really not," May bluntly said. "Just get here and we'll do the rest."

"Oh, thank you, May. You're a natural at this stuff, May, a natural, I tell you. You're a wizard!"

08

TOP SECRET

"Greetings! Greetings, fellow friends! Welcome to our top-secret, absolutely confidential treehouse meeting," Bea exclaimed, jubilantly throwing her long arms into the air.

Cheers and chatter ran in waves throughout the crowd, the attention of the attendees far from the presenter.

"SILENCE," roared Oliver with a wink, who stood up abruptly from the log that he sat upon.

The chitchat abated and all heads turned in Bea's direction. "Thank you, kind Oliver." Bea bowed, pretending to be elegant.

The treehouse was a remarkable place. It was large enough to house the Bean children and was held together by the many memories the children had made in its keeping. There was a rectangular table that sat in the front of the low-ceilinged treehouse, doubling as both a project table and podium where the presenter often stood. The back shelf was lined with colourful books, playing cards, costumes, and jars full of crayons, pencils, and paintbrushes. They hung garlands of leaves and flowers from the rafters, and little lanterns that they lit during evening meetings. Atop the table sat a homemade gavel. It was made of an old branch and a river rock that was held together with a surplus of twine. The gavel was saved for constructive meetings and complicated verdicts.

Bea fumbled with her clipboard. "Okay, I'm going to call for attendance to ensure that we have no imposters," she proclaimed with a laugh. "Rose?"

"Here," waved Rose.

"Flynn?"

"Aye!" Flynn nodded lazily.

"Luce?"

"Here," smiled Lucy.

"Pops?"

"What?" Poppy asked, oblivious to what was going on.

Bea ignored her and called, "Oliver?"

"Ai. Ai."

"Perfect attendance, eh?" Bea said in her Canadian accent, which received the most eye rolls of all the accents she toyed with.

"Ready to get down to business then?" she asked, glancing over her clipboard. The attendants offered agreeable nods and Bea began.

"Now for our first presenter, everybody, please welcome to the stage LUCY JEAN BEAN!"

Applause pierced the silence, and all were well engaged, as most everyone loved top-secret meetings as much as Bea. Lucy arose, skipping to the podium, where she took Bea's place.

"Thank you, Bea," she grinned. "Okay, as you'll notice, Evie is not here today. And if you're wondering, Bea and I did plan this meeting around the fact that she'd be at the market at this time."

Flynn yawned involuntarily and Lucy hurried to the action of the story. "Last night we stumbled upon Eve. She couldn't hold herself together. She explained that she felt all the work she does for us was . . . uhh . . . what's the word?"

"Inadequate?" piped up Rose, who was easily the most intelligent, for her age, in the family.

"Yes, that's the one. Which is silly because she does heaps and heaps for us! So Bea and I were talking, and we thought that we must do something big for her!"

A bluebird flew to the open window of the treehouse and perched itself on the sill to join the meeting.

Poppy giggled at the bird's assertiveness and hoped it would choose to stay. "Welcome, birdy." She smiled.

"After lots of talking we found a brilliant idea! Could you tell it, Bea?" Lucy looked to Bea, who sat on a stump in the front row.

"Happily!" Bea bounced to the podium. "I called May last night for some advice, and she suggested that we take Eve to London! She's in dire need of a break, and we could visit May and Arli too!"

"In London?" Flynn asked.

Lucy grinned mysteriously. "And we are going to surprise Eve about the whole thing!"

"Eve? Surprise? I don't see it," Rose chuckled bluntly, revealing the fear that Eve, who basically had eyes on the back of her head, would quickly discover their secret.

Flynn perked up on his stump somewhat abruptly, as if the stars had aligned within his mind and everything began to come together. "If we're going to sneak Eve onto a train to London, then that means WE'RE GOING TO LONDON! WITH HER? Wait. We are going to London, right?"

Bea laughed at Flynn's excitement. "Flynn Maximus! You are one sharp lad," she joked. "I'm afraid you've cracked the case."

The crowd erupted with excitement and applause.

"What does Dad think?" Rose asked.

"He thinks we're quite right to give Eve a break."

"And what do you suppose we'll say when we kidnap Eve and hop on a train?" Rose questioned, clearly a step ahead of the rest of the crew.

Oliver scratched his chin in wonder, searching for the answer that was deep below the surface.

"Blindfold her?" Flynn suggested loudly.

"Guard Eve's eyes?" Rose howled, for she knew how quickly Eve would tear a blindfold from her face. "We might as well use blow darts."

"That will be the challenge, Rose, but I've talked to Dad and he'll help us get on the train without too much trouble. It should be fine."

"Dad isn't coming?" Flynn raised an eyebrow.

"No, he thinks it'll be good to have some cousin time with May and Arli," Bea added. "Also, May told me that there will be a dance in London that week."

"Really?" Rose was quite jealous that Eve was old enough to go to one and see elegant Londoners waltz.

"Yes!" Lucy nodded her head quite rapidly.

"Well, it's not exactly a ball," Bea explained. "She'd have to be royalty to waltz in the opera hall," she added, laughing.

"Oh," Rose nodded, feeling much less disappointed, for it sounded like she wouldn't miss much.

"And," started Rose, whose head was yet still exploding with questions, "how would we get her to the dance?"

"Oh, Rose," laughed Bea maliciously, "that's the least of our worries! We'll have already trapped her in London, and she will not be able turn around when she's miles from home. On the other hand, we must stress the fact that this will only work if NONE OF YOU, and I mean none of you, say a word to Eve about London or surprises or even travel." But by that Bea meant Poppy, who had not yet mastered keeping secrets. "If you must talk about London, then talk about how they are doing in football. Understand?"

Everyone nodded eagerly except Poppy, who was humming a little tune and twirling her strawberry hair in her tiny fingers.

"Poppy?" Lucy asked kindly.

Poppy snapped out of her little world and listened to her sister's gentle voice.

"Do you know what's happening?" Lucy asked.

"Umm . . . well. There is this silly frog named Tom. He would not stop following me around, but now I can't find him anywhere. It's quite strange, have you seen him?"

Oliver laughed out loud, for he was not yet used to Poppy's peculiar cuteness.

"BUT do you know what WE'RE talking about?" Rose piped up, who was most definitely used to Poppy's distracted remarks and was probably tired of them.

Poppy looked at Rose with an oblivious expression, clearly stating with her face that she was only concerned about the frog named Tom and not about secret plans to bring Eve to London behind her back.

"Poppy." Bea knelt down beside her spirited sister. She tucked a strand of Poppy's wild hair behind her ear and whispered, "Why don't you go find Tom? I thought I might have seen him in the garden. You should go find him before he hops away."

Poppy nodded exuberantly and then raced down the rope ladder that led to the vast meadow. The children watched as she hopped like a bunny through the garden, her hair flopping as she went along.

"It's probably better that she doesn't know at all," Rose stated bluntly as she watched her hop away. "She's not one for keeping secrets."

"That's true," agreed Flynn.

"Now, for what she'll wear to the dance," started up Lucy. She crossed the treehouse to a little stand-up cabinet. She told her siblings to cover their eyes, and then with a loud creak, she opened the wooden door.

"And open."

They opened their eyes, only to see a fashionable gown that flowed with a familiar air of beauty. It was long and rose-coloured, with cap sleeves and a scoop neckline that would look nicely with a string of pearls above it. It was no princess gown, but to the children it seemed like a work of art.

"Stunning," gawked Rose, who was not easily impressed.

Lucy beamed at her approval. "I know you're wondering where I found it. It was Mum's old dress when she and Dad were young. I saw him looking at it the other night. I asked him what it was and he told me that it was Mum's favourite gown. She wore it all the time before she had us, and when she died, she wanted us girls to have it . . ."

Rose's jaw had now dropped nearly to the floor. Bea's eyes wide, and the boys nodded in approval.

"Now, seeing that Rose and I are too small to wear it . . ."

"I could fit into it if I wanted," mumbled Rose under her breath.

"And I'm much too awkward and messy to wear something so elegant," added Bea, "Eve's our only option."

"She'd do it justice," smiled Flynn, who missed his beloved mum immensely and felt that Eve was the only one of his sisters who could properly fill her shoes.

"It's perfect, Lucy," grinned Oliver in approval.

Lucy wore the look of contentment on her sleeve, her heart beating with the promise of their plan.

"Our plan, it's going to work," exclaimed Bea in jubilance, feeling the same joy that Lucy felt. "Hands in the middle," she shouted.

Each Bean placed their hand in the middle of the circle. Bea's left hand on the bottom, each child stacked theirs on top like a pile of flapjacks. A sandwich of confidence, electricity, and approval, she placed her right hand atop the pile of hands and shouted in unison with her siblings, "To Eve!"

Their hands flew into the air like fireworks filling the sky with sparks of hope and good intentions with their beloved sister in mind. Eve didn't know it yet, but something was coming. Something extraordinary.

09

ABOARD THE TRAIN

The night before the children left for London, Bea met her Dad in the sitting room, where the two reviewed the plan for the next day.

"How do you suppose we should get Eve on the train without her going berserk?" Bea inquired.

"Stay calm and tell her to follow your lead if she asks too many questions," Dad suggested. "We'll get everything packed before we wake her, so there won't be time for inquiries. I visited with Arli and he will meet you at the gate."

"Alright," Bea exhaled. "I think I'm ready." She sat up on the sofa, looking confident.

Dad chuckled. "We best get to bed. Big day tomorrow."

"Right."

The two parted their ways, with Dad's alarm clock set for five a.m., trunks packed and a plan so thorough that chaos couldn't find its way in.

Five a.m. came and left as gracefully as it arrived and Dad and his children lay still in their beds. At five-thirty the cock crowed loudly on its perch, and Dad shot up in his bed. He looked at the clock beside him and jolted out of bed, headed for Bea's room.

"Bea!" he shook the post of her bed.

"What time is it?"

"Not five a.m.," Dad informed cautiously, as if he were treading on thin ice.

"Have we missed the train?" Bea tossed the covers from her body and leapt out of bed.

"We might barely make it." Dad frowned.

"Well, what are we waiting for? I'll get the lunches packed."

"I'll get the others." Dad saluted and turned on his heel to wake the girls.

Though their plan was solid, things hardly went as planned when there were six children trying not to wake Eve and a scatter-brained captain behind it all.

The children darted from place to place, trying to complete the many tasks that came with travelling as quickly and quietly as they could without waking Eve and spoiling the surprise. Thank goodness Eve slept as deeply as she did, because the "quiet" part was quite a daunting task for the Beans. Bea rushed from room to room doing several feverish tasks, from buckling Poppy's shoes and braiding Lucy's hair, to slapping lunches for the train together and making up beds. Rose, who was not, by nature, a morning person, had to be woken again and again by the shaking of her bed. Oliver hauled heavy trunks to the pickup and Dad caught burnt toast that shot out of the toaster with a frustrated groan. Flynn tried to keep his face tranquil as his sisters rushed from place to place shouting orders, crossing checklists, and directing traffic at the loo.

"Rose, hurry up! I'm going to pee my trousers!" Poppy complained as she stood on the door.

"Flynn," Bea whispered between clenched teeth, "are you doing anything? I need your help with the sandwiches."

Flynn rushed to his sister's side, a perfect servant with a steady hand.

"Oi, Flynn! Did you pack your football so we can play in the park?" Oliver waved.

"Oh, good call. Did you, Flynn?" Bea joined in.

"I want turkey and crisps on my sandy," Poppy commanded Flynn as she twirled around the kitchen.

"Yes, I've got it," he nodded as he slapped the turkey down onto the bread.

With the bustle of grabbing last-minute items and snacks, the Bean children almost forgot to wake Eve.

Bewildered and wrapped in her robe, she stepped out into the kitchen. "What is going on?" she yawned.

"Eve, hurry!" Rose chanted. "Get yourself dressed!"

"Why?" Eve loathed being left in the dark, but what she loathed even more was being ordered around. It was her job to give orders.

"Because! Just go!" Bea shot from behind the counter.

"Flynn, what's going on?" Eve asked her brother.

Flynn shrugged as he walked away, and Eve felt more excluded than ever.

In mild irritation, she shuffled away to her bedroom, where she got dressed and ready for the day, whatever it had in store for her.

"Eve, are you ready, love?" Dad pounded on her door.

"Ready for what, Dad?" She stepped out of her bedroom, wearing her red button dress with a cosy cardigan over top.

"Oh, nothing!" He waved her off. "Quickly now, Evie. Quickly." He handed her a coat and led her out the door to the pickup, where the others were already bundled up and piled in the bed.

Blindly she followed, with a million questions colliding in her head. "Where are we going?"

The whole family ignored Eve, and blank stares filled the truck bed. Dad hopped in the driver's seat and began driving down the lane. The children bit into their toast awkwardly, not sure what it was they were supposed to say to Eve as Dad sped down the road as if in a hurry and Eve had no idea why.

"I've had enough!" Eve roared. "Everyone seems to know what's happening except me! So will someone please speak up already?"

Flynn looked from Bea to Eve, then to Bea again. "Should we tell her?"

"Tell me what?" Eve swallowed loudly. It was her duty and obligation as the oldest Bean to make plans. Curiosity was an unfamiliar and unwelcome feeling to Eve, for certainty was her usual state of mind.

"I will tell her," Bea spoke up. The family nodded their heads in approval, and Eve looked at her sister with a raised eyebrow.

"Eve," Bea cleared her throat, "you've been working so hard, especially since Mum . . . since . . . you know." It was still a difficult task to address her mum's death, especially in the company of her younger siblings. "We owe everything to you. And maybe it was all a huge mistake, but we planned a little surprise for you—"

Eve interrupted, "You did?"

"We did," Bea smiled. "But that's all I'm willing to say. At least for now. So you must be patient." Bea commanded.

The sharp morning breeze swept past the children in the bed of the truck as they made their way to the Windermere Transport Station with barely enough time to spare. Their train ready to lurch into action, Eve had no time to ask more questions.

"Ready, loves?" Dad helped his children out of the truck.

"Ready for what, Dad? Where are we going?" Eve was struggling with her patience.

"You'll see, Evie. You'll see," Dad assured as he watched his children climb aboard the train. Flynn was the last to step toward the train and Dad stopped him in his tracks.

"Flynn." Dad found Flynn's eyes.

"What is it, Dad?"

"Your sisters might go a bit mad today. You'll be ma boy and keep things smooth, won't you?"

"Indeed I will, Dad," Flynn valiantly promised, for he was used to looking out for his sisters.

"I knew I could count on you," Dad smiled as he shoved his only son onto the train and watched them slowly pull from the station in a cloud of smoke. The sun barely awake, the world quiet, he waved his young adventurers farewell.

MAY & ARLI'S FLAT

10

LADS IN LONDON

Flynn watched as his father faded and the train propelled forward. Dad's figure, now smaller than the length of his thumb, departed under the archway and disappeared amid dawn. Flynn lay his head against the windowpane as Oliver slid the compartment door shut. Oliver, Rose, Poppy, Lucy, and Eve (who strangely slept better when anxious) drifted off. Poppy claimed Bea's lap as her pillow, and Bea pulled out her novel. As for Flynn (who wasn't tired), he watched. He watched the countryside fly past his very eyes, observing attentively as the world woke up in its familiar golden glow. It awoke gradually, taking one step at a time. First, the trunks of the trees caught the contagious light, then the moors, then the homes in the distance, until the light danced in the sky. He saw gardeners tend to their crops not far off the tracks, and before he knew it, the world seemed entirely awake. Everything shot past his view like arrows in the wind, but somehow every detail could be caught.

"It's beautiful out there, isn't it?" Bea smiled, looking up from her book.

"Yes, brilliant," he agreed.

"What are you most excited for when we get to London?" she asked, stowing her book away.

"Football in the park obviously. You?"

"Oh, I'd fancy to find a new book, or to run through the park as fast as I can. But what I'm secretly out of mind about is seeing all the people. There's so many people in London, and I want to watch them hurry by."

"You're mad," Flynn teased his sister.

She chuckled heartily. "I suppose I am . . . and I'm okay with it."

Flynn turned back toward the window. "There's nothing wrong about it, just don't let Eve or Rose find out your secret wish."

Bea laughed. "Well, isn't that obvious?"

The hours on the train passed slowly but rapidly all the same. Thankfully, Eve slept so they didn't have to reveal the full surprise. They reached Kings Cross Station with a screeching halt and all the children seemed to break into a broad smile as they watched Eve awaken. Poppy spotted "Aunty May" out the train window and began waving excitedly to get her attention. Eve looked out the window and began her squealing, "Is this Kings Cross?" She was shaking with excitement. "Are we in London?"

The others turned to Eve, a shade of exhilaration and pride upon their faces.

"Yes, Evie," Lucy beamed.

"This is London," Oliver added as he retrieved Eve's trunk from the rack and handed it to her.

"You did all this for me?" Eve was astonished.

"How could we not," Bea piped up, "after all you've done for us?"

Eve stood there for a second processing it all as her family stepped out of the compartment door. They practically skipped off the train, moving their legs at last. Poppy leapt into May's arms with a yip.

"Hello, Poppies darling!" May held her youngest cousin in her slender, ladylike arms. After a long moment she let go of Poppy, dropping her to the floor.

"May!" Eve jumped. "Did you help with all this?"

"I barely lifted a finger, Eve. These lads have done it all!"

"Oh, thank you, May." She hugged her cousin.

May was a tall and slender woman with short ginger hair that bounced above her shoulders with a frivolous air. She wore an elegant pencil dress with a cardigan over the top. Her pale blue eyes were the kind that dreamed of an elegant life but deep down sang the song of a farm girl still stuck in her wellies.

"Come this way! This way to the flat! Pip, Pip." She gestured like a hen gathering chicks. "I can't wait to show you lovely chaps the city. It's astounding. Arli, can you help Lucy with her trunk?" May blurted rapidly, forgetting to take a breath.

Arli quietly nodded at his spritely wife, for after nearly a year of marriage, he'd learned it was best to simply smile and nod. Arli looked opposite his wife. He was short and stout with a firm grip and a willing heart. He wore a neatly trimmed cap of light brown hair and saw the world behind a pair of round spectacles.

Poppy emerged from the train station to smells and sounds that overwhelmed her. She gazed at the tall buildings and the busy sidewalks in awe. She was a girl of many words, yet at the sight of London she was speechless. The other Beans, having been to London once before with Mum and Dad, referenced their blueprint of memory. They quickly mixed in with the people rushing from place to place, and it was intimidating yet exciting. Eve, however, had another emotion to add to her excitement. She was simply overflowing with gratitude for her family.

May and Arli led the children to their flat at 105 N. Sapphire Street. The building was a few stories tall with a blue door on a peach canvas, dressed in a skirt of painted bricks, and enclosed by a picket fence. Neatly trimmed rosebushes lined up the front steps, inviting them in. They climbed the steps and May showed them to her humble flat. She slammed her body into the door as she entered. "You've got to show the door who's in charge," she advised. "It tends to get jammed."

The children pushed into the living space. It was small and square, with a big bright window that gave a view of a grassy area across the way. Cousin May showed off her humble flat like it was the Taj Mahal.

The decorations on the walls were lively and rambunctious, almost haphazard. Eve assumed that her loving cousin had difficulty choosing between her treasures and ultimately decided to *make* room for every single one. She showed the children to their room up the narrow and creaky flight of stairs. "Girls," May bounced, "this will be your bed." The bed was made with quilt after quilt, layered atop the other to make a comfy cushion. "And, boys, this will be yours." She motioned to a nearly identical quilt pile beside the other. "Get comfortable." She winked and bounced on her heel as she turned out of the doorway.

The Beans unpacked their trunks, only making the untidy house less tidy. Then, anxious to explore, they followed May and Arli out the door for their long-awaited picnic in the park. Flynn, with his football tucked under his arm, assumed the role of leader without appointment. May and Arli barely kept up with Flynn on their brisk walk. When they reached the park, they laid the gingham blanket neatly out below the cover of an imposing tree. They quickly ate, and when they finished, began exploring. Lucy hunted for trees lofty enough to climb and was pleased with what she found. Flynn, Oliver, and Arli dribbled the football, Rose danced, and Poppy and Bea chased the pigeons and kites. As for Eve, she ascended Primrose Hill to see the view of the city. She reached the top out of breath, but not necessarily because of the steep climb. It was entirely because she couldn't believe her eyes.

"Wow," she said aloud as she gazed at the city's breath-taking skyline and the handsome people who sat about the hill, gazing as she did.

"Beautiful, isn't it?" a noble and kind voice asked from beside her.

Eve glanced over her shoulder to see a handsome young man near her. His hair a soft milk chocolate and his eyes a gentle brown. He was finely dressed and strong, but it was not his rugged looks that lured Eve in.

"It looks as if it could be in a painting," Eve analysed thoughtfully.

The handsome stranger laughed under his breath, "I've never thought about it that way. But you're quite right, miss."

"I can just see it hanging on an elegant wall in Paris, can't you?" Eve smiled at him.

"Yes," he chuckled softly. "Are you an artist yourself?" he inquired.

"Not of the painting sort, unfortunately," she sighed.

"I see," he nodded. "Then what kind of art do you excel in?"

"Food is my canvas," she twinkled.

"Hmm, the loveliest kind of art," he sang. "What do they call you, Ms Artist?"

"Eve Marie," she grinned.

"Eve Marie," he paused, as if memorizing the way it felt to say it. "What a beautiful name."

"Thank you. Marie was my mother's name."

"Was?"

"She passed away about six months ago," Eve explained in a reverent tone.

"I'm sorry. It's hard to lose a mother," he sighed.

"Have you lost one yourself?" Eve gazed into his honest eyes.

"When I was young," he told, "but my father and I get along well."

"I'm sure you miss her very much," Eve added in her sweet voice.

"Thank you," he smiled at her for long seconds, and she smiled at him.

"What do they call you?" Eve asked.

"Henry." He dropped his shoulders and outstretched his hand for Eve to shake, which she did. "I'm glad to have met you, Eve Marie."

"And you," she swayed.

He glanced at his wristwatch and apologized in his kind tone, "I'm terribly sorry, but I've got to get back to my father. It was good to chat with you."

Eve agreed, smiled, and waved Henry away as he started down Primrose Hill. In a daze, she pivoted on her heel and wandered back to the tree where May sat.

"What's that look?" May eyed her cousin with a suspicious air.

"Look?" Eve laughed. "What look?"

"I think you know," May teased, "tell me at once!"

"I think I've met someone," Eve let out.

"Someone handsome?" May yelped, for she didn't mind a bit of gossip.

"Yes!" Eve gasped softly. "Incredibly!"

"Oh, Eve! Tell me more!" Impatient, May perked up, and Eve began reenacting her conversation with Henry.

After soaking in the open spaces of the park, the Beans left to tour the city. The hours spent about London passed like minutes, and the Beans seemed to grow more and more enchanted with the city. The feeling was quite peculiar and fresh to the Beans to be frank. Running around a city full of charming and important people, who seemed to have such zeal as they marched along the streets, could have intimidated the tourists. But not the Beans. There was something about chasing pigeons through the park, galloping through crowded streets, and scanning shelves of shops that were stories and stories high that left the children feeling big. The peculiar thing is that in a place where they were just one small group in a crowd of thousands, they felt as grand as the London Bridge. Perhaps it was the uncanny way that the Beans made everywhere they went feel like home.

Each Bean chose an activity to do that day.

Rose wanted nothing but to see the Royal Opera House, where she would one day dance if she couldn't dance in Paris.

Flynn, who was not one for sightseeing, had only one wish, and it was already granted when he ran through Regent's Park chasing his football.

Oliver hoped to skip stones into the harbour and watch the massive ships.

Bea and Lucy dreamt of the bookshop, and when their wish was granted, they soaked it up like a sponge, memorizing all the colourful books stacked neatly on the shelves.

As wonderful as the bookshop was, Bea's greatest joy came from watching the people. She took notes in her head of their mannerisms, stowing them away for characters in her later stories.

Poppy, who was fuelled by lollies, begged to visit London's best sweetshop, which none of the others were opposed to.

After nearly a full day of sightseeing, exploring, and shopping, Arli, who was tasked with time, had forgotten to check his pocket watch. It was when they were standing at the dock skipping stones into the sunset, that May shot up, realizing it, "Arli!"

"What is it, dear?" Arli asked, clearly side-tracked as he watched his stone skip thrice across the waters.

"What time is it?"

"It's time," he gestured.

"Time for what?" Eve looked toward her cousin.

"Oh, Eve! I thought they told you already!" May glanced in surprise.

"No," Eve shrugged.

"Oh, blimey! I suppose we got caught up in the day of fun and forgot all about telling you!" May laughed as they started down the street toward the flat.

"What?"

"Well, there's this dance in London tonight and we thought you might fancy attending. You know, a bit of a dawdle never hurts."

"Like a ball?"

"Not necessarily a ball, but one of London's neighbourhood dances. Everybody loves them."

"You mean it?"

"Yes, of course!"

"But I don't have a dress better than this one," she looked concerned.

"Never fear," Oliver laughed, "Cinderella may not have a suitable dress, but she does have squirrels and birds."

The others roared in laughter, because it felt quite funny to be compared to forest animals.

"What?" Eve didn't get it.

"All I'm saying is Lucy may have found something dashing," Oliver elaborated.

"Did you, Luce?" Eve turned to her sister.

"You could say that," she humbly admitted.

"You're a regular heroine!" She couldn't believe how her family had done all this for her.

The journey back to Sapphire Street was a jubilant one. Eve's grin seemed to widen as each block passed, and every so often she'd ask to ensure she wasn't sleeping, "I really get to go to a dance in London?"

They answered in annoyance, "Yes, Eve!"

But she didn't care one bit that her repeating questions bugged them. It had been her dream to gallivant around London since she was a girl, but the fact that they'd planned to take her to a dance took her over the edge. Despite her bursting excitement, loud and persistent was the question in her mind, "How did they manage all of this without me?" And the even louder follow-up question, "Do they even need me anymore?"

POETRY in LONDON

11

UNDER THE STARS

(8 years earlier)

"One day, I will gallivant around London," Eve wished out loud, twirling in a flowing dress that was two sizes too large for her, "like I have lived there all my life, and fancy people will know my name. Oh, what a life!" Eve spun as if she was wrapped up in her dream.

Eve, Bea, and Rose were prone to dancing in the attic as young girls, assured that they were alone with their imaginations.

Eve was but a few days older than ten, and Bea, at eight, pulled her astronaut helmet from the overflowing wooden chest full of endless costume possibilities for the children. Bea pulled the helmet over her head. It was much too big for her and seemed to swallow her up as if she was literally falling into space.

"And I'm going to the moon." She stretched her arms into the sky like she was reaching for the stars themselves. "I'll write books about my adventures and all my alien friends."

Rose, innocent yet just as feisty, popped out from behind the coatrack, wearing a tweed business jacket paired with a ballet skirt. "And I am going to Paris to dance and rule the world." She twirled.

(Present day)

Eve Marie stood in front of the mirror, blinking back at her reflection. Eve was energized by the thought of wearing her mother's beloved dress about London.

"You look stunning, Eve," May smiled contently.

"You think?" Eve twirled, lifting the rose-coloured dress as she spun.

"You look just like your mother, Aunt Marie," May added as if she could read Eve's mind.

"Really?" Eve's eyes sparkled with the lingering fragrance of hope.

"Just like her."

Bea, pleased her plans were working out so perfectly, whispered in her sister's ear, "You're about to gallivant around London like you've lived here all your life."

Eve laughed softly, remembering the time that her foolish dream once ruled her whole world. An hour before her departure, Eve requested to speak in private with the *big girls*, otherwise known as Bea and Rose. Lucy and Poppy walked away with their heads held low, wishing they were just a few inches taller so they could be admitted to the coveted club. When the door shut behind the three girls, Eve gasped, overwhelmed. "Our childhood dreams seem so silly now, don't they?"

"I suppose they do," Bea said, for her dream to make it to the moon had drifted off into outer space since the day she learned that it wasn't made of cheese.

"But they shouldn't, not when they're at our fingertips," Bea decided, whose plans to be a writer seemed nearer every day.

"Hmm," Rose nodded, hoping her days in Paris would come quickly.

"It's odd though," Eve whispered, "I've wanted this for as long as I can remember, yet I'm petrified."

"You have no reason to be," Bea assured.

"Yeah, I just wish . . .," Eve paused "I just wish . . . I had someone to do it with me," she mumbled thoughtlessly. "Wait . . .," she started, as if trying to catch the idea that shot across her brain.

Bea, who caught Eve's idea before she could verbalize it, shot up from the bed. "Eve, no!" she yelled.

"Bea, you're old enough. We could go together! It would be such great fun! Just two sisters out on the dance floor." She grabbed her little sister's hand. But Bea, who was clearly not on board with the *new* plan, jerked away from Eve's grasp.

"Bea, you might enjoy it!"

"No, Eve. It's not really my cup of tea, thanks."

"But I do so much for you," she batted her eyelashes, recycling Bea's own words.

"Oh, Eve! Don't make me retract my words!" Bea whined, dodging her sister's persuasive brown eyes.

Rose broke into a million giggles watching her cornered sister. Eve's pleading left Bea wailing helplessly as she weighed the options. *"Should I sacrifice my sister's happiness or my dignity?"* Bea asked herself.

"Oi, Bea! It could be fun, you never know," Rose roared in laughter.

"Oh, shut up, Rose!" she snapped. "I could use some backup here!"

"Bea! I'll do anything for you! Anything you ask," Eve hadn't given up yet.

"Alright!" Bea shouted in compliance.

Rose was now on the floor, rolling in laughter. Eve leapt into the air, forgetting she was wearing a dress, as Bea sat with her head in her hands in fear of what she'd agreed to seconds before.

She believed she was not built for a room full of pretty and put-together people. Even though it was but a neighbourhood dance, Bea didn't imagine it that way. She did not like sparkling cider except for Christmas dinner. On all other occasions, she preferred milk. She was under the impression that any dress that you couldn't wear with wellies shouldn't be worn, and on top of it all, she held fast to the opinion that dancing should be spontaneous, not planned. Bea finished cataloguing all the situation's flaws and decided she loved her sister too much to stand by her stubborn precepts.

The girls were so caught up in their laughing fit that they didn't notice Oliver coming to the door. He knocked on the door and called out, "Girls!" When no one answered or acknowledged him, he spoke up, "Girls! People!"

Bea reached for the door, and at the sight of Oliver, her face awoke like a lightbulb had been switched on in her head. "Oliver," she suggested, looking toward Eve.

Oliver looked from Bea to Eve in a state of perplexity, his eyebrow rose to maximum heights.

"Oliver is the answer! I'll only go if Oliver goes." Bea crossed her arms and stood back-to-back with Oliver.

"Oh boy," Oliver turned to walk away, like coming upstairs in the first place was a big mistake. But before he could slip away, Bea gripped his arm and pulled him within whispering distance.

"Oliver, please come. Eve wants me to go to the dance with her and I just can't do it alone. She'll get snatched up by some chiselled man and I'll be all alone. Best friends stick together."

"But I can't even talk to ladies!" he spoke up. "I've never even really seen one." He hesitated on the last part of his comment, partially aware of the line he'd just crossed.

Eve jumped up with a pointed finger. "What about us?" she barked.

"Oh yeah." He hid behind Bea in fear. "I guess it can't be that bad," he stumbled.

"So you'll come?" Bea asked, clutching Oliver's arm.

"Sure," he muttered unenthusiastically.

Bea relaxed immediately. She threw her long arms around his neck without warning. Even she didn't know it was coming.

Oliver, half surprised, half afraid of what he'd just agreed to, stared blankly at Rose as he awkwardly patted Bea's back. As expected, May was elated when she had two more people to dress. Oliver dressed in one of Arli's old suits, which was much too baggy and short for him, but it would do. And Bea dressed in one of May's dresses, which fit her perfectly.

The night was breezy but not cold. The sky was a deep midnight blue covered with stars that resembled the accidental splattering of a paintbrush dipped in white. It was a beautiful night, the kind that Bea and Oliver wished they could spend outdoors. But Bea's love for her sister and Oliver's love for his new friend sent all three toward the event in good spirits.

The dance floor was in the centre of a high-ceilinged building with a parquet floor. Sconces hung on each wall, filling the room with brilliant light. Handsome young people filled the room, already partnered up to the classical yet spirited music in the background. The refreshment table was dressed in dainty dishes, sparkling punches, and fragile appetizers.

"Well, we're here," Bea swallowed harshly, trying to hide the thick fog of fear she was wrapped in.

Eve, who had practiced spinning across her bedroom floor since age five, had to blink twice to make sure she wasn't stuck in a dream. "I'm finally here," she sang dreamily.

Not long after arriving, Eve was asked to dance and slipped into the crowd, leaving Bea and Oliver to stand as wallflowers. Bea suffered through a few songs and then pulled Oliver into an empty coat closet, for fear often wins before it can be moulded into courage.

"Woah," Bea dropped her head into her hands, "those people are so intimidating."

"And beautiful," she added. "Are they even having any fun?"

"I wonder, Bea, I do."

"Who even knows what are in those sandwiches? They are much too fancy to be eaten," Oliver scoffed.

"I hope Eve is doing okay." Bea ignored Oliver and poked her head out of the closet to see if she could locate her sister.

"I'm certain she's fine, Bea. She's dancing in a place filled with London boys. Isn't that, like, her dream?"

"I just hope it is everything she imagined." Bea leaned against the wall in distress.

Across the room, Eve Marie was having the time of her life.

"This is better than I ever imagined," she thought to herself.

She danced with a German boy who knew more English than she did. Blond hair, blue eyes, and heaps to say about himself. Then a ginger boy from Brighton. His nose was a bit crooked and his teeth a bit crowded, but he knew French like her and kept calling her "belle."

The appetizers were pure artistry, the sparkling cider a delicate indulgence, and the only thing that could make the night any better was if Bea and Oliver were having fun wherever they were. It was then in the middle of that happy thought that her stomach clenched as she saw who was approaching her. Scarlette Beaulieu was part English and part French, and possibly the most manipulating witch who'd settled in London after a short-lived life in the country. Her raven black hair flew behind her and her cold eyes narrowed in Eve's direction as if she were penetrating Eve's soul. Eve choked on her sparkling cider as Scarlette approached her. Her long legs and the etched scowl on her face caused Eve to break out in hives.

"Well. Well. Well. If it isn't Eve Bean," Scarlette snapped in her mocking tone, her cronies Abigail and Charlotte following closely behind.

"Evening Scarlette," Eve's voice cracked in fear.

"Ha!" Scarlette croaked. "What brings you to London?"

"Erm . . .," Eve stuttered helplessly.

"I presume your mummy forgot to inform you."

"Inform me of what?"

"That stupid farm girls aren't welcome in London," Scarlette barked.

Eve backed away. "I'm visiting my cousin, and I've been to London once before when I was young," she whispered in disgust.

"Oh, is that right?" Scarlette mocked.

"Do you miss your mummy, Bean?" Scarlette and her cronies stepped even closer to Eve.

Eve was now trembling from head to toe. How dare they talk about her mum that way? She blinked back her tears, searching for a single ounce of courage when moments before she was on cloud nine. She wished Oliver and Bea were here to rescue her. Where were they anyway? She scanned the room for support but found none.

Scarlette's breath was cold and cutting. "It must be hard trying to chase your idiot of a father around all day. And I won't even mention those helpless children." Her cold eyes locked with Eve's.

Eve tried to stand up. She tried to defend her family, but when she opened her mouth to speak, her tongue was tied, and the only thing that seeped out from between her lips was cold air. She stood there flushed in the face accepting her fate as the London dance was, in fact, a dream.

"Eve?" a familiar and pleasant voice drifted into Eve's ear. "Is she bugging you?"

Eve glanced over her shoulder to see a handsome young man standing above her. It was Henry from the park! In a flash of light, Scarlette and her cronies marched away with a snooty eye roll and an expression of utter disgust.

Eve turned to face him. "Henry!" She paused, finding his eyes.

"Eve! What a coincidence." He offered his noble hand, which Eve gratefully accepted.

From that moment on, Scarlette was forgotten. The two took the dance floor and it felt to Eve that her whole world had stopped. She'd already forgotten about all her troubles, including Scarlette. They blended in with the other couples on the dance floor and began to sway like they did, but to Eve it felt as if they were flying across the dance floor like it was made of ice. And before she could help it, Eve was caught in a moment where she saw the world fly past her eyes at the speed of light, and yet inside the moment everything was still, slow, and every detail could be captured.

When the music changed and the dancing halted, the two caught their breath and stood face to face. And it seemed the same crazy idea was theirs to share.

"A stroll?" Henry asked, offering his arm once again.

"Let me tell my sister and then yes," Eve beamed and rushed off to find Bea and share the news that she'd found Henry.

Caught actually enjoying some cider, Bea was compelled by the story. She was tempted to follow and spy on Eve, which she refrained from due to the respect she had for her sister. Eve quickly returned to Henry, who stood at the open doors waiting for her, and then with a smile they began down the sidewalk, under a blanket of a million twinkling lights.

"So, Eve," he began, "where'd you learn to dance so well?"

"I'm embarrassed to say that my fourteen-year-old sister taught me," she laughed. "Even so, I'm proud to say I'm the *only* one of my sisters that passed her tedious course."

"And why is that?" Henry asked.

"Let's just say the others find choreography to be restricting. Especially Bea," Eve tipped her head in laughter.

"Your family sounds delightful," Henry decided.

"They are something, for sure, and I owe everything to them," she said.

"I know how that feels," Henry smiled.

"What's your family like?" Eve wondered.

"Well, my father brought me up, with help, of course. He employed a wonderful orphan named Juliette when my mother left, and the poor girl gave me everything she had. She still lives on the estate with us and has a son of her own now."

"How wonderful," Eve grinned in admiration.

"Yes," Henry agreed. "Both Father and Juliette give me more than I deserve."

For a few more blocks, they walked and talked. Finding easy conversation, their route returned them to the dance.

"Eve Marie," he paused, "I've had a marvelous time with you tonight."

"Thank you for saving me from that dreadful Scarlette, Henry. It is a debt I hope to oneday repay."

"You already have, Eve." He brushed one of her fly-a-ways behind her ear. "And I too know of the sheer cruelty of Scarlette. I wouldn't wish her saltiness on anyone." He smiled.

"She's pretty bad, isn't she? I haven't seen her since grade school and she only grew meaner."

"Blimey, yes," he laughed. "Look, my father is expecting me soon, but you promise you'll write?" The two had exchanged addresses for letter writing on their stroll.

"Yes, of course," Eve promised.

"Good." Henry took her hand. "Let me bring you back to your sister." He led her close to the dance floor but stopped her and whispered, "I have something for you."

"You do?"

"Yes." Henry pulled a primrose from his pocket. "I plucked it from the garden at the park right after we met earlier today. I hoped I'd see you here to give it to you." He smiled. "And here you are."

"Oh, thank you, Henry!" Eve blushed.

"No, thank you." Henry leaned in and kissed her softly on the cheek.

"Until next time." Eve waved as he vanished out the doors and into the breezy London night.

Eve stood dazed, starstruck by the enchanting events that had taken place.

Anxiously awaiting Eve's return and watching the door closely, Oliver and Bea swiftly rushed to her side. The walk back to May's was spirited, to say the least. Even after recounting the events of the evening with her cousin and Rose, Eve still didn't feel tired. She lay in bed wide awake, her mind swirling as she replayed the moments with Henry repeatedly as if she'd never tire of remembering them.

12

BEHIND LOCKED DOORS

Oliver knew two things about his parents. First, he knew they were explorers. Second, he knew they loved him very much. He felt that deeply. Love, though, wasn't quite enough to let them live to raise him. Their death was so unexpected that all their baby boy had to remember them by was a battered old stuffed elephant, now worn to shreds, and his father's leather briefcase that was in the car with him the night he'd passed.

Both items accompanied Oliver to the orphanage and were returned to him when he was old enough. The briefcase had proven to Oliver to be of no use. It had been locked since the day he first held it and hopes of getting it unlocked had waned. At the orphanage, when Oliver couldn't sleep at night, he would often sneak out onto the roof and try every number combination he could think of, yet the briefcase remained locked.

Like a loose but not yet lost tooth, the briefcase always seemed to be in the way of other thoughts. In the dark of the night, Oliver would try to imagine what lived inside its leather walls. He hoped there was a picture of his mother and father. He didn't know what they looked like. He imagined his mum to be tall and pretty. He hoped she had lots of spunk. As for his father, he believed him to be like any other man who carried a briefcase, with dark passionate eyes and a knack for words.

Perhaps the briefcase was jammed full of diaries from his mum and dad's adventures, or maybe old travel receipts. It crossed Oliver's mind on rare occasions that it could be full of shillings, but he didn't like the thought of that much.

Oliver's secret hope was that there was a map inside. He wished to find a record of their travels so that he could escape to where they'd been. He'd planned it all out. He would find the people that they'd once known, and those people would tell him everything he'd ever wondered about his parents. And by the end of his trip he would feel like he had known them all along.

"Ahh." Oliver closed his eyes, daydreaming and inhaling that transfixing thought.

There were endless possibilities, many of which Oliver entertained in his mind, but heavier than all the possibilities was fear. The fear that seeped in his mind like cold, black fog. The unlikely possibility that the briefcase was full of rocks and empty sheets of paper or nothing at all. Oliver didn't know which was worse.

"Oi, Ollie Wollie!" It was Poppy, skipping down the hall.

Without much of a warning, Oliver shoved his father's briefcase under his bed feverishly, but he was too slow. Poppy entered the room clumsily with her stuffed bunny "Dotty" tucked in the front of her trousers like a joey in a kangaroo pouch. Her strawberry hair flying in every which direction, like always. She tumbled onto Oliver's bed and began asking the long string of questions that was expected nearly every time she visited the room.

"Ollie, what was that you were shoving away?" was her first curious question.

"Oh, nothing, Poppy! Just ole rubbish," he lied.

Poppy figured if she wasn't going to get anything out of her first question then she'd better rephrase it. "Well, why were you looking at it?" she pushed on, toying with Dotty's ears.

"I was just bored," he laughed. "But now that you're here, I don't have to worry about that! So tell me, Poppy, to what do I owe this pleasure?"

"Huh?" Poppy had decided Oliver was acting strange.

"Why are you here?" Oliver restated kindly.

Poppy ignored Oliver's redirect and bounced back to where she'd begun, "Ollie?"

"Poppy?"

"What is really in that box?"

Oliver sighed as he searched for a suitable lie. It was no use ignoring Poppy's question. Her curiosity was relentless.

"Poppy," he put the mystery box on his lap, "this box is magic."

He was interrupted by a welcome knock at the door. It was Bea.

"Ooh-la-la!" she cheered in a French accent. "Did someone say *magic box?*"

Poppy, who was the only Bean who didn't tire of Bea's "funny voices," chirped up, laughing, "Yes, Beazy! This box is magic!"

Bea had already sat down across from Oliver, highly intrigued. She pulled her little sister onto her lap, fully prepared for an explanation.

"Well, you see," Oliver cleared his throat, "this box is filled with . . ." Oliver was stuck.

"Magic fairies," Bea rescued him.

Poppy gasped.

"Yes, yes. And over the centuries the box has been passed from hand to hand in hopes that one day the fairies could be returned to their home, which they were stripped of long ago. One day, Poppy, I hope to return them to Fairyland or find someone that can." Oliver valiantly raised his hand to his forehead in a wave of commitment and honour.

"Really?" Poppy asked, gobsmacked. "Can I help?"

"I would like that very much."

"Can I see them?" Poppy pestered.

Oliver hesitated, and Bea swept in.

"Poppy, long ago, when the fairies were captured, a spell was cast on them. The fairies will be locked in the case until they are returned to Fairyland! Only then can the spell be broken. So for now, we just have to believe."

"Wow!" Poppy gasped yet again, and then went off, with a spark in her step, to tell the news to her pets.

"Don't tell Eve that we just lied to your sister!" Oliver raised his hands into the air as if ready to be handcuffed.

Bea chuckled. "I'm not an idiot. Besides, it's not a lie, just a story. And stories help—"

"Imagination," Oliver completed her sentence.

"Right," Bea nodded.

A wave of contented silence washed over the room for long moments until Bea broke the silence, plagued by her own curiosity.

"Oliver, what's really in the briefcase? I hesitate to believe it's magic fairies."

Oliver gulped loudly at the elephant in the room.

"Oliver, you know you can tell me anything, right?"

Oliver nodded, avoiding Bea's stare as if she was a dragon who breathed fire when she locked her eyes with some other creature. But Bea was much wiser than to let her best friend stay hidden behind locked doors, so she grabbed his briefcase, set it gently on her lap, and began, "Oliver, that means you can tell me what's inside." She tapped it softly.

Oliver flinched at the substance of her plea, and then after anxious silence and the gathering of courage, Oliver began. He told of his worries held inside the briefcase. He explained how he used to hold it and wonder what it would be like to see his father hold it. He told of the many times he'd tried to open it and how his efforts were all for naught. He told her what he wished would be inside and wondered aloud whether he'd ever discover its contents. Bea listened to it all, her eyes unwavering.

"You know, Oliver, I might know how to help you."

"Is that so?" He was intrigued.

"Yes, but not without the helping hand of my most trusted business consultant."

"How professional," Oliver decided.

Bea called for Rose, who entered the bedroom with a businesslike air.

"You summoned me." She folded her arms, leaning against the door.

It was then that Bea whispered something suspicious in her sister's ear. Rose nodded in approval, and Bea chuckled in excitement as Rose ordered Oliver, "Stop sitting around and get your shoes!"

Oliver shot up abruptly and followed the girls to the door.

"Where are you off to?" Lucy asked, nestled against the windowsill with her sketchbook.

"It doesn't concern you!" Rose snapped in her sharp older-sister tone.

And Bea, who didn't believe in leaving her younger siblings in the dark, knelt next to her sister.

"We're going to meet a friend and then stop at the bakery for a treat. What would you like us to snatch you?"

Lucy's eyes lit up, "A chocolate croissant please."

Bea crossed her heart with a smile and followed the others out the door. The day was pleasant and tranquil. The December breeze still against a slate of freshly fallen snow. The sun hung in the sky, surrounded by gentle wisps of clouds like an old man's greying hair. Oliver put one foot in front of another, wondering what was going through the girls' heads. Where could they be taking him? What kind of friend were they off to see? Would this friend really be able to help him? He doubted it, but what he did know was that it was best not to ask. He'd discovered in the month living with the Bean children that spontaneous adventures were meant to remain surprises. So being the clever boy that he was, he didn't ask.

"This is the place," Bea stopped abruptly, after about two miles of walking, in front of an eccentric-looking cottage.

"This is the place?" Oliver questioned.

"Yes," Bea sighed.

From the look of it, the cottage belonged to a crook. The exterior was painted a vibrant pink and was drowning in climbing ivy and overgrown shrubberies, dusted by snow. A decrepit fence surrounded the overgrown yard with oddly shaped signs posted on it.

"Beware of the exploding dingleberries," one of them read in slanted and slightly loopy cursive.

It seemed the snowy lawn was crawling with garden gnomes and mystical figurines. Beside the bird bath yet another sign was posted. "You only find what you seek," it read in the same mysterious penmanship.

"Does your friend happen to be a . . . witch?" Oliver whispered.

"Oliver, don't be daft—" Rose assured. And Bea interrupted, "She very well could be."

Rose approached the backdoor purposefully. The door was an electric turquoise that clashed terribly with the house. Oliver believed the colour scheme would have looked good on a cupcake but that was about it. The sign posted on the door read, "*In aura est amor,*" a Latin phrase. Just below that, in English, the sign stated, "Taste the air." Rose knocked, and a mystical-looking woman draped in colourful shawls that resembled curtains approached them.

Her hair a vibrant red, it hung in coils of untidy curls. She wore about thirty bracelets per arm and a billowing skirt beneath her shawls. Tea in hand and a haunted smile painted on her face, she welcomed the trio into her chaotic office. The shelves were lined with oils and other flasks of mysterious substances. Her desk was covered in crumbled paper, dried paint splatters, and glitter spills. Colourful scarves seemed to burst out of the drawers, and the room was bombarded with a thick fog that smelled of incense.

"Now, what brings you lovely and luminous creatures here today?" the woman asked in a dreamy and slightly eerie tone.

"Erm . . . we were hoping . . . erm?" Bea started to answer her question but was disrupted by the image right before her eyes.

The woman had slithered across the desk toward Oliver, who had rightfully recoiled.

"Who's the lover boy?"

"I'm not a—" Oliver asserted, but it was too late. She had already begun tracing her long emerald fingernails up and down his face.

"He's very handsome." She tossed his thick hair, and he felt his face burn with disgust and embarrassment.

"Pepper! Do you mind?" Rose barked.

Pepper narrowed her eyes in Rose's direction. "Is he your lover boy, Rose?"

"No!" Rose jumped from her chair, shocked at her nerve.

"Then I guess he's my lover boy," Pepper smirked devilishly, not once considering that Oliver's loyalty could have been to the other sister. Which it wasn't.

"I'm not your lover boy!" Oliver swatted her away like the pest that she was.

"Oh, I see." Pepper stepped back, clearly offended. She bit her tongue in anguish and turned to the girls. "What brings you to my lair? Potions, home remedies, fashion advice? I see you two could use some help," she scolded.

Rose inched toward Pepper, clearly angered by her behaviour, and Bea thrust her back into her seat.

"Pepper," Bea rested her head on her hand and whispered loudly, "we've got a request for the lock doctor. Is she in?"

Pepper smiled maliciously and then vanished for a moment. She reappeared in a lab coat, spectacles as thick as jam jars hooked on her slightly crooked nose, and a big red bag with the clasp held tightly in her grip. She sat down at her desk again and opened the mysterious red bag.

"Where's the patient?" she asked in a new and businesslike tone.

Oliver wondered what had just happened but figured he had nothing to lose. He slammed the briefcase on the desk and Pepper studied it—if that's what you would call her tracing its lines with her cheek.

"Ah," she started up in her wispy voice, "I see."

Bea, Rose, and Oliver stared at her as she scribbled feverishly onto a piece of parchment with nothing to fill the silence but the sound of her scratching her chin and an occasional "Hmm."

She picked up her pen and gazed up at the dream catcher that hung above her head and then she began, "Let us call upon the spirits." Pepper stretched out her hands for the others to grab and closed her eyes. When they finally gave in, she sang an out-of-tune incantation.

Spirits from the past,
Why have you gone away?
My humble plea at last,
Is to hear the whispers you must say,
We are hungry and yet we fast,
Don't leave us in the dark today,
Oh, spirits, come to play.

She ceased her dramatic screeching, and her customers couldn't have been more grateful. Oliver shuttered in horror, hoping this witch's trade was worth tolerating the preamble. Pepper thrust her hand into her red bag and fished around. She retrieved a butter knife, a stethoscope, a hammer, a bottle of glitter, and a swirly straw.

"The spirits requested." She motioned to the strange objects as if they'd understand.

First, she placed the stethoscope on the face of the briefcase. She wailed, thumped, and cried as she listened to its "heartbeat."

"Peculiar, yes, very peculiar," she shrieked.

Bea, Rose, and Oliver, who were wise enough to refrain from asking questions, sat there silently, with their mouths slightly agape.

Pepper then took her glitter and dumped it on the leather. She pressed her lips firmly into the glitter and muttered a jumble of strange sounds. Oliver winced at the sight of her puffy lips on his father's case.

"Oh!" She shot up suddenly, grasping her chest as if a bullet had just shot right through it. "That's it!"

She then slid her butter knife between the cracks of the briefcase and pounded her hammer harshly into the knife so that the briefcase was forced open. She took a deep breath, bounced back in her chair, and wailed, "That was exhausting!"

13

OPEN DOORS

Oliver's heart raced at the speed of a jet. His palms grew clammy, his face ghostly, and his forehead sweaty. He reached out to open the briefcase but his hands trembled. All his wonders, concerns, and fears were moments away from being washed into the abyss forevermore, and he couldn't even steady himself to grasp them. He whispered into Bea's ear, "Can we do this someplace else? Some place that doesn't reek of incense?"

Bea chuckled and nodded. As she often did, she thrust a bill on the desk, thanked Pepper for her "service," and strut out the door, glad to escape the haphazard office. Oliver held the briefcase in his anxious grip as Bea led the way to Mr Brown's Bakery, where they'd open the mysterious box.

Thunder raging inside his chest, Oliver's mind was fixated in a loop replaying one thought, "What if?" He wiped the sweat off his forehead, hoping his fear would wipe away with it. His whole life he'd wondered, wished, hoped, and now he could taste closure, yet he was petrified.

Bea and Rose sat across from Oliver at the table as he outstretched his trembling hands to open the lid. He used his left hand to steady his right arm and then he opened it. His eyes grew wide with surprise at the sight of what had slept inside the leather walls for so many hopeless years. He felt frail and helpless, yet empowered and maybe even moved. A square photograph lay gently atop everything else. It was a brilliant image. A picture of his mother and father holding a bright-eyed baby boy in their arms. They were standing atop a cliff that overlooked crashing ocean waves. His mum was not quite as he expected her, but far more than he ever imagined. Short dark hair hung happily at her shoulders. She had soft hazel eyes with warm golden flecks in them that breathed both passion and adventure. Something about her eyes reminded him of Bea. She wore a striped shirt and a contented smile. His father wore a cap of mousy red hair and a determined look. His eyes a deep ocean blue that were both kind and mysterious, identical to Oliver's eyes. Oliver caressed the picture gently; he felt a keen sense of knowing them as he looked into their eyes.

"Well?" pestered Rose, who'd apparently been waiting too long for Oliver to speak up.

"Oh, sorry." Oliver had almost forgotten Bea and Rose were there. He'd been swept up too suddenly to notice them. He angled the open briefcase so his friends could enjoy the view, and they then decided it was safe to inch closer.

"Woah," Bea's mouth hung wide open as Rose snatched the photo impatiently from Oliver's grip.

"So this is them," Rose blurted

Bea turned to enjoy the photo still in Rose's hand, "Oh, Oliver! They look lovely. You have your mum's hair and smile. And your father's eyes," Bea analysed it looking from Oliver to the picture and then back to Oliver again.

"Blah, blah, blah," Rose mocked, "what else is in here?" And she dove into the case as if digging for treasure.

The three teenagers sat at the square table unaware of the customers that shuffled in and out of the shop for what felt like a quick hour, searching through the briefcase. Oliver studied his father's old compass in his palm. Rose pulled out a Moroccan purse, a tin of stale mints, a travel guide, and a bandana. Bea gripped a mysterious leather-bound book with the word "Adventures" imprinted on the binding. She flipped it open to see slanted letters scratched onto the opening page *"This book belongs to Benjamin 'Benji' West,"* it read. Giddy with excitement, she immediately showed it to Oliver.

"His name was Benjamin," she announced, "but he went by Benji!"

Oliver beamed. "Does that seem fitting, Bea?" Oliver asked, for Bea was the expert at the "naming strangers" game where the players dub strangers with the name that *fits* their appearance.

"Like a glove," she smiled. "Now let's find your mum's name. I'm sure it's here somewhere." She searched.

They flipped through the leather-bound book, quickly scanning each page. In doing this, they discovered many things, but Mrs West's name was not one of them. Tucked inside the case pocket, however, held fast against the lid with bronze snaps, Oliver found a bundle of letters tied together with a frayed red ribbon. Oliver untied the knot and exposed the first letter. It was addressed in sloppy yet strangely comforting penmanship to *"Mr Benji West."* In the left corner it read, *"Kate and Oliver West."*

"Kate," Oliver vocalized, observing the way it sounded for the first time. "Kate and Oliver."

Bea wondered what it would feel like to discover the name of a lost mum for the very first time.

"Could you read it for me, Bea?" Oliver asked, feeling that her voice was the only one that could do a handwritten letter from his mother justice.

Bea nodded, honoured, and unfolded the parcel of yellowed parchment.

"Dear Captain," she cleared her throat.

Oliver closed his eyes, picturing his mother bent over a roll-top desk. He pictured her hand moving up and down the page quickly, without taking a break.

How is Greenland? Kiss a penguin for me. Is James healed and ready to return yet? I'm sure he's grateful to have you there to take care of him. Give him my best wishes. Tell me all you have to say. Hearing about your adventures is almost as rewarding as being on them.

I got a job as a governess in a fancy estate on the outskirts of Keswick. It's fifteen minutes by bike to get there every morning, and it is a lovely, scenic ride. You will love the rolling hills here. They are brilliantly green and endless. The estate where they live looks like it's been ripped from the pages of a magazine, so I must tread lightly to avoid breaking things. The job pays enough, and I started on Monday. Two children: Michael who's ten and is exceptionally smart for his age. And you'll be glad to know that he loves sports. We play football on the lawn every day. I'm getting quite good with his help. Then Merci, who's eight. She's a talking machine and a bit of a princess, but is very sweet. She adores Ollie. They both do. Their mother doesn't like messes, so I've become quite good at hiding them.

Vern is well. Still caged up in his shack, and I don't think he'll ever come out. He's become too comfortable with his private life, I suppose. I keep telling him to get over it and enjoy the world. He says he's "enjoying it just fine in his little corner." You know Vern. Never listens. What a delightful, nincompoop.

I miss you more than I can express, so does Ollie. He points at your picture on the wall and says, "Pop, come home!" I remind him each time that you'll return soon, and his smile returns. He can hardly wait to see you. He's grown so much. We manage without you, but that doesn't change the fact that we miss you terribly.

Bea gulped as she began the next portion, *Three more weeks, my Captain. Three more weeks and we will begin our next grand adventure—raising our son. We'll escape somewhere new with him as often as we can, and it will be, in one word, stupendous. He's an explorer just like us, Captain. I can tell.*

Now, as much as I love being Ollie's tour guide, I'm so excited to show you Keswick. I've already scheduled a nanny for the day after your return. I will give you the grand tour of our new home, and you will love it.

Three weeks, Captain. Three weeks.

Love,

Kate and Ollie

Bea tucked the letter back into its envelope and turned to Oliver. His eyes swelled with sadness, longing, and misery. It was deep and silent, but she knew. After all, she was a writer, and writers understood even the most complicated of emotions. She reached her hand across the table and gripped Oliver's. Rose put her hand awkwardly on top of Bea's and hoped it would help. After all, sympathizing was not ballet, which came so naturally to her.

"They died on their first date back together," Oliver stated.

"How can you be sure?" Rose questioned.

"They died when I was with the nanny, I know that," he paused, and then whispered the thing that stung the most, "I would've died too, if I were with them."

"But you didn't," Bea whispered back.

"No. But so what if I did?" he scoffed. "I'd be with them now."

"Oliver!" Rose shot up.

"Oliver," Bea began, "it's a truly tragic thing that your paths only crossed for a short time."

"I just wish I could have known them. It would be an entirely different story if they'd died when I was like ten. At least I would have remembered them," Oliver said without blinking.

"You know more now than you ever did." Bea tried to shine a light on the darkness. "And I believe that they still live inside of you."

He was silent.

"You can't . . . ," she stammered.

"Can't what?" he asked, fiddling with his napkin.

"Disregard that. They loved you. They still love you. And more than anything, they wanted you to be happy."

THE BEANS OF LAVENDER LANE

He went silent again.

"They wanted to give you the best life."

"But they couldn't."

Bea sighed once again. "You're entirely missing the point."

Oliver let out a sad laugh. "What's the point?"

"You cannot change what happened. No one can." She gazed off into the distance. "But you can make it your duty to write the middle and end of your family's story. You have control over that."

"And?"

"Show them that their love is enough."

"How?" Oliver was curious.

"Make something extraordinary with your life. Make them proud."

Oliver looked up from his napkin and faced Bea.

Perhaps she was right.

14

WACKY WORLD

It was mid-April and the Beans had been anticipating spring for long months. When it finally came, they were simply overjoyed. However, blue skies only lasted a week until they were replaced by grey, rainy ones. The thought of sunshine became a far-fetched idea, and even Lucy and Poppy who loved to jump in puddles and Bea who loved dancing in the rain grew tired of the reoccurring storms. Moreover, it didn't help matters that Eve persistently wound up at her corner desk drafting letter after letter to Henry. If not there, she was seen at the window looking longingly out into the distance as if searching for something. Flynn was seriously concerned that all this "thinking" would negatively impact her cooking.

After six days of clouds and solemn afternoons, Flynn and Tommy were sitting in the attic, playing cards thoughtlessly. Tommy dropped his ace of spades to win the game; however, victory was far from his mind. A beam of sunlight struck the attic window, the raindrops dried up on the glass, and immediately things changed, as if time had stopped. He jumped to his feet and cheered.

Flynn fled to the window, where he inquired, "The rain stopped?"

"Indeed it has, mate."

"Tommy, do you know what this means?"

The two boys grinned at each other like it was Christmas morning. They shouted in unison, "Wacky World!"

Wacky World was the two lads' iconic secret hideout. It was gifted with this fitting name when they stumbled upon the battered old treehouse near the duck pond the previous summer. The day they stumbled upon the sanctuary, they discovered they were not the only visitors to the duck pond. An odd-looking rooster with its eyes practically bulging out of its head squawked around the pond as if warning the ducks of serious peril. Determined to make the ducks listen, the rooster squawked on relentlessly. And after all his efforts, the ducks remained uninterested. So as a last hurrah, the persistent rooster perched up on the mossy sign posted at the south end of the pond. He bawked and crowed, clearly exploding with things to say. However, the creaky old sign proved to be less than satisfactory as a soapbox. The rooster got a little too animated and his little chicken feet slipped on the moss and he flung into the air. He plummeted into the pond, losing half his feathers on the descent. It was then the boys insisted on calling their new hideout "Wacky World," after the peculiar rooster. It was also that day that Flynn and Tommy came to the consensus that animals must have personalities.

The two boys rushed down the stairs, skipping half the steps as they went. They raced into the mudroom and jerked their shoes on.

"Where are you going?" Lucy chased them out the door, clearly dying to get out of the house.

"None of your business!" mumbled Flynn, waving Lucy away.

"Flynn, just tell me!"

"I said none of your business!" Flynn reminded her, much more sternly this time.

"Wait, Flynn!" Lucy called, slipping on her blue wellies. "Can I come?"

"Lucy, no."

Lucy was not in the mood to take no for an answer. "But, Flynn. I'll do anything for you!" she wailed.

"Ugh, fine," he muttered, "but you have to do my chores for a week."

"Done," she agreed as if it was a bargain, and chased her brother out the door.

It was a glorious thing, the sun. It could change the whole story in a snap. One moment everything could be dreary, and the next, the children would be tripping down the moors with adventure looming on the horizon.

The trio hopped through the garden like a couple of jackrabbits foraging carrots, except this time they were hungry for excitement. It was a good thing Lucy had long legs and could keep up with her brother. It was Tommy whose trousers kept falling down, assigning him the role of caboose. They skipped through the meadow, past Poppy, who'd been talking to her pets long before the sun had come out. They raced yet faster over each of the hills until they reached the picket fence that wrapped around the perimeter of the property. They were at the edge of their yard now, and from where they stood the cottage looked like a dollhouse. The three of them leaned against the fence to catch their breath.

"Can you hop fences, Lucy?" Flynn asked through gasps.

She nodded affirmatively, too honoured that she was on one of Flynn's sacred adventures to ask why they'd be hopping mean Mr Petosa's fence. Little did she know the plan was not only to hop Mr

Petosa's fence, but to make it to the other side of his pasture so they could reach Wacky World. She was smart enough to know tagalongs weren't granted the right to ask questions.

"Good. Then I'll take the lead." Flynn squinted into the distance. "If you see Petosa, then it's full sprint from then on, understand?"

Again, Lucy nodded in agreeance, and Tommy rolled his eyes. They'd never seen Petosa on trips to Wacky World before, and Tommy was starting to believe that there was really a sweet lady who made jams that lived in the house. Perhaps Mr Petosa's reputation was just another one of the Bean family stories.

Flynn led the way as he swung his leg over the fence. Lucy slid expeditiously through the posts, and Tommy followed. They looked left and then right.

"All clear," Flynn whispered, crossing his fingers that it would remain that way, and tiptoed on.

Occasionally, Flynn would stop and turn to his followers at the sound of a rustle or the squawk of a bird.

"Come on, Flynn," Tommy pleaded, "he's just a spineless old man. What can he do?"

However, Flynn knew something Tommy didn't. He knew what Mr Petosa was capable of, and perhaps it was the old man's capabilities that worried him so much. As the three explorers clambered up the last slope, Flynn peered over the hill and his heart dropped at the realization of what was on the other side. "Oh no," he mumbled under his breath, "I thought we had at least another week." It felt as if literal lightning had shot through his veins as he turned to Lucy and Tommy. "RUN!" he yelled.

And run they did, continuing bravely toward Wacky World.

SHELBY EVE SAYER

Their alarm at the top of the hill did not go unnoticed. Ziggy, the blood-thirsty sheepdog, who came out of his pen every spring around sheep grazing time to protect the sheep, immediately perked up. All seven Beans were convinced, even Dad, that Mr Petosa fed Ziggy mischievous children for breakfast. As Flynn turned his head to see Ziggy bounding up the slope toward him, he asked himself, "I wonder how long it will be till I make the menu." He hoped he had more time but time wasn't always kind, he remembered his mum saying. He tried to close his mind, because thinking and running for dear life never went together.

Tommy screamed at the top of his lungs as they sprinted through the pasture. He claimed screaming made an adventure extra thrilling, but who knows whether he would have said that very same thing at the end of the day.

Ziggy ran like the wind, chasing the children with a furrowed brow and a deadly look in his eye.

Lucy had only heard stories of Ziggy Petosa, the great and terrible. Stories she'd been convinced were only legends. But the stories had clearly been true as one larger-than-life Ziggy was hot on her trail. Instinctively she ran as fast as her long legs would take her. *Thump, thump, thump,*" She heard her feet match her heartbeat as they pounded against the ground. It was awfully hard to run in wellies.

The sheep moaned and bleated between bites of grass, in a state of perplexity as they watched the commotion unfold. Mr Petosa must have listened to the confused moans of the sheep, the ferocious barks of Ziggy, and the shrill shrieks of Tommy long enough to stand silent. He came limping around the corner of his stone home with a cane in one hand and a hose in the other, ready to fire.

"What do you nitwits think you're doing in my pastures," Mr Petosa shouted, "haven't you ever heard of trespassing?"

108

The trio ignored him, for he was the least of their troubles. They whizzed around the corner out of Petosa's sight and through the thick, shaggy grass. The relentless Ziggy was now nearly nipping at their heels.

Flynn, who was a whole pace ahead of Lucy and Tommy, hopped over the wood fence at the back of the pasture that marked the edge of Mr Petosa's land and the direct path to Wacky World. He roared at the other two, "Keep running!"

Lucy leapt into the air as high as she could, tumbling over the fence, not worried about any scrapes and bruises on the descent when considering the alternative.

Tommy, who lagged seconds behind Lucy, then leapt toward freedom. He closed his eyes in fear as he muttered between gritted teeth, "P-please, please." But Tommy's luck had run out. Ziggy blasted into the air as Tommy did. It was a close call, it really was. Ziggy's sharp teeth caught hold of Tommy's shirt tail in midair. Tommy could feel Ziggy's teeth dig into skin and was sure he was done for.

"Tommy, no!!!!" Lucy reached toward him, almost in slow motion.

Tommy whimpered, still closing his eyes as if trying to pretend he was someplace else. Flynn, who was quick as a whip in critical, doomsday situations, reached for the trail snack he'd stowed away in his pocket—carrots. He hoped Ziggy was hungrier for a carrot than his best mate.

"Oi, Ziggy," he hollered as he dangled the two carrots above his sweaty nose.

Though Ziggy was blood-thirsty and cruel, he was still a dog, and dogs love to play fetch.

"Come 'ere, boy!" Flynn called, still dangling the carrots.

Ziggy dropped Tommy and sat up quite abruptly. It was almost comical as he wagged his tail at the sight of the freshly picked treat. It turns out Ziggy had a taste for naughty children *and* garden treats. Flynn threw the carrot like a Frisbee toward Mr Petosa's house and Ziggy jolted after it like a bolt of lightning.

"Come on, Tommy!" Lucy motioned, helping him over the fence "Are you hurt?"

"Only shook a bit." He rubbed his back where Ziggy's teeth had been.

The three of them were now over the fence but still far from safe. Mr Petosa was coming toward them as flustered as ever. He blabbered on and on about how he'd never seen such insolent children, and how they'd surely be punished for such behaviour. He rambled on, slipping in a few choice words that all Beans knew not to use. Perhaps he was a spineless old man, but he sure had some nerve.

With no intent to be polite, Mr Petosa's words met the children's backsides as they vanished into a grove of trees. With the unfounded fear that Mr Petosa could hop fences too, the trio didn't cease sprinting until they reached Wacky World itself. As they wove through the trees, Lucy wondered if her brother was still simply escaping or had an actual destination.

"I see it!"

Tommy collapsed against a nearby tree and began to wheeze. "What ju–s–t happened?" Tommy bellowed between wheezes.

"You alright, Tommy?" Lucy asked once she had sufficient breath to speak. She'd always worried about Tommy like a brother. He was Flynn's best mate, which practically made him Rose and Flynn's triplet.

"I have the ver-yy same questio-n," he gasped, turning from Lucy to Flynn. "Mate, you totally saved my life," he delivered in soberness.

Flynn, who was awfully quiet, rendered a small fake smile and turned to face the duck pond.

Lucy, who gave credit where credit was due, turned her head toward her brave big brother. "You really are a hero, Flynn." She patted his back.

"No. Not really."

Flynn was too ashamed to be worried, and so he hid his choking panic. Flynn hated being wrong, especially because it was such a rare occurrence. His pride hurt, and most of all, he worried his little sister could see that. He hated feeling exposed and vulnerable. He was supposed to be the resilient big brother, especially after he'd promised Dad to be strong for his sisters. And it was his duty to shield them from danger of all kinds. Instead, in the name of adventure, he'd broken that promise.

Tommy, who finally caught on, piped up, "That was an adventure mate. We made it past a child-eating dog and Petosa in one day. We've never done that before."

With that, the three headed toward the pond. It wasn't long before Flynn forgot what he was sulking about and was sucked into the lure of Wacky World. The children danced around the duck pond and laughed in the makeshift treehouse until it was too unsteady to occupy. It was in that treehouse that Flynn, Tommy, and Lucy became oblivious to the world around them. They forgot about mean Mr Petosa, Ziggy, and even more concerning, they forgot about getting home before sunset.

15

SHADOW-CAST MEN

"My children." Dad smoothed the newspaper on his lap and faced his children with a stern look in his paternal eye.

The embers crackled in the fireplace behind Dad's armchair as the shadows crawled up the bookcase. Dad's face was half-lit in firelight, while Flynn and Lucy stood as still as statues at the foot of his chair.

"You worried me sick."

"We are sorry, Dad," Lucy soberly said.

"And Mrs Dee was worried sick for Tommy's sake. And can't you see how I would be held responsible for his absence . . . and his injuries?" Dad explained, his voice growing sterner by the minute.

"Yes, Dad." Flynn nodded in shame.

"You've got me in quite a pickle, children. Quite a pickle . . ."

A single tear fell silently down Lucy's cheek. *"It's all my fault,"* she thought.

"Mr Petosa was, in one word, *incensed* by your insensitivity. And I have to say I'm not too proud of you either. Trespassing? Whatever made you think that was okay? What a stupid, foolish, daft thing to do!" Dad raised his voice. "My children, leaving without telling me, causing heaps of trouble, and worrying me and everyone else SICK! What do you have to say for yourselves?" Dad thrust his newspaper down and it hit the floor with a slap.

The peak of Dad's angry voice, the dark shadows, and the slap of the newspaper against the floor were too much for Lucy to manage. At once, she burst into tears.

With one glance at his horrified daughter, all the exhaustion, worry, and anger drained from Dad's countenance and all he felt was guilt.

"Lucy," Dad jumped to his daughter's side and reached for her arm.

Instinctively, she jerked from his grasp and jolted off to her bedroom. Seeing Dad like this was unfamiliar, and Lucy knew well enough that she had played a part in his anger and worry, and that alone was too much to bear.

"Oh, Flynn." Dad collapsed back into his chair. "What have I done?" He dropped his heavy head into his hands.

"Dad, I've done the worst of it." Flynn dropped onto the sofa, feeling remorse for his own sins.

"No, my son. I should have—"

"I should have asked before I went," Flynn interjected.

"I should have understood a boy's need for adventure," Dad and Flynn spoke over each other, barely paying attention to what the other said.

"I should have known the sheep dog would be out," Flynn thought aloud.

"I shouldn't have let that perturbed mother of Tommy's get to me," Dad scoffed.

"I should have been smarter," Dad and Flynn said at the exact same time.

Both looked up from their thoughts and into each other's eyes.

"The Bean men," Dad considered, "never quite content with themselves. Always the first to notice their faults. Always half as good without the women."

Flynn raised a curious eyebrow. "Dad, what do you mean?"

"I'm ashamed of myself, son, and broken without your mother. Things like this never happened when she was here." Dad's heavy heart seemed to weigh down the whole room.

"Dad, if Eve or Bea were here, they would say something perfectly meaningful," Flynn said. "And I don't quite know what to say."

"Then say nothing, son," Dad suggested with a sombre smile.

"You're a good dad, Dad," Flynn tried, thinking something was better than nothing. "Despite all your faults," he added.

"Flynn," Dad broke into a sad laugh as he stood up, "one day you will be a better dad and man than I ever could, ma boy." He messed up Flynn's hair. "I suppose I've got to make things right then, don't I?"

"Yes, Dad." Flynn nodded.

"Alright, wise guy that did get carried away today," he reminded, "that's what I'll do." Dad smiled as he slipped down the hall to Lucy's room, on his way to turn the upside down right side up again.

16

BIRTHDAY BUNNY

(Two years earlier)

"Hoorah! Hooray!" Poppy squealed as she skipped around the sofa.

She shook the brightly wrapped parcel in her hand and tried to guess what might be inside. The purple paper was so shiny she could practically see her reflection on it.

"Open it, Poppy! Open it!" Flynn shouted impatiently.

Poppy held it tightly in her embrace as she wheeled around the room. "What could possibly be inside?" she wondered.

When Poppy finally settled down beside Lucy on the sofa, Lucy read the words on the tag aloud, "To my bunny, love Mummy."

"Go ahead," Mum Marie motioned to Poppy.

Poppy peeled the paper back vigorously, stripping the parcel of its clothes.

"It's a box!" Poppy chirped, her strawberry pigtails bouncing as she did. For a four-year-old girl with as much imagination

as Poppy had, a box was a glorious gift. Her family chuckled, and Mum Marie rushed to her side.

"Not quite, dearie," she smirked. She held Poppy and together they opened the flaps of the cardboard box.

Poppy peered inside, the anticipation bursting out of her chest like fireworks in the London sky. A beautifully sewn bunny lay sleeping at the bottom of the box. The bunny had a grey body with purple ears, embroidered sleeping eyes, a sweet smile, and a purple polka-dotted dress draped around her body. A matching pair of bunny ears with a headband attached lay next to the bunny. Poppy immediately embraced her newest friend. She squeezed and kissed its head with all her might.

"Dotty," she pronounced. "I will name her Dotty."

"It suits her, darling," Mum Marie smiled. "Does that mean you like her?"

"Oh yes, Mummy!" Four-year-old Poppy leapt into her Mother's arms, and Mum Marie slyly slid the matching bunny ears onto Poppy's head, completing the picture. And for one moment, it was just the three of them. Dotty and her mummy, Poppy. And Poppy and her mummy, Marie. It was a circle full of mummies who loved their Bunnies. And from the tip of Poppy's flappy ears all the way down to her toes she believed, she believed that of all the circles in the world, this one was full of the most love, which also made it the warmest.

(Present day)

Today was the most important day of Poppy Bean's life. It was her birthday. After all, it wasn't every day that a little girl turned six. She sprung out of bed the second she heard the first bird chirp, and rummaged through her dresser drawer searching for her special notebook. It was a gift from Bea on her last birthday, given in hopes that Poppy would become a writer too. But Poppy had not filled it with very many words, much less stories. Her notebook was full of doodles, ideas, and an occasional scribble here and there. She flipped to page twenty and reviewed her research.

In the month leading up to her birthday, she had asked everyone she saw about what it was like to be six. Everyone that is, from Bob the butcher to her own father. Dad announced that it was a time of "creativity and discovery," both words Poppy couldn't spell.

Eve whispered something about responsibility and ownership. Rubbish, Poppy hoped.

Oliver told of the pranks he pulled on the other orphans during his sixth year and assured Poppy, "Six will be a hoot. Just like you are!"

Bea rambled on and on about how, "Six was magical." She told stories of learning how to make toast for the first time, writing her first stories, riding a bicycle all by herself, and much more, but Poppy couldn't write that fast.

"It's just the same as any year!" someone blurted. Probably Rose.

Flynn claimed that he couldn't remember being six because it was so "terribly long ago."

Lucy smiled as she pondered the question, as if remembering a good memory, and then frowned as if remembering a sad one. Then she smiled again, told a quick story, and wished Poppy good luck.

Poppy tried to imagine what a much older and wiser version of herself would have said to the new six-year-old. But her squint wrinkled up her nose as she tried to picture what she'd look like in ten years. Poppy rushed back to the dresser, shoving her notebook back into the drawer where it belonged. Her eye then wandered to the little frame perched on the dresser. Perhaps the woman in the frame would know the answer.

"Mummy?" Poppy asked the picture, "Will I like six?"

She imagined her mummy nodding at her and whispering comprehendible words into her ears. She'd fill them with birthday wishes and perfect promises that couldn't help but come true. Poppy set the frame down gently and set off skipping to the kitchen, where her first birthday wish came true.

Eve was in the kitchen making Poppy's favourite breakfast: strawberries with whipping cream wrapped up in a scrumptious crepe. Yum!

Eve smiled warmly at the birthday girl the way her mum once did, and pointed to the table. "Dad left you a message."

Poppy slid to the table where Dad's note sat, "H-a-p-p-y B-i-r-t-h-d-a-y m-y Popsies!" Poppy sounded out the first sentence, "I h-o-p-e t-o-d-a-y i-s," she stopped on the long word she hadn't learned yet. "What's this one?" she asked her sister, who knew practically everything.

"That one's stupendous." She smiled as she flipped a perfectly golden crepe over on the skillet.

"Stupendous," Poppy repeated, deciding whether she liked the word or not.

"L-o-v-e D-a-d."

"He'll be home as soon as he can to celebrate, Pops." Eve flipped another crepe. "And he told me to tell you that he's sorry he can't spend the whole day with you."

"That's okay," Poppy said, fumbling with Dotty.

Eve deserted her crepes and wrapped Poppy in her arms. "This one is from me," she whispered, "and this one's from *Mum*." And she kissed Poppy's wild head. "Happy birthday, Poppy."

Poppy's birthday unravelled into a day of excitement before she could decide whether five or six was better. She gobbled up her crepes and was gifted several happy wishes by her siblings between bites. When her plate was cleaned off, she slid on her special bunny ears, her polka-dot wellies, and without a bit of hesitation she marched out the door. Within moments she was skipping into the May sunlight, chasing birds and rabbits alike, while singing her favourite nursery rhymes all along the way.

After a few minutes of lolling around, Poppy decided it was time to get to work. For months she'd been planning it. "Poppy's Birthday Parade," and it was going to be the theatrical event of the century, no doubt about it. She'd been training her pets for weeks to be able to march in sync across the meadow, and they were nearly ready. Poppy figured that if circus trainers could get elephants to walk through fire, then anything was possible.

She started by dressing the goats, Daisy and Duron, who were the finest set of goat twins in Grasmere according to Poppy. She'd crafted a pretty flower crown for Daisy and a festive jingle bell sash for Duron. Then, she'd dress Bess the cow. For Bess, she would use her grandmother's old sun hat, which would fit Bess and complement her wise nature. She didn't need to worry about dressing Petey the rabbit, for Eve had helped her sew a bowtie for him that he was already wearing. Lastly, she would adorn Ramsey, her clumsy dog, with moose antlers. As for the hens and chicks, she figured they were cute enough costume or not. Plus, chickens didn't like to be dressed. She'd learned that one the hard way. Kitty the cat was also best left alone, since while a beautiful cat, she also had claws and a cemented opinion about things.

Poppy turned to review her final stage directions with the pets. She enforced and reinforced the drill rules with all the animals before they began dress rehearsal. She got a deliberate "Moo" from Bess, a "Baa" or two from the goats, and a simultaneous "Ruff" from Ramsey. Clearly in a state of readiness, she turned to get her last prop from Dad's garden shed. But on the way to its hiding place, she saw a pair of dark eyes peering in her direction through the holes in the fence. She blinked twice and the mysterious set of eyes vanished. "How odd!" she thought as she found her sparkly director's baton wedged between a terra cotta pot and a garden shovel. She slammed the garden shed door shut and glanced over her shoulder once again. Sure enough, the set of eyes had reappeared. Without thinking twice, Poppy tiptoed purposefully to the fence.

The eyes had disappeared yet again. "Hello?" she asked, sticking her lips through the hole in the fence. She listened for a reply but there was none. Poppy knew that she had not imagined the eyes. True, she did have a powerful imagination, but she always knew the difference between pretending and an actual situation. So sure as she was, she persisted with her hellos.

"Hello?" she shouted. Still no reply.

Poppy didn't give up. She dragged Bess over to the fence, who was the perfect footstool. "Moo," Bess belted out as Poppy mounted the cow. Poppy peered over the top of the fence to see a timid boy about her age curled up in a ball on the other side. His skin like rich chocolate and his head was covered by an array of tiny knots.

"Hello," Poppy smiled, "I'm Poppy."

The boy looked shyly at the dirt.

"What's your name?"

The boy stared blankly at Poppy.

"Do you have a name?"

The boy nodded shyly.

"Me too!" Poppy yelped. "What's yours?"

The boy giggled softly at Poppy's goofiness.

"Do you talk?" Poppy blurted impolitely.

The boy nodded, his eyes still fixed on his toes.

"It's my birthday!" Poppy bounced, running out of things to say to the boy.

The boy stood up suddenly and quite bravely. "Happy birthday," he whispered softly, "I'm Danny."

"Hi, Danny," Poppy beamed, "I'm six now. How old are you?"

"Seven," the boy muttered.

"Oh, I'll be seven . . . next birthday," Poppy counted, using her fingers as a reference.

The boy nodded and smiled shyly.

"Would you like to play with me?" Poppy asked impulsively.

The boy nodded yet again, looking Poppy in the eyes this time. And Poppy helped him over the fence and onto Bess's back. The two climbed safely down and ran toward Poppy's playhouse. On the way, they crashed into Bea and Lucy, who were carrying a plate of biscuits.

"Poppy!" Lucy waved. "We're going to bring some biscuits to the new neighbours," she pointed to the house next door.

"What is your name?" Bea asked Danny, kneeling at his level.

Danny dodged her eyes and hid behind Poppy, who was inches shorter than him.

"It's okay, Danny. These are my best sisters," Poppy assured.

"Hello there, Danny," Bea smiled. "Would you fancy a biscuit?"

Danny nodded and selected a biscuit from the plate.

"Did you move in next door?" she asked as Danny bit into his biscuit. He nodded and she beamed, "Welcome to Lavender Lane."

17

POPPY'S PARADE

Danny felt at home with Poppy and her finest furry friends. He didn't have any animals of his own. His older sister, Aiysha, was terribly afraid and his mother was extremely allergic to dogs and cats. Though Danny had no experience with pets, he'd always longed to have one. He loved animals. Perhaps he was drawn to them because he didn't have to explain himself much to them, or possibly because of how free they seemed. Danny loved to watch them run wild. Sometimes he wished he were an animal, like a wild horse or a wolf. Then, he could run for days and days without anyone to tell him what to do, and above all, wolves didn't have chores or demanding older sisters.

Poppy introduced her new friend to every one of her pets and said, "You know, I've been looking for a little extra help with the pets. Would you like to be my apprentice?" Poppy offered, feeling proud to have used such a big word. Five-year-olds never used words like *apprentice*. "You could be an apprentice to Poppy's Pets Incorporated?"

He gladly accepted with a firm handshake and wrapped himself in the light that accompanied belonging.

That morning, Danny and Poppy rehearsed the birthday parade more times than they had fingers to count. They gathered all the props, fed each pet a full-course meal, and went over each drill several times. It was tedious work for certain, but the pets were finally fully prepared. They were "circus ready," as Poppy described it. Poppy and Danny sat against the playhouse after rehearsal, just awaiting Dad's arrival with anxious excitement.

Dad's truck rolled down the lane and Poppy bolted inside to be there to greet him. His arms were so full of goodies that he nearly toppled over. He held a homemade birthday masterpiece crafted by Mr Brown himself and a stack of presents. Poppy was delighted to see him, and the three girls lined up behind him. Mr Brown's three daughters happened to be Poppy and Lucy's greatest friends. Claire was the oldest at eleven years old. Poppy believed she was almost as kind and pretty as Lucy. Paige was the middle daughter at age eight, and spunky and bright like Poppy. The youngest daughter, Lila, was usually found behind Claire's leg in social situations. She was nearly five and loved animals almost as much as Poppy.

"Happy birthday, Poppy!" the three sisters shouted in unison.

Poppy hugged all her guests and was thoroughly pleased her audience had grown. Despite any plan they had for gifts and hellos, Poppy promptly ushered them to the playhouse with a rushed explanation, where Danny and the pets were waiting bravely. Jitters shot up Poppy's spine as she stood atop the dirt mound that overlooked her audience.

"Welcome to Poppy's Birthday Parade!" Poppy cheered enthusiastically. "Featuring Danny and the Pets." She bowed and hit the record player in the same motion.

Danny opened the gate at the start of the music and the animals rushed out at once. At first, everything ran smoothly. Petey obediently followed his trail of carrot chunks. Ramsey struck one foot in front of the other following Danny's whistle. The chicks clung to Poppy's side as chicken feed sprinkled from her pocket. Bessy "mooed" along to the music, and Kitty, as expected, scampered off into the wood.

The audience clapped and cheered, and Poppy was overwhelmed with joy. She was sure she'd mastered the daunting task of teaching animals to march. She closed her eyes for one moment to take it all in, and the next moment her family was shouting, "Poppy!"

She opened her eyes to see her pets going berserk.

She heard Flynn shout, "That nasty dog," and turned to see Ziggy leaping over the fence and racing toward Petey the rabbit. It was a known fact that Ziggy couldn't resist fresh rabbit. Danny leapt up in an attempt to guard Petey from the beast, but Ziggy was ruthless. He knocked Danny to the dirt and raced after Petey.

"No!" Poppy screamed as she took off after Petey and Ziggy. Poppy loved all her pets but not as much as she loved Petey. Petey was her fondest friend, and it wasn't just because he was a bunny. She couldn't lose him, not when he had so much left to live for. She ran as fast as her little legs could carry her, with tears spilling down her face.

She ran and ran and ran until she couldn't run anymore. She'd made it over the fence and into Mr Petosa's yard and kept up with Ziggy most of the way, but it was not enough to save Petey. She lost Ziggy in the flock of confused sheep and certainly lost Petey.

When Poppy was sure it was too late, she dropped to the hard earth and broke into a tempest of tears. Her parade fell apart, Petey was going to be captured by a rabbit-loving predator, her newest friend had been tackled and scratched by the same predator, and on top of it all, her costume was dirty, torn, and soaked in tears. Had she spoiled everything? It was her birthday, the day she couldn't wreck with her mischief, and now she'd ruined that too.

She wondered what her mummy would have said if she were here. Would she have been disappointed?

Poppy cried harder yet, the tears streaming down her face.

"Little girl!" she heard a gruff voice bellow from behind her. She squinted through her tears to see a blurred Mr Petosa standing there.

"You shan't be here. This is my pasture!"

Poppy didn't realize that she'd trespassed too! She bawled even harder than she thought she could and shoved her tears into the grass, hoping that if she couldn't stop the storm she'd better put it to use and water the grass. She hoped her mum wasn't watching from the clouds today. She wouldn't want her mummy to see her six-year-old daughter all tragic in front of mean Mr Petosa.

"It's . . . my . . . birthday," Poppy sobbed.

And Mr Petosa wasn't sure what to say. After all, children were never his expertise.

"Oh," Mr Petosa sighed, lost on what to do.

"I'm six," she wailed.

"Well . . .," Mr Petosa racked his brain for a fitting response but couldn't find one. "Well, six-year-olds don't act like this."

Poppy burst into an even louder set of tears.

"You should really act more grown-up," he continued.

Poppy was a lost cause, and Mr Petosa's shrewd remarks were no help.

"She's perfect, thank you," a booming voice called. It was Dad. He narrowed his eyes at Mr Petosa in fury and swept up his tear-sodden daughter. "I'd invite you and your dog to stay away from my children," Dad spoke in a voice both calm and stern.

Mr Petosa stamped his foot and limped back home.

For a moment Poppy pitied Mr Petosa, but promptly returned to pitying herself. She cried into her Dad's shirt as he gallantly carried her to safety. When they were securely in their own yard, Dad sat down in the meadow grass, Poppy still in his arms. He brushed her wet waves from her face and whispered softly, "I'm so sorry, Poppy girl."

Poppy whimpered a little softer.

"Your show was marvelous, darling. Truly. And that evil dog deserves to be dead," he growled.

Poppy had never heard her father say such things, and in some strange way it was refreshing to see him not be tempered for once. One could suppose that Dad did unfamiliar things when his children were hurt. Poppy chuckled at the thought between tears.

"That's my happy girl," he smiled. "My happy, brave, smart, sweet, spunky, and strong six-year-old."

Poppy sat up, quieting her tears. And when she'd gathered her strength, she asked, "Daddy?"

"Yes, my love?"

"Do I need to act more grown-up?"

"Good heavens, no!" Dad dropped his hand in Poppy's lap. "Poppy, you don't need to act more grown-up, and don't you listen to anyone who tells you so. They are just jealous of your spirit, because they will never have what you have. Frankly, I feel sorry for them."

"Why?" she peeped.

"They grew up far too fast. And once you grow-up, you can't go back."

Poppy pondered that thought silently, and Dad interrupted.

"Poppy, I've been thinking lately . . . about your mummy."

Poppy looked into her father's kind eyes.

"Do you know how proud she would be of you?" Dad asked, and Poppy shook her head.

"She would be so proud of the little girl you've become. She really would." Dad's eyes swelled with tears.

"I wish she was still here to watch you."

Poppy grabbed his hand, and he chuckled softly.

"You must promise me something, dear."

"What, Dad?"

"You must keep being who you are, darling. Because you fill our lives with so much colour. So much." Dad planted a kiss atop his daughter's head.

Poppy wiped away her last tear and jumped into the arms of her beloved father. When they finally let go, Dad whispered in her ear,

"Everyone is inside with a surprise. Do you think you could come in and be our colourful girl? It wouldn't be a birthday party without a birthday girl."

Poppy nodded, perked up, and Dad led her home. They entered together, hand in hand, to see the picture of her family and friends laughing in a tone of giddy anticipation. Everyone was crowding around Flynn, and as Poppy approached, they parted the seas, clearing a path for Poppy to walk to her brother. In his arms sat the best birthday gift Poppy could have asked for. The return of an old friend. There sat Petey with a purple ribbon tied around his neck. Poppy jumped in joy and was baffled with surprise. She snuggled Petey to her cheek and kissed him about a hundred times. "How?" she squealed at Flynn.

Flynn shrugged heroically, and Poppy leapt up for a hug. She practically squeezed the life out of him, but he deserved it. He'd saved her most cherished friend; he was her hero.

The rest of the evening was painted with joy. Eve had cooked Poppy's most favourite supper. She was showered with hugs and laughs, Danny stayed for presents, Mr Brown's cake was scrumptious, and she had Petey back. Poppy smiled from ear to ear as she climbed into bed that night.

"I'm going to love six, Mummy," she whispered to the picture of her mother as she lay down to sleep.

And sleep she did, dreaming of the best birthday she'd ever had.

18

FIERY FLAMES

The blue sky was beautiful and awake, and the girl beneath it was just as radiant. She moved through the midmorning air like a graceful dove that just kept spinning. Rose had dreamt of flying across the stage in the famous Ballet de l'Opéra in Paris since the day she learned to dance. Mum once said she danced before she learned to walk. Rose was always aware of how proud her mother was of her. After all, it was her mother's dream before it was hers. But then Dad came along, just a tourist in her mother's city who fell in love with a French girl with a pair of ballet shoes and a wild dream. And just like that, her dream drifted off to the place where the abandoned dreams go.

It wasn't until Rose came along that Mum Marie remembered what it felt like to dance. And though she claimed she didn't miss it because she had a family in return, Rose was never fully convinced. When her mother died, Rose vowed to complete her mother's dream—or in Rose's mind, erase her mistake. She was not going to sell herself to love like her mum had. Not now. Not ever. She'd locked her heart since she'd discovered the five positions of ballet and had no intention of unlocking it.

"ROSE!" Eve dashed outside.

"What?" Rose blurted, clearly irritated. She was working on her pirouette and Eve had totally interrupted her.

"Guess what?"

"Tell me already!" Rose zipped.

Eve ignored this for she was far too happy to let Rose's irritation dampen her excitement.

"Henry is coming to visit from London. He's going to spend the weekend with us! Henry!" Eve spun into the air.

"Here?" Rose questioned.

"Yes!" Eve squealed. "Isn't that marvelous?"

"I suppose," Rose shrugged.

"At least pretend to be happy!" Eve squinted, obviously offended. "He could be your brother-in-law you know!" And then she was gone.

"Bluh!" Rose gagged as her sister left. She was not ready for brothers-in-law's or even talk of them. Besides, Eve wasn't even nineteen yet. She was far too young and foolish to be blindsided by love! Rose had to find a way to keep her sister away from love. Her best thoughts usually came when she was dancing, so she hit the old record player and began spinning again. Spinning, leaping, and tiptoeing, as if plateauing atop the May breeze.

. . .

Two days passed and Rose thought of no way to keep Henry from Eve. The preparations for his arrival were in full swing and she realized the visit was truly happening. Eve was covered from head to toe in flour for she was making her lemon tarts for Henry. Bea and Oliver were pretending that the brooms were swords as they fenced down the hall—not much sweeping was taking place. Poppy, Lucy, and Danny were making signs to welcome Henry, and Flynn and Tommy were in the attic making a list of questions to ask the mystery boyfriend. They had to ensure he was good enough for Eve, but more importantly, they had to ensure he would not distract her from the kitchen.

Once the house was spit-spot, and once Eve had been defloured and properly dressed, the Bean children piled into the pickup and were off to the Windermere train station. That is, everyone except Rose. Rose had locked herself in the girls' room with her favourite dance theory book, although not much reading was taking place as frustrations were building. She secretly wished that her family would never return with that monstrous Henry, at least not with him in one piece. Rose was starting to believe that she did not only dislike romance but that she LOATHED IT!

Soon enough, the cottage was again full of commotion and chaos, and Rose was forced to leave her room.

"Rose! Come out here and meet Henry!" Eve hollered.

Rose took a deep breath in an attempt to release her angst. She smoothed her clothes and marched out with her nose held high. Eve flashed her the "be nice" face and Rose ignored it. Henry was tall and strong. His hair a milky brown and his eyes were honest and kind—the classic prince.

"Hello, Rose," Henry smiled. "It's lovely to meet you." He outstretched his hand for her to shake, and she dodged it.

Clearly embarrassed, Henry reached for a bouquet of fresh red roses from the counter and handed them to Rose.

"Isn't that sweet, Rose! He got you flowers to match your name!" Eve clung to Henry's arm.

Rose considered accepting them, she really did. And not just because they were pretty, but also because it was so vital to Eve that she accept them. But the fire within the chamber of Rose's soul burned far too strong to ignore, stronger than the rules of courtesy and politeness burned themselves.

"I thought you were *Eve's* boyfriend." The soul fire had won.

Rose thrust the bouquet into Henry's hands and turned to leave. Henry's face flushed pink with embarrassment, and Eve abandoned his arm to scold her sister. "Rose!"

Rose slammed the door in Eve's face.

"Rose!" Eve didn't care if the door was slammed in her face or not as Rose had crossed the line. She burst into the room and shouted, "Get back to the kitchen and apologize!"

But Rose was in no form to apologize, especially not to a man who intended to take her sister away.

"You know," Eve was fuming, "he got flowers for all of us girls! Red roses for you, pink roses for me, daisies for Bea, lilies for Lucy, and poppies for Poppy. And that was a very kind thing to do." She was now red in the face, fuming. "That was no way to act to a kind man, especially . . . especially . . ."

"Especially what?" Rose interrupted.

"Especially a man that I so happen to be in love with!" she shouted.

"Oh please!" Rose shouted back.

"Excuse me?"

The rest of the crew sat awkwardly in the kitchen pretending they couldn't hear what was unfolding on the other side of the wall.

"Go back to your charming prince, CINDERELLA!" Rose screamed at the top of her lungs.

Eve was near tears and absolutely appalled. "I WOULD RATHER BE ANYWHERE THAN HERE WITH YOU!" Eve yelled, biting back the tears. And then she was gone, just as she'd gone before.

Rose was left in silence, with only her thoughts. And she remained in that state for two whole days. Remorse demanded authority over her entire being, and she sat paralyzed in her own sins, haunted by the ghost of her fiery heart. She sat in her room, quiet and isolated. She was visited by Flynn, Bea, and Oliver on separate occasions, but she quickly shooed them away. Dad thought about confronting her but decided that he'd try "time" first to see if it would soften her up. She didn't come out for meals and avoided Eve and Henry at all costs. In her room, she sat stewing and wishing her mum was there to tell her how to climb out of the hole she'd buried herself in. But help was distant, and her soul too racked to find peace. The only thing that felt familiar was the bitter loneliness that her rage often brought.

19

TWO HALVES

Silence is a precarious creature and can do many uncertain things. It can heal broken wounds, cleanse the worries of the soul, and provide an abundance of perspective. Silence also has the capability to inflict unquenchable pain. Since Rose was cruel to Henry, Eve and Rose became two islands separated by a raging sea. Rose's heart had bathed in silence but not of the cleansing sort.

Though she craved peace and quiet most days in the rambunctious cottage, peace and quiet evolved into a reoccurring haunting nightmare she'd inflicted upon herself. She spent the two whole days watching the sunlight dance on the carpet and wished she too could dance. But as the shadow of remorse often occludes, Rose could not hear the music. Her guilt was far too monstrous.

Her thoughts were interrupted by an urgent knock at the door.

"Go away, Flynn!" she shouted.

The door swung open but it was not Flynn on the other side. It was Dad who emerged through the shadow.

"Is Flynn being obnoxious again? I cannot believe that boy," Dad stated in his usual lighthearted tone.

"He never stopped being obnoxious." Rose rolled her eyes.

"What will we ever do with him? You'll be happy to know he's in the yard, and so are the others," Dad chuckled and then invited himself into the room. He sat beside his daughter and said nothing.

Rose quickly grew impatient and blurted, "What is it, Father?" Rose was the only one in the Bean family who called him "Father."

"What?" Dad was startled.

"Why-are-you-here?" Rose said slowly to ensure her father could understand. "You've come to scold me, haven't you?" Rose had dealt with parents long enough to know when she was about to get in trouble.

"No, no. Of course not, Rosie!" And Dad was the only one that got away with calling Rose "Rosie." She'd always thought it sounded rather weak.

"Can I tell you a story?"

"About what?" Rose wasn't in the mood for a story.

"About your mother." Dad looked his daughter in the eyes.

Mention of Mum left Rose interested, but she couldn't let Dad know that, so she shrugged and moaned, "All right!"

Dad chuckled as if he could read his daughter's mind and then began.

"When we first started dating, we were just foolish children."

Rose could imagine her father being a foolish child, but her mum not quite.

"When she first came to Grasmere, I made sure to introduce her to all of my mates."

"Why?" Rose wasn't sure why he was telling her all of this.

"One, I thought she was the most marvelous thing that ever happened to humanity, so I imagined everyone should know her. Two, I thought others would be amazed that a gorgeous Frenchie girl would give a goofy country Brit boy a chance. And I rather liked watching people experience confoundment." Dad chuckled his jolly chuckle, reminiscing on his boyhood self.

Rose's father was a lot of things but a show-off was never one of them. She looked at him in disgust and he replied, "I know that sounds absolutely mad—"

"It is." Rose stuck her nose out.

"Yes, I suppose it was. I was smitten!" He flailed his arms in the air. "Don't say I didn't warn you about love."

Rose rolled her eyes as Dad continued.

"Everyone loved her. *Loved* is probably an understatement. In fact, do you know what my father said when he met her?"

"What?" Rose asked.

"He said, 'She's perfect, Max. What I don't understand is why would she marry you?'" Dad tried to imitate Grandad Bean's gravelly voice.

"They loved her beauty, kindness, and fairness. But most of all, they loved her humour."

"Humour?" Rose had never thought of her mother as a particularly amusing woman.

"She just said things."

Rose glared at Dad.

"She was stubborn, quick—oh boy, was she quick." Dad took a hollow breath and then added, "And fiery."

"Like you," he whispered.

"No," Rose muttered, and Dad disagreed.

"You are your mother's daughter."

"No, Father."

"No what?" Dad was legitimately curious.

"I am not like Mum!" Rose shook her fists in the air.

"And why would you say that?"

"I'm terrible, Father. Terrible!" Rose swallowed loudly.

"Rosie," Dad tried to stop her, but that was his first mistake.

"Oh yes, I am! Don't you see what I've done? Are you completely blind?" her voice went brittle. "I've broken my sister's heart. And hers is not the first I've broken. I've broken many others, and I'd be lying to say I'm finished. I can't help it most of the time. I'm just angry."

"Rosie, dear. Slow do-w-n," Dad tried to steady her trembling arm, and she swatted him away.

"I won't SLOW DOWN! Because I can't. I cannot let go of my convictions no matter how hard I try, and before I know it, they've turned into radioactive explosions that CANNOT BE STOPPED." Rose wasn't done.

"Rose, look at me."

"NO! I won't look at you, because I'm not finished. I'm a reckless, ruthless, restless monster who can't stop or slow down. Half the time against my will." Rose was speeding up now and was far from slowing down.

"My love," Dad tried once more, "just listen."

"I'M NOT DONE!" she screamed as loud as her voice could go.

Dad went silent and gazed into his daughter's dragon eyes.

"Eve may never talk to me again." she said, much quieter this time. A single tear fell down her face and her father wiped it away with his thumb.

"Will you listen now?" he whispered kindly.

Rose nodded, and he solemnly started up.

"Your mother had two very powerful halves of her soul."

"Oh great." Rose rolled her eyes. Here came another long story.

"That isn't fair," Dad's voice was now stern and disciplinary, which Rose respected. She went silent.

"One half was obedient, good, kind, and always fair. This side, from time to time, was quite bossy." Dad laughed. "The other half of her soul was stubborn, fiery, passionate, and extremely strong-willed.

This part had the tendency to say regretful things and occasionally explode. Sound familiar?"

Rose nodded shyly.

"Marie had five daughters. But two of them are much more like her than the others. Do you know which two?"

Rose nodded, less shyly this time, for this was common knowledge to all who knew the Beans.

"Eve owns your mother's sensitive and obedient side. She took one half of your mother's soul." Dad nudged his daughter. "And you, you are your mother's living fire. You have her passion, stubbornness, and pride."

Rose was starting to catch on.

"And you know what else? Your mother's soul that was split in half was always at war with itself." He took another hollow breath and began again, "Yet over time she learned to love both halves and became the confident, controlled, and radiant woman you knew her to be."

Rose sighed, for she knew what her father was to say next.

"If your mum was here, she'd tell you this exact thing. She would say that you need to find a way to respect Eve. And you need to use your fire for good and not to burn other people."

Rose said nothing for she knew her father was quite correct. Admitting it was the thing she couldn't handle.

"Rosie?" Dad looked her dead in the eyes.

"Yes?"

SHELBY EVE SAYER

"I must tell you that you have more passion in your eyes than most people can find in their entire being. And passion will take you places that others could never dream of."

"What about Bea?"

"Bea is passionate in a different way. Bea could fall in love with any way of life. But you, Rosie, you're different. You have convictions that you cannot forget, and you are fiercely protective of them, no matter what. Do or die."

Rose liked the sound of this.

"And that, my love, is a gift. And you must promise to never lose hold of that. You just need to begin to tame it like Mum did."

"Promise," Rose answered sincerely, and for the first time in two days she smiled. It was small and subtle, but a smile nonetheless.

"One more thing, dear."

"What?" she asked, forgetting her father was there.

"I love you more than you could ever know."

"Promise?" she asked.

"Promise." Dad smiled, stood up, and then slipped away, leaving the familiar trace of magic that lingered in every room he left.

GARDEN OF

green beans

rosemary

parsnip

potato

basil

radish

onion

peas

rosemary

carrot

tomato

LAVENDER LANE

145

20

HEAVY CURRENTS

The sunlight sliced through the open window, tempting the two youngest Beans sitting inside of it. It was bothersome to be stuck inside on a rainy day, but it was unbearable to be stuck inside on a glorious day like this one! They'd begged their older siblings to let them go play in the swimming hole, but Eve was firmly against Lucy and Poppy going alone. Since it was only the first of June, the water level in the river was still awfully high and fast. And though Lucy could watch after Poppy, Eve was still uncertain.

And of course, the vote of the older, more responsible children carried more weight.

"They always get to make all the decisions," Poppy wailed.

"I can be responsible," Lucy thought aloud.

"And you're way nicer about it than Rose," Poppy pointed out.

It didn't matter anyway, because Rose was engrossed in practicing ballet for her next lesson and didn't have time for their foolish adventure.

Flynn couldn't come because he was with Tommy in the attic discussing a particularly breath-taking girl named Jane.

Oliver and Bea pinkie swore to take the girls to the stream after their bicycle adventure. They were always on bicycle adventures lately and it was starting to interfere with family plans.

"If we *must* be chaperoned then at least Bea and Oliver agreed to take us," Lucy reminded Poppy.

"But, Lucy, they might not be back for a long while! I can't wait that long."

Looking from their lousy dollhouse to the beaming rays that danced on the walls then to Poppy, Lucy felt a sudden rush of adrenaline. It was this adrenaline that led to rebellion.

"Let's go," Lucy pronounced. "We can show them that we are responsible."

"Yes!" Poppy squealed, who loved it when her older siblings listened to her ideas.

They rummaged through the dresser looking for their swimming costumes and pulled them on without any consideration for detection. Lucy's was baby blue with white polka dots and Poppy's bright purple. Poppy slipped on her wellies and Lucy buckled her favourite summer sandals to her feet. They tiptoed down the hall and snuck out the backdoor that led to the meadow. They broke into a gallop, headed for the wood, feeling freedom at last. Rose was practicing on the edge of the meadow and caught them out of the corner of her eye.

"And where do you think you're going?" she inquired with a condescending tone.

"Off to the wood!" Lucy hollered over her shoulder as she zipped by.

Rose shrugged as she transitioned smoothly to the next position.

Poppy and Lucy shot through the meadow with their eyes riveted to the stout sign posted at the entrance of the grove of trees. The girls painted it with Mum long ago and it read "The Wood" in Mum's beautiful script. They weaved through the meandering forest, their arms spread out like airplane wings as they brushed the vegetation that lined the trail. The sun forced its way through the cover of the treetops, fuelling their flight. They belonged amongst nature and its wild music.

The sound of the babbling brook broke through the trees and Lucy chanted, "We're almost there!" The brook ran into a wider body of water, almost the size of a river, and the water deepened as the girls skipped farther down the road.

Poppy came to an abrupt halt and whispered between pants, "We made it."

Lucy ran to the trunk of the tree she loved to climb best, just before the river. She took a hollow breath and scaled its strong limbs.

Poppy, who was not quite strong enough to climb such tall trees, sat on the muddy shore and dipped her little toes into the crisp water.

"How does it feel, Poppy?" Lucy questioned, focused on which branch to perch her foot on.

Poppy giggled and answered, "It's a little chilly!"

She splashed her feet in the water and then bravely stepped into the quick moving current before fully warming up to the temperature.

Lucy, who was focused on her tree climbing, didn't notice Poppy wade into the water.

The water was deeper than expected from the spring runoff and it hit Poppy all at once. She was just beginning to learn how to swim and had no business in the quickly moving runoff with no life vest. It all happened too quickly—she was caught in the current. Realizing she was in trouble, Poppy believed she could make it safely to the shore. She fought to keep her head above the water and paddle toward Lucy, but the current was strong and seemed to pull her in. She felt her strength weaken as the water rushed around her. It was too much for her to bear.

Flailing and afraid, she called out, "Luc-y!"

Lucy's heart dropped instantly, seeing her precious sister.

"Poppy, no!" she wailed.

The cold water shot up Poppy's nose and she began to cry.

"Luc-yyy!"

Lucy jumped down from the middle branch with a surge of adrenaline that surpassed the one that got her into this predicament.

She hit the muddy forest floor with force and tumbled into a somersault descending from the limbs above. Enveloped in sheer panic, she grabbed a low-hanging branch near the edge of the water. She knelt on the shore as she knew better than to wade in, bending nearly in half to extend the branch to her sister. A flood of water pushed Poppy further off her footing. Lucy nearly fainted in a panic.

"Poppy, please!" Lucy began to cry too. "Poppy be brave! Gra-b the branch!" She trembled helplessly.

Poppy outstretched her frail arm and wrapped her blue fingers around the tip of the branch.

For a split-second Lucy thought she had her, but the branch wasn't strong enough to hold a girl and it snapped in half. Horrified and helpless, she screamed a blood-curdling shriek.

"HELP! SOMEBODY HELP!" Her voice broke and tears streamed down her face as she looked at her sister, who was now too far for Lucy to reach. Poppy tried to fight for her place above the current, but the force of nature was too powerful.

Lucy's high-pitched scream carried through the trees where all fell silent; even the birds stopped their chirping and took notice. Across the meadow, Rose heard the scream mid-pirouette. She heard fear and knew the scream. All at once lightning struck and she broke into a sprint. Running faster than time itself, she broke through the forest and toward the brook. Her hair broke free of its bindings and sailed fearlessly behind her back.

"HE-LP! Poppy, I can't lose you!" Lucy pleaded as she watched Poppy's strawberry head bob up and down, still fighting for air. Lucy tried to get herself to leap after her drowning sister but fear paralyzed her. Blurry eyed, she cried out, shaking as her muscles went limp.

Poppy couldn't fight against the current any longer. Her limbs went still as she slipped under the surface of the water. She could feel her breathing cease, but matching the fire of death himself, Rose broke through the trees like a torment of flame. She didn't think and dove into the cutting water after Poppy. Lucy's stone-cold eyes registered hope as she saw Rose dive after Poppy. Still trembling, Lucy leaned over the edge as if to guide Rose to Poppy. Rose fought against the rock bed toward Poppy, who lay lifeless on the bottom. Rose's chestnut waves danced in the water, and she wrapped her strong arms around Poppy's torso and lifted her from the silty riverbed, where she had become wedged against a large boulder. She lifted her from the pressure of the current, fighting against every force of nature that said she'd lose the fight. Providence was on her side as she reached Poppy and gained solid enough footing to hoist her atop the water. The view of the shoreline blurred and faded. She laid Poppy on the dirt floor and pulled herself up out of the river.

Taking one look at sobbing Lucy, she shouted with force, "Go! Go get someone!"

Lucy ran, and she ran fast.

Water dripping from Rose's clothes, she leaned over her still sister and laid her ear on her heart. She had no heartbeat. Innately, Rose placed her hands one atop another on Poppy's tiny chest. Her heart racing but her mind clear, she began chest compressions.

"Come on, Poppy! Come on!" Rose begged.

After several chest compressions, Rose gave her innocent sister some of her breath. And with no sign of life, she began chest compressions once again.

"Come on, Poppy. Please." Her eyes swelled with tears and she let them fall onto her sister's grey skin.

Rosemary Bean put everything she ever had into saving her sister, praying that it would be enough to let her live.

Oliver, Bea, and Lucy broke through the trees as Rose was offering breath.

Brave Rose inhaled as deeply as she could and then exhaled, filling Poppy's lungs. Oliver, Bea, and Lucy held hands, looking toward the heavens as there was clearly no alternative, putting every ounce of their faith in God and in Rose. Praying that he'd spare Poppy's life.

Rose returned to compressions, her tears now raining on Poppy's face.

It was as if Poppy sensed her siblings couldn't catch a breath of their own. Her eyelids fluttered and she began violently coughing up water. Turning to retch, Poppy rejoined life. Rose fell to her back, her heart still racing ten times the speed God intended it to. Poppy retched once more, and tears poured out from all, half thankful, half terrorized for what had just happened. Lucy embraced Poppy's numb legs, warming them with her hot tears.

"I thought I lost you, Poppy," Lucy muttered between cries.

And Poppy uttered her first, very weak, words since life had been restored, "I'm here now."

Her frail words hugged Lucy's broken heart and Lucy smiled feebly.

Bea scooped Poppy into her arms, rocking her back and forth, while Oliver comforted Rose.

"You saved her life, Rose! You are a he-ro—" Oliver's voice broke in gratitude and fear as he grasped Rose's pruned hand.

"Come on! We have to get her warm!" Bea shouted, wrapping her shivering sister in her warm arms.

Oliver ripped his shirt off and offered to carry Poppy. They covered her half-naked body in his shirt and carried her through the meadow and back toward the cottage, moving as quickly as they could.

Eve stepped in the front doorway for she'd just returned from town and had no idea what had happened. She was instantly struck with dread at the sight of Poppy in Oliver's arms. She dropped her shopping bags and raced out into the meadow, leaving the door wide open.

Flynn and Tommy came down the stairs two steps at a time to see what Eve's scream was all about.

Poppy's skin regained most of its colour as the others learned of the horror of the last hour. As they tucked her into her bed, their neighbour Dr Boris came running in with Flynn, who'd gone to fetch him. Having checked her vitals, he assured the worried children that she wouldn't need to be hospitalized unless conditions worsened.

"She will probably be down for a few days, but Poppy is young and strong. Her shock will probably last longer than anything else. You are all very lucky lads. Very lucky. I will check back in when your father is home," Dr Boris stated, closing Poppy's door behind him so she could rest.

The children moved to the living room, where they waited for Dad. All but Lucy, that is. She couldn't leave Poppy's side, nor could she stop the tears. Rose stared blankly in shock; her mind couldn't process the events that had just taken place. Flynn sat next to her thinking about what would've happened if his brave twin sister hadn't been there to save his baby sister's life. When Dad came home, he swung the front door open, dropped his briefcase, and raced straight to Poppy's room without greeting his children. Leaving the door wide open, he knelt by her side and let his head fall onto her sleeping torso.

The Bean cottage resonated with emotion, thanks to God, amazement, and terror. After nearly losing Poppy, they hugged her harder and loved her more than they ever had before. For the thought of almost losing another Bean was unbearable, and they each silently hoped they would never be asked to face that sorrow again.

21

SHOCK

A tense kind of quiet filled the Bean cottage the following day. Poppy spent most of the day in bed and the others stayed within her reach, including Dad, who took a sick day from work to be with his children. Being so close to tragedy and avoiding it was hard to process for all the Beans, but Dad was especially impacted. How did they get so lucky? How could this happen to his little girl? And most pressing of all, how had she gotten into this predicament in the first place?

Even a fly on the wall could sense Dad's uneasiness. He sat and stewed on his thoughts all day, making his children nervous. To the Bean children, it was a relief when after Poppy had gone to sleep Dad spoke.

"Meet me in the sitting room in five minutes," he told them without giving them a choice.

Doing as they were told, the children gathered in the sitting room and sat on the edge of the sofa, nervously awaiting Dad's preamble.

"Something is weighing on me," he finally admitted after several seconds of gathering his thoughts.

The children blinked back at him.

"Wh-what? An-and . . . why? But . . . how?" Dad asked in near gibberish.

"What?" Rose was the only one brave enough to ask for more clarity.

"Yesterday, in the wood, Poppy, vibrant Poppy, almost dying . . . h-ow . . . how did it happen? I must know!" He quaked and so did the room.

At this, Lucy burst into tears and fled to her room. Lucy was a strong girl, but nearly losing her sister and feeling responsible for the tragedy would break anyone.

This time, Dad didn't follow her. He had to know what had happened in the wood. He would comfort Lucy later.

"Will someone speak up and explain?" Dad asked in a softer but equally demanding tone.

"We promised to take the girls to the swimming hole after our bike ride but they didn't listen!" Bea defended herself.

"We would have protected them," Oliver added.

"I wasn't paying attention," Rose admitted, "but they aren't my responsibility."

"I wasn't either," Flynn said.

"Dad," Eve spoke up, and Dad listened.

"I should've been here to prevent it . . . it is my fault . . . I should have been here." Eve's chin fell to her chest. She felt almost as much remorse as Lucy.

Dad, realizing this line of questioning was not going to be helpful, looked at each of his children and love returned to his eyes. "No," he whispered. "Eve, it is not your fault. Same goes for each of you. You are all asked to do SO much." Dad's eyes filled with emotion. "We've dodged tragedy, thanks to God and thanks to our brave Rose, who is the saving fire that promises Poppy a bright future, just as her past has been." Dad found a smile for his heroine daughter, and Rose adjusted her posture, accepting the compliment with dignity.

"Poppy will be okay. And so will we," Dad barely hesitated on his last promise.

"Indeed we will," Bea agreed in a low whisper.

"We've overcome much worse," Rose reminded them.

"Yes, Rose, we have," Dad reflected. "You are all such courageous children—no, young people." His eyes traveled from Flynn and Oliver to his daughters.

After a moment's silence and pondering, Rose stood up and announced, "I'm going to talk to Lucy," and she disappeared down the hall.

"Lucy," Rose blurted in the dark.

Lucy was curled up on the rug, she couldn't stop crying. Rose joined her on the rug and Lucy fell into her arms.

"It's all my fault," Lucy moaned.

"You know, Lucy," Rose started, "I think quite the opposite."

"You have to say that!" Lucy cried hysterically.

"No, I don't. I'm not forced to say anything. I'm entitled to my own words." Rose stuck her nose out. "And I have actual evidence, Lucy, despite what you may think."

Lucy continued to cry.

"Poppy really wanted to go to the swimming hole, did she not?" Rose inquired.

Lucy said nothing.

"Did she not?" Rose repeated louder this time.

Lucy nodded between wails.

"And you went with her, did you not?"

"I wanted to show . . . I was . . . responsible enough. That . . . I could be taken seriously," Lucy confessed.

"Ahh." Rose grinned. "I've been there," she empathized. "There is no shame in wanting such things, Lucy. Nobody blames you for that. The entire family is in the sitting room as we speak, equally doubting their own actions."

Rose cleared her throat. "When she began to drown, you called for help, did you not?"

"Yes," Lucy wailed.

"Well, Lucy, here's my claim: Poppy has double the mischief of a normal child, and on top of that, Poppy is decisive. She makes up her mind quickly and sticks to it. A Bean family trait. If you, Lucy Jean Bean, were not with Poppy yesterday, she would have gone alone. I am sure of it. And if she had gone by herself, without telling anyone, she would surely be gone, and we would have no idea where to find her."

Lucy flinched at this thought.

"But you, Lucy, were there to call for help. Which brought me. So, Lucy, you saved Poppy just as much as I did. That's my consensus."

Strangely, this calmed Lucy.

"But I could have avoided all of this if we'd never gone at all," was Lucy's rebuttal.

"Don't be daft, Lucy!" Rose laughed. "Yesterday, you encountered what Bea would title 'a call to adventure.' And for us Beans that is irresistible. Another Bean family trait. Yesterday's events were inevitable."

Lucy's cries ceased. She sat upright and reported, "Thank you, Rose, I feel better."

Rose nodded, stood up, and left Lucy alone with this new thought.

22

A MAP TO NOWHERE

Many months had passed since Poppy's life was threatened in the wood, and for a while, things around the Bean home were different. It was an unspoken understanding that risks were not to be taken. It was the birth of 1956 and things seemed to be changing quietly without any warning whatsoever.

Bea felt the impact of this quiet and gradual change, and it troubled her because in her mind the shift endangered childhood. But Bea was armed and ready to fight for it. Childhood meant imagination and reaching exhilarating heights that practical adults simply didn't understand. Heights sensible people couldn't dream of. There was something magical about living boundlessly with no limits or fence posts. Something infinite about chasing dreams, disregarding society norms and bad weather, and Bea was not going to trade that mentality for the alternative. She was determined to save childhood, and she was going to accomplish it through her pen.

That rainy January morning, Bea scooted under the roll-top desk in the attic where she found herself most days. The window was barely cracked open and the soft pitter-patter of the rain on the metal roof was the background music to her magic making. She started at the top of the page and began scratching away. Left to right. Left to right. Today she wouldn't be bothered. Today was dedicated to writing, to creativity, and to a pull that couldn't be ignored.

"Oi, Beazy! Are you up there?" It was Poppy skipping up the stairs to the attic.

"Yes, Poppy, I am." Bea tried to sound enthusiastic but felt caught rather than pleased to see Poppy.

"I'm off to feed the chickies. Can you come?" Poppy flashed Bea her most convincing puppy eyes.

"I'm busy now, Pops. Have you asked Danny?"

"He's in Keswick." Poppy curled her lip to emphasize the feeling of loneliness.

"I guess . . . I could take a break," Bea thought aloud, feeling generous.

When Bea could finally wriggle away from Poppy, she returned promptly to the attic, where she continued scratching away. Feverishly this time, she wrote in hopes of catching up on all she'd missed while feeding the chickens with Poppy. Fifteen minutes passed before another set of feet came tiptoeing up the steps. This time it was Lucy.

"Off to organize the treehouse. Care to come?" Lucy asked.

"I'd normally love to but . . ." Bea sighed.

"Got to a good part?" Lucy was the most understanding of Bea and her writing. She loved books almost as much as Bea and would hate to interrupt her sister mid-masterpiece.

"Yes." Bea grinned, glad to be understood.

"I'll ask Eve." And Lucy tiptoed away.

Bea dropped her shoulders and began for the third time. "*The charm*," she thought. At last, she was completely alone with her pen, paper, and thoughts. But she was badly mistaken, for not one but two pairs of feet came tromping up the creaky attic steps.

"Ah rats," Bea snapped, wondering if a moment alone was too grand of an ask.

Flynn and Tommy stepped into the light. "Eve is off with Lucy somewhere." Flynn swayed cautiously.

"And we're hungry," Tommy added.

"How good of a sandwich can you make?" Flynn raised an eyebrow less cautiously.

Of all the things that had changed in the past year, Flynn's constant hunger was not one of them.

"You can't be serious." Bea glared. She could hold her frustration for her two adorable little sisters, but Flynn and Tommy were neither adorable nor little.

"Bea!" Flynn whined. "We both know you can make a mean sandwich!"

"I'm flattered," Bea said sarcastically.

And Tommy, who didn't know the difference between sarcasm and sincerity, blurted, "So you'll make us one?"

Bea gave both Flynn and his dim-witted crony a nice long stare.

"Oh come on!" Flynn gasped. "It doesn't even have to be a sandwich!"

"Flynn," Bea stood up from her chair, "if you blockheads are still here in ten seconds then you'll have bigger fish to fry."

"Ooh! Fish sounds good." Tommy couldn't keep up.

Flynn, who had enough brains for both boys, grabbed his mate by the wrist and yanked him down the stairs.

Bea's head fell onto the desk and she said a silent prayer that this would be the last of today's interruptions.

"Where was I?" she asked herself, and recommenced. Every word felt like a story itself. The words danced across the page with eloquence and passion. She was stuck in a trance, trapped in a writer's daze, and she could not be disturbed. Or so she thought. Perhaps she should have knocked on wood to secure her luck.

Yet one more trot up the attic stairs intruded on her trance, and she picked up her pen midsentence but didn't dare look away from her page.

"Oi, Bea," the voice hollered.

Bea knew the intruder by his voice. However, his usually crisp voice was rather pitchy.

"What?" she asked, at the end of her fuse.

"Oh." Oliver hopped away from her, pretending to be afraid, though he really wasn't. "Should I go?" he shrieked in a teasing tone.

"That would be grand," Bea whispered.

But Oliver wasn't convinced.

"Not happy to see me then?" Oliver clutched his chest, pretending to be offended. Both he and Bea knew he was amused rather than offended. In the year that he'd lived with them, Bea had learned that offense was something Oliver was incapable of experiencing. Every passive-aggressive comment along with the overt put-down rolled off Oliver like water off a duck's back.

"Oliver." Bea tried to pace herself.

Though cool-headed, Oliver was a trained professional at driving others away from their intended task.

"No time for your handsome friend?" Oliver stroked his hair.

"Oliver!" Bea lunged toward him, about to burst.

"Who are you and what have you done with the kind and patient Beatrice Bean?" he questioned, and Bea pinned him to the wall, her pen tucked safely behind her ear.

"Too bad, for I had something rather exciting to say," he sang.

Bea let go of him somewhat abruptly, and he dropped to the floor dramatically.

"I forgot what it felt like to breathe," he gasped.

Bea folded her arms and sat facing him. "Oliver?"

He raised an eyebrow.

"Do you like your neck?"

"Uh . . . sure?" He laughed in confusion.

"Well, don't get too used to having one," Bea stated abruptly, sounding an awful lot like Rose.

"Whoa. I didn't know you could talk like that, Bea," he laughed, clutching his neck.

"Sorry," she giggled, realizing she'd gone too far. "Now, tell me the secret and you will never have to worry about your safety again!"

Oliver let go of his neck and grinned his familiar mysterious grin. His eyes sparkled with a mixture of nervousness, and utter exhilaration, as he opened his mouth to share the news. He pulled his father's briefcase from behind his back and Bea sprang into the air.

"It involves the briefcase?" her voice cracked as it always did when she got excited. She didn't notice him bring the case up the stairs as he had crept up on her.

"Yes," Oliver nodded fervently, matching her tone of voice.

Bea's imagination ignited and her mind quickly jumped to a list of possibilities. She pushed them away, trying to focus only on Oliver. He opened the briefcase. "Ahem," he cleared his throat. "I was bored and looking at the inside of the case, and was sliding my finger across the leather." He demonstrated on the inner lid. "And I found this."

Bea's mouth dropped. Oliver slid his hand into a discreet pocket that they'd never noticed before. He pulled out an envelope that was labeled in slanted lettering: "Confidential."

"You must be joking!" Bea shoved Oliver to the ground in surprise, nearly knocking the wind out of him. "Have you opened it?" She helped him up.

"Not without you of course!" He was shocked that she'd imagine him doing such a thing without her.

"Is that so?" Bea was flattered.

"Will you open it for me please?"

"I wouldn't dare!" Bea scoffed, but secretly, she wanted nothing more than to open it.

"Go on." Oliver motioned. "I insist."

"Really?" Bea's voice cracked again, and she peeled the envelope open in one greedy rip.

"Whoa gently now," Oliver whispered.

She giggled as she slid out a square piece of parchment. In purple ink the name "Vern" was written, with a strange address inscribed below the name.

"Do you know a Vern?" Bea asked.

"No, but he was mentioned in my mother's letter to my dad. Remember?"

"That's right. What did she say about him again?"

Oliver pulled the letter out from between the pages of his dad's travel journal. Aloud, he read the line, "Vern is well. Still caged up in his shack, and I don't think he'll ever come out. He's become too comfortable with his private life I suppose. I keep telling him to get over it and enjoy the world. He says he's "enjoying it just fine in his little corner." You know Vern. Never listens. What a delightful, nincompoop."

"We have to find out who he is, Oliver. He might know something about your parents," Bea said with wide eyes.

"Agreed," Oliver nodded.

"One moment," Bea said over her shoulder as she tore down the steps and rushed in and out of Dad's room, snatching up the map of England that he kept in his dresser on the way out.

"What's the address?" she asked, out of breath.

"Forty-four Winona Road, Mungrisdale, United Kingdom," Oliver told her, and the two scanned the map.

"Mungrisdale!" Oliver pointed.

"No way! It's only two towns over!" Bea jumped

The two friends examined the minute dot on the map. It was in the middle of nowhere but also unbelievably close. Oliver looked hopefully at Bea, and she proclaimed without a second blink, "Go get your things!!"

"We're going, aren't we?" Oliver didn't need Bea to answer; her eyes said it all. Oliver grabbed the map, some snacks, and the car keys, while Bea scribbled a note on the back of one of Eve's stray recipes. It read,

We left to solve a mystery.

We'll be back ASAP and will call with updates when we can get to a tele.

Love,

Bea & Oliver

Without another thought, Bea and Oliver were rolling down the lane in Dad's pickup, gone on an adventure, visualizing what grand possibilities could await them at a nondescript tiny dot on a map.

23

VERN

Dad's pickup meandered through the hillside, and Bea and Oliver were filled with anticipation. They drove until the snow-covered fields, once crawling with civilization, turned into fields of sheep bleating at the birds. And once the roads turned to dirt and the only sign of human life was a telephone box and wooden bench alongside the road, they knew they had followed the map correctly. They continued down the main road until they found the Mungrisdale Petrol Station. Bea hopped out of the truck to ask for directions to Winona Road.

"They said to continue straight for five miles and we will find a gravel road on our left," Bea directed.

Oliver nodded in understanding, and they rolled down the road. They found the short gravel road with no trouble. Winona Road led to a red-planked shack. Bea and Oliver could only see a sliver of the shack as it was hiding behind a wall of overgrown shrubberies dripping with frost.

"Do you think he's still here?" Bea whispered as they hopped out of the truck.

"Yes," Oliver nodded. He'd spotted a stack of freshly chopped wood leaning against the shack.

He approached the screen door with a certainty that Bea didn't expect. In his palm, he clutched a picture of his parents as evidence of his purpose. Something felt familiar to him about this place but he didn't know what. He studied the stack of clean-cut wood as they approached the door. Someone lived here. He just knew it.

Oliver pounded his fist against the screen door with a determined gusto. No one came, nor was there audible movement from inside the house, but Oliver didn't surrender. Something had brought him here and he was going to find out what.

"Oliver." Bea rested her hand on his shoulder.

He brushed her away. "No, not yet."

He pounded harder on the door. No reply. Just before Oliver looked for another way in, he called out, "I know you're in there VERN!"

He was surprised to hear the brave voice that came out when he opened his mouth. This realization bolstered him.

"And what are you going to do about it?" a gruff and somewhat croaky voice bellowed back.

Bea flashed him a hopeful smile, which Oliver returned. His voice like thunder, he shouted into the door, "Come out here and we'll see."

"Some nerve!" the voice croaked back. "Who are yer, the Interpol?"

"We mean no harm!" Bea shouted through the crack in the door.

Bea and Oliver could hear the man approach the door from inside of the shack. His footsteps were like falling timber that hit the ground with an alarming thump. The screen door swung open and a large-bottomed man stepped out. Patches of ginger-grey hair were planted randomly across his balding head. One of his eyes was beetle black and lazy, the other a deep blue. He wore a scraggly beard and a look of self-inflicted solitude. His nose was large and disproportional to his face, yet there was a part of him that felt familiar to Oliver.

"What do you fools want?" Vern scratched his scraggly beard.

Suddenly Oliver's body went numb and he couldn't speak.

"Who'd you say yer were?" Vern raised an eyebrow at Oliver.

"I didn't," Oliver studied Vern's face.

"Well, who are yer?"

"I'm Oliver," Oliver hesitated.

"Oliver who?"

"OLIVER WEST!" Oliver puffed out his chest, and for the first time he felt proud of his name.

And then there was silence. Vern's eyes swelled red, and he gazed at Oliver with a glare that was difficult to explain or predict.

"You got parents?" The man's face went pale and his body froze.

Oliver had gone cold too. All he could do was stare at Vern's face and wonder. Bea saw this, so she stepped in. She snatched the photograph of Ben and Kate West and thrust it into Vern's view. Vern took one look at the photo and then went white as a sheet. His heart rate spiked, and next thing you know, he fell sideways onto the dusty floor with a thud, out cold.

Bea and Oliver rushed to his side. They tried to pick him up, but Vern was a colossus of a man and they simply couldn't lift him without their arms turning to jelly. They dragged him across the floor to the little sofa beside the window. The small room was filled with a leather armchair, a torn sofa, about a million cobwebs, and a coffee table, covered by empty gin bottles strewn everywhere. Together they rolled him up onto the cushions. Oliver perched his head up on a pillow and Bea searched the tight kitchen for a cloth, which she doused in cold water and laid across the man's forehead.

Able to confirm he was still breathing, the two of them waited impatiently for Vern to awaken. Bea tried to put on a brave face for Oliver yet she was deeply frightened. For all they knew, Vern could be a dangerous man and they were sitting ducks. Within a few minutes, Vern's eyes slowly fluttered open. He took one look at Oliver and then lost consciousness once again. Oliver shook him back to life, gently sat him up, and ordered him to pull himself together.

In search of words, Vern gave up and reached for a flask of whiskey instead. He gulped it loudly and depended upon it like it was air. Oliver snatched it from his hands after a few gulps and Bea replaced it with a glass of water from the tap.

"Drink this," she nudged.

Vern protested, but when it failed, he took a few cautious sips, then set it on the coffee table, never once taking his eye off Oliver.

"Who are you?" Oliver asked, his voice painted in wonder.

The man took a deep breath, the kind you could hear travel through his whole body, and mumbled, "I'm not exactly the right person to tell yer that."

"You're the only person," Bea broke the silence.

This truth put Vern's wheels in motion, no matter how slowly they moved.

"You have the same fearless look your father had," Vern began. "And you've got yer mother's smile. She was the best of all of them women. It's a ruddy shame . . ." His voice croaked, and he reached for his whiskey, which Oliver slid out his grasp.

"You can't escape," Oliver stated, handing him water, "not anymore."

Vern drank slowly and then started up again, "Last time I saw you, boy, you were just a lad. You could barely even walk. It's a shocking miracle tha' yer here." And for the first time Oliver spotted a ray of light in Vern's functional eye.

"Who are you?" Oliver badgered.

"There's no easy way to tell yer this," he stumbled to his feet, "so I must show yer." He limped to the closet and returned with a cardboard box in his hand.

"What's this?" Oliver and Bea joined Vern on the floor.

He flipped through the box for a few moments and then pulled out a photograph of a stout and stalky teenage Vern back-to-back with a teenage version of Benjamin West. Oliver studied the photograph for long, silent seconds. *"Who is this man?"* he thought. *"And what is he doing with my father?"*

Oliver couldn't shake the feeling that now in his presence half of him was enthralled with Vern and his story and the other half hated him; he didn't know why.

"When Benji and I were boys, we vowed to always be there for each other," Vern choked on his voice, "I only wish . . ."

"That you could have kept the promise," Oliver heard himself say.

"Yes."

"Tell me more," Oliver demanded.

"We practically raised ourselves. Our mum wanted daughters and spent almost every day—"

Oliver interjected, "Your mum?" He shot to his feet. "Wait."

"I know what yer thinking. I got all of their rotten genes. Your dad was the handsome one," the man laughed awkwardly.

"You're my—" Oliver questioned, and Vern awkwardly reached out.

"Yes," Vern nodded.

"Uncle," Oliver muttered. "Family." He didn't know whether to say the last part with joy or anger.

"I'm so sorry, Oliver . . ." He started to tear up.

Oliver had dreamed of having a family his entire childhood and now he was discovering that he'd had one this whole time and that Vern had never come for him And that made him want to hate him.

"You're sorry?" Oliver's voice broke. "Did you not even mind that they'd died and that—"

Vern shot up. "I broke that day . . . in ways that haven't ever been fixed!" he roared.

"But you didn't even mind that I was motherless, fatherless, and locked up in a child prison with no one to love me?" Oliver leapt to his feet, facing Vern eye to eye. "No! You didn't even try, did you?"

"I thought you dead," Vern wept. "I'm so sorry, Oliver."

"Sorry isn't going to cut it anymore!" Oliver screamed. "It just isn't enough."

"OLIVER! Look around," his so-called uncle pointed to the empty bottles of rum around the room. "You did this to me! Losing you and your parents turned me into a ruddy alcoholic like my father was!"

"Well, I'M REALLY SORRY ABOUT THAT!" Oliver thrust one of the bottles of rum on the wall and watched it shatter into a hundred fragments of glass. Hot tears ran down his face and perilous thoughts jabbed his already swollen heart like daggers. He could not, would not, look his traitor of an uncle in the eye, not after all he'd *never had* because of him.

"Oliver," Vern gasped desperately, "I thought I'd lost everyone I'd ever loved."

"Well, I never had anyone that could love me," Oliver's eye twitched in anger, "because of you!"

"I was wrong. You are still here." Vern leaned toward his nephew.

Oliver's face went numb. He didn't want to be loved by a man who was responsible for depriving his childhood of love.

"I never stopped loving you," Vern uttered.

"IS THAT SO?" Oliver swatted Vern away. "Say, where were you sixteen years ago when I needed you? When we all needed you."

Oliver paused. "You could have been a hero, but you will NEVER be a hero. Will you?"

"I'm so sorry, Oliver. I'm here now. Now that I know," Vern pleaded.

"It's too late."

Oliver turned to leave, but he wasn't finished. "Don't expect me to leap into your arms when they weren't open when I needed them most!" Oliver shouted and then busted out the backdoor away from Vern. He didn't care that he was running to a field of snow and frigid January winds as any place was a haven compared to being with his uncle. Or should he even call him that?

24

FRIGID WINDS

Vern looked solemnly at Bea. He didn't even know her name, yet she'd brought Oliver back into his life. The nephew whom he'd presumed dead like his parents. Yet he wasn't, and she had proved him wrong. Vern had believed that to be a miracle. A long in coming miracle, but a miracle all the same. But now, as he saw his brother's son in his backyard looking grown up, devastated, broken, and poor all at the same time, he wasn't quite sure. Vern couldn't distinguish a miracle from a curse.

"Will he hate me forever?" Vern couldn't hide the despair in his voice.

Bea fumbled with her hands in her lap. "No, he won't." She laughed quietly, remembering a moment on the car ride. "On the way here, Oliver and I were trying to imagine who you might be. We considered every possibility, but the most nefarious of them all was the fear that you could be a serial killer and we would never even know."

Vern half chuckled under his breath.

"An uncle is quite the upgrade," Bea smiled. "You know, he spent a lot of time growing up, dreaming about what it would be like to have a family. And the reality that he had one all along is earth-shattering. He is probably just shocked. And nothing will heal like time can," she added hopefully.

"You seem to know him well," Vern chortled. "How'd you get so lucky, miss?"

Bea smiled wide and said, "I'm no miss, I'm only Bea."

"What a lovely name, Bea."

"Thank you, sir."

"Call me Vern."

"Alright."

"Now, Bea, how'd you come to know my nephew?" Vern seemed sincerely interested.

"It's actually a funny story," Bea chuckled. "It has to do with runaways, garden goons, and apple thieves."

"My favourite," Vern smiled weakly, and Bea went ahead to tell him the long version of Oliver's arrival on Lavender Lane.

"Sounds jus' like Benji," Vern grinned at the end of the tale. "He'd get in a passion and the next thing you know he'd be gone on another endless 'venture. I was eternally grateful when Kate took charge of Benji. He was a lot for a brother like me to keep up with. But she was just as restless as he was."

"Tell me more." Bea was on the edge of her seat.

"When Benji and I were lads we hardly saw our parents. Mum was a seamstress and married to her work, and Dad was married to his gin."

"That's sad," Bea whispered.

"Not for us," Vern's face lit up. "We could be gone for days and they'd never know. We were living mud balls, always in the wild or on a secret mission. I could've died happy in those days, but not Benji. He had dreams as big as they got, and when he found Kate . . . they only got bigger. They often invited me to join them, but my health got a little shaky. I went when I could handle it. They were always so good to me. Especially Kate. She was on the hunt to find me a lady. I'm relieved she never found one." Vern chuckled. "Then Ollie came around and it only got better. They were such parents, loved him with more love than I'd ever seen in my life, and you could just tell that Ollie loved them too. They were his whole world. When they . . ." Vern stuttered on the thought of their death. "You know . . ." And Bea nodded empathetically.

"My life fell apart. But if I'dda known . . ." A giant tear splattered on the coffee table. Bea handed him a handkerchief. "If I'dda known Oliver was still here . . . I'dda ran across the world to find him."

"I don't doubt it," Bea pitied the poor guy.

Vern shook his tears away and said to Bea, "Enough of this!" He leaped to his feet. "You hungry?"

"Let me help you," Bea followed him into the kitchen.

She was surprised to see a wide assortment of food in the refrigerator. Vern pulled out squash in three different colours, a steak, a bundle of potatoes, and fresh chives.

"You cook?" Bea's voice was soaked in surprise.

"I know what you're thinking, Bea," he chortled. "I don't look like much of a chef, do I?"

Bea laughed, glad to know he understood. "It's the only thing I do that makes sense to me," Vern explained and Bea nodded, wide-eyed, for she knew exactly what he meant.

"Can you roast potatoes?" Vern asked, rinsing his sausage-like fingers in the sink.

"Yes, sir!" She nodded confidently and waited for her turn to wash the potatoes in the sink.

The small galley kitchen was filled with the sound of knives on cutting boards and the sizzling and searing of steak.

"He's lucky to have you," Vern said as he looked out at Oliver through the kitchen window.

"Huh?" Bea jumped at Vern. She was too focused on dicing potatoes and hadn't been watching him.

Vern snorted. "You're good to him."

"Oh!" Bea laughed. "Well, he's good to us. I was feeling that my life wasn't quite thrilling enough to be in a story book until Oliver came along. And if housing a runaway orphan who craves adventures as much as my siblings and I do isn't thrilling, I don't know what is," she explained to him.

"I don't read much but that's a story I'd read," Vern winked.

When the cooking was done, Bea jumped up in a panic. She'd forgotten to call her family when she arrived at Vern's.

"Oh no!" she yelled.

"What?" Vern jumped.

"I forgot to call my dad."

"Oh, Bea," Vern took a deep breath, "I thought you dropped a knife on yer foot or something."

Bea giggled, "Sorry, can I use your tele?"

"By all means." Vern pointed to the telephone on the small table by the sofa and Bea feverishly dialled the home number.

"I'm going to take this out to Oliver. Hope yer Dad isn't too furious," Vern wished her good luck.

Meanwhile, in Vern's backyard, Oliver sat with his knees to his chest, his mind rocked in bitterness. Melting icicles dripped from the gutter and cold droplets splattered on his head, making him shiver. He didn't know how long he'd been sitting there but he would've stayed there for a lifetime if it meant he'd never have to look Vern in the eye again. And he meant that. At least he thought he meant that. Right before he could decide whether he meant it or not, a pair of footsteps approached him from behind. He hoped they were Bea's and believed they were, until he glanced over his shoulder to see not Bea but Vern approaching him with a plate of steaming food in his hand.

"I don't want to talk to you," Oliver belted out.

"You don't have to talk to me," Vern slowly but sternly stated. "You don't e'en have to look at me. But you must eat. Now that's nonnegotiable."

"I'm not hungry," Oliver protested, but it was too late. Vern had already shoved the plate onto Oliver's lap.

"Eat," he ordered, and Oliver slowly did so.

Silence filled the pasture except for Oliver's quiet chewing.

As much as Oliver resented Vern, and as much as Vern knew it, he wouldn't abandon his nephew, not again. He waited until the very last trace of supper was cleared from his plate before he considered leaving. Oliver handed his uncle the emptied plate, which he gladly accepted, but even still, Vern didn't move a muscle.

Finally, Oliver broke the silence. "Did you really think I'd died too?" he quietly asked. Clearly Vern's good cooking warmed Oliver up to the idea of talking.

Vern immediately replied with sadness in his voice, "Yes. I checked the flat where you used to live. It was empty, like yer'd never even lived there. You see, it took me a while to realize they were gone. I've been in hiding since I was about twenty for reasons I'm not proud of. Yer mum and dad were respectful of my wishes to stay hidden, so they didn't write or reveal my location to anyone. They visited about once a month, and yer mum promised to come by for supper af'er your dad got home. I was going to make toad in a hole. When they didn't come, I got worried. Yer mum always kept her promises."

Oliver listened but he still couldn't look his uncle in the eye.

"I should've been smarter but I thought I did everything . . . that it was hopeless. Not that any of that should be defended. You deserved better. So much better."

"You're right about one thing," Oliver muttered.

"What?"

"That I deserved better," he stated bluntly.

Vern took this as a note of progression. He'd never even dreamed of hearing him speak and here he was, next to him, his brother's son, speaking in full sentences and agreeing with him even if he did despise him.

"How's Bea?" Oliver asked.

Vern chuckled softly, "She's 'mazing."

Oliver laughed, "Yes, she is."

"She told me about how you ran from the orphanage, 'ow her family took you in. That was very brave of yer, Oliver."

"Does she think I'm despicable?"

"Hardly. In fact, I think she thinks a little TOO highly of yer," Vern teased.

"What? Did she say something?" Oliver jumped a bit.

"Was there something to be said?" Vern played.

"I guess not," Oliver tried to conceal his obvious fascination with the subject.

"Well, I'm glad yer stumbled upon her because I can tell she's given yer a chance to . . . a chance to . . ." Vern searched for the right words.

"Have a childhood," Oliver completed the sentence.

"Exactly," Vern nodded. "She reminds me of someone."

"Who?" Oliver jumped again.

SHELBY EVE SAYER

"Your mum."

That statement hung in the air for a minute with no movement or words to displace it. Oliver sat there trying to hide the smile that begged to come out. Vern stood up with the cleaned-off plate in his hand and said, "Come in when yer ready. It's freezing out here, and Bea and I are going to make a li'l dessert. I'll avoid you as much as possible if it would make yer feel better."

"You don't have to," Oliver whispered almost inaudibly but Vern heard it. Perhaps today really was a miracle.

25

THE APPLE THIEF & THE GARDEN GOON

Bea and Vern were icing cinnamon buns when Oliver came in through the screen door, wrapped in a conversation about the potatoes in Idaho, which Vern just so happened to know all about. Bea was laughing, as always, and they didn't even notice Oliver coming in.

"Hello," Oliver sidled up beside them and that's all he could say.

That simple "Hello" snapped Bea out of her head cloud and she leapt into Oliver's arms.

"You came in!" she beamed as if he'd been in a long coma.

"Yes," he said, holding her tight. He didn't even make a joke about how tightly she was squeezing him.

Oliver had loads of time to think about Vern in the hour he'd stayed outside after dinner and had made up his mind about many things. Letting go of Bea, he addressed the first.

"Bea," he smiled at her, "do you think I could talk to Vern alone for a minute?"

Bea nodded and started out the door to go for a walk. Usually she'd be tempted to eavesdrop but this wasn't one of those times. As she walked, she replayed in her mind the events of the last hour. She felt there were ample signs things would work out between Vern and Oliver, and was busy cataloguing them. Soon Bea was lost in her thoughts, skipping down the country road with the cold breeze dancing in her hair. The fields resembled a unified ocean of white that seemed to stretch beyond the horizon. It left the impression that the world would never end.

"Bea!" It was Oliver, chasing after her.

She turned and smiled at him with the kind of smile that she didn't even realize she was wearing.

"Why are you smiling?" Oliver looked at her suspiciously.

"It never ends, Oliver. It goes on forever." She presented the view to him. "And I could chase after it my whole life and never run out of things to see."

"Let's get you home," he teased, but deep down Oliver felt the exact same way. He, too, wanted so badly to live a life of chasing skies.

"And why are you smiling?" Bea glared in his direction.

"I'm not!" He tried to hide his joy but it was impossible, so he gave up. "My parents loved me so much," he admitted. "They were unstoppable like we are. They could go for ages and never rest. Mum was always laughing." He looked at Bea. "And Dad was always running. Together they had dreams, and I was one of them. One of their many dreams." Oliver's eyes reflected the view of the fields. "Can you even believe that?"

Bea could believe it. "That's the most wonderful news, Oliver. The most extraordinary."

Soon Bea and Oliver were tripping down the road, not able to help from skipping. Back to the car they went, bidding Vern farewell. Both felt palpable excitement to share the day's events with Lavender Lane. When they rolled up to the cottage, Poppy and Lucy came sprinting out the front door toward them. They wrapped themselves in a gigantic bear hug and then it was off to the treehouse for a mandatory meeting. Bea and Oliver had so much to tell, and they illustrated every detail for the others. The eyes of the Lavender Lane audience widened as each piece of the mystery unfolded.

"Your uncle?" Rose couldn't believe it, and neither could anyone else.

"That's marvelous!" Eve exclaimed, in awe.

"Does that mean you'll leave us?" Flynn jumped up in a sweat.

"Come on, Flynn! Don't be so anxious to get rid of me," Oliver teased.

"I don't want you to leave," Flynn admitted. "Are you going to stay?"

"Course I will," Oliver nodded. "This is my home."

With the assurance that Oliver would stay, the news that he had found a living relative, celebration was called up. They caught Dad up and celebrated that night with biscuits and grape juice. At the tail end of the festivities, Bea snuck away into the attic to catch up on all the writing she'd missed from the spontaneous excursion. She returned to her lucky notebook, her favourite pen, and began to do what she knew best. Suddenly she was wrapped in a whirlwind of words that she grasped as they buzzed on by. The world was blurred around her and her soul was alive with imagination and colour. Unaware of how long she had been writing, she simply knew that while the world had gone dark her mind was still at noonday.

"Hey," a crisp voice whispered from behind.

Bea dropped her pen to the floor. "Oliver," she jumped. "You scared me!"

"Sorry!" He laughed, picking up her pen and handing it to her.

"That's alright," she sighed and got back to work.

Oliver opened the attic window that led to the rooftop and he sat halfway out of it.

"Bea, come here."

"Give me, like, two minutes. I have to finish this thought."

He waited two minutes, then five, and at minute ten Bea was still furiously writing.

"Bea?"

"What?" Bea asked, half-listening, half not.

"Which story is more important?" He snuck up behind her. "This one," he pointed to her notebook, "or yours?"

Bea had never thought of it like that. "Mine?" She hesitated.

"That's what I thought." Oliver gave her his hand and he led her out the window. "You've got to see the world tonight," he demanded smoothly.

The two friends climbed onto the rooftop where the world was asleep.

"Wow," Bea whispered in awe. "I didn't even notice the stars," she laughed, "and I love the stars."

"Bea?" Oliver muttered between teeth.

"Oliver?" Bea turned to him.

"I still can't get over today."

"Me either," Bea agreed. "Can you believe you found family?"

"No, it still feels so surreal," he replied.

"You know, at the orphanage, I used to come out on the roof like this all the time and look at the stars."

"What would you think about?" Bea could almost see Oliver doing this.

"What it would be like to have what I have now." His smile was soft as he said this, like the brush of the wind through the sleeping trees. "A year ago I had nothing. And I wondered what it would be like to have something to live for. To have a purpose. Now I know."

Bea's eyes brightened at the thought of Oliver's triumphs over struggle.

"I have a home. I have a . . ." He paused and then said without a stutter, "A family. I now have knowledge of my roots, adventures, and real, happy memories. I have a purpose." He paused again, for the gratitude he felt overwhelmed his tongue. "You gave me that, Bea. And that is truly a marvelous gift."

Bea's eyes were filled with emotion. Not the kind of emotion that is damp and sad. And certainly not the kind of emotion that is rambunctious and dramatic. The kind that is quiet and joyous that comes only from giving and seeing the fruit that comes from it.

Bea gazed at the stars, thinking of the mischievous apple thief that became a brilliant friend.

26

FIRELIGHT AND STAR GLOW

Flynn sat in the corner pretending to read the *London Times* but secretly listening to Bea and Dad's conversation.

Bea asked, "Dad, when you married Mum, what did Kit think of it?" Kit was Dad's younger sister, his childhood best friend and Bea's favourite aunt. She had remained a spinster all her life, but Bea certainly felt the title was a misnomer.

Dad scratched his chin. "Well, I don't know, Bea. I guess she was used to her brothers getting married. After Edwin and Charles, I assumed she was accustomed to it. I guess, I've never really thought about that before."

"Oh." Bea nodded.

"Why do you ask?" Bea usually did not ask complex questions like this one.

"I don't know, just thinking about what it will be like when Eve gets married," Bea replied as she tossed an orange into the air and caught it.

"You know, we still spent time with Kit. A lot of it. Sometimes we would go on hikes, just me and her, and we would talk about old times and laugh. We'd laugh a lot," Dad added as he scrubbed the dishes in the sink.

Bea laughed, trying to picture her dad and aunt as children. "Sometimes I wish I could have been a fly on the wall in your childhood home."

"Hmm," he chuckled thoughtfully. "I think you would find that we did a lot of the same funny things that you lads do. Visiting my childhood would only remind you of yours."

"Ahh," Bea nodded as she understood, and she was more in love with the childhood she had lived than she thought possible.

"Bea," Dad looked up from the dishes, "could you read Poppy a bedtime story for me tonight?"

"Sure, Dad." Bea set out to the girls' bedroom happily, for bedtime story duty was her favourite chore.

"Flynn?" Dad perked up, realizing his son was camouflaged in the corner and had been there the whole time. "Since when do you read the paper?"

"Since always," Flynn fibbed.

"You don't say," Dad chuckled in astonishment. "In that case, could you give me a summary?"

"Erm . . .," Flynn stuttered.

"That's what I thought. Brilliant eavesdropping tactic, really. I would do the same thing when I was a boy. Uncle Edwin was an unruly boy and Mum was constantly scolding him. Which made quality entertainment for Kit and I."

Just as Flynn was appreciating his dad's understanding, Oliver, Rose, and Lucy came bursting into the house.

"Flynn!"

"What?" Flynn dropped his newspaper.

"Tonight's perfect for a Bean family fire, come help us build it," Rose commanded.

"Alright," he smiled broadly. "Let me see if Bea's done."

And then, careful not to let Poppy hear of the plan, all five of them headed to the little fire pit in the back of the meadow that had grown old with them.

The evening sky was a deep navy and beginning to burst with stars. The March air was weightless and cold. Oliver and Flynn chopped wood for the fire, while Rose and her sharp eye disappeared into the wood in search of proper kindling. Bea arranged the wood the boys cut into a log cabin of sorts, and Lucy tucked wads of newspaper in between the logs.

When Rose returned from the wood, her hands were empty but her eyes were wide with disgust.

Bea was the first to notice the change in emotion. "Rose, have you been kicked by a mule?" she asked, and the others turned to look.

"I caught them snogging." Rose looked as if she might gag.

"Who?" Flynn jumped.

"The deer?" Oliver joked.

"Not the deer, you daft fool! The lovebirds!" Rose scolded.

"Eve and Henry?" Lucy's eyes enlarged at the thought of her sister snogging.

"Eve and Henry!" Bea and Oliver burst out into belly laughter.

"Did they notice?" Bea asked through giggles.

"No, they were, like, really snogging." Rose was still shaking from trauma. "I made a run for it!"

"I've got to see this." Oliver lurched toward the wood and Rose caught his sleeve. "No!" She jumped.

Flynn's mouth hung wide open like a drawbridge, still in obvious shock. He was with Rose, he did not find snogging amusing.

"Say something, Flynn!" Rose pushed.

"She's going to marry him," Flynn uttered, his eyes still wide open and his face still ghostly.

"Ugh . . . marriage . . .," Rose coughed.

"You think she will?" Lucy asked her older siblings as she stared blankly at the heightening flames.

"I think she will," Bea said as she thrust another log into the embers.

"But she's younger than time," Rose debated.

"Yeah!" Flynn sided with his sister.

"I'm not sure time cares," Bea whispered in a much more serious tone this time.

"Why should it?" Oliver thought of Eve and Henry's marriage as an imminent reality and was not sure how their age could ever change that.

"Who will play mum if she moves to London?" Lucy asked.

"And who will cook?" Now Flynn was seriously concerned.

"And who will keep Poppy from bugging me?" Rose gulped.

None of these questions intimidated Oliver, as he knew exactly who would handle all these daunting tasks.

"Well, isn't it obvious?" Oliver shouted into the orange light, wondering why they were all so blind.

Everyone turned toward him, curious as to what they were missing.

"Hardly," Bea said, with a look of bewilderment.

"Bea," Oliver threw a stick into the fire. "You can."

"Well, can she make Mum's roast?" Flynn shot up, his faith in Bea clearly lacking.

"Flynn, for the last time, it isn't always about food!" Oliver laughed under his breath.

"I'm a man. And it's always about food!"

"If Flynn's a man, then I'm seriously worried about humanity." Rose rolled in laughter and colour returned to her face.

Laughter won again, as it always did, and the fear of losing Eve to marriage drifted into the cool air. In laughter, they had forgotten their disgust with snogging and looming marriages, and remembered what bonfires on Lavender Lane were really about.

The subject quickly switched to the proper way to peel a banana, which apparently was a very controversial topic.

"Monkey's peel them from the bottom up!" Rose shouted. "And they're the professionals!"

"Take it from the experts!" Flynn roared.

"But the top part has a fancy little handle," Oliver argued.

"Are they more slippery based on how you peel them?" Bea blankly asked, and nobody was quite sure what she was asking.

"Are bananas actually slippery?" Rose doubted.

"Or is that just in cartoons?" Lucy asked.

"Cartoons are always accurate!" Bea said and meant it.

Then Flynn ran to the kitchen to fetch a banana so they could experiment.

Amongst all this debate, Eve and Henry approached the curious scene.

"What is going on?" Eve shook her head.

Bea jumped up and suspiciously asked, "Where'd you come from?"

"The wood." Eve tossed her hair and joined them around the fire.

"What were you doing in there?" Oliver added, quite obviously trying to imply impropriety, and Rose swatted him like a fly.

Eve blushed and Henry awkwardly kicked the dirt, for both of them were weak liars. A gift and an ailment. That night, as the fire died out and the children nestled in their beds, Flynn lay awake, his mind spinning.

"You won't get away with this!" Oliver karate-chopped the air, for he is quite a sleep fighter and Flynn lay silent with his eyes locked on the shadowy ceiling.

Was Eve really going to get married and leave Lavender Lane? Part of Flynn hoped she would not. What would it be like without her? Eve was not like the other sisters. Eve understood Flynn perfectly. She did not tease or joke like Bea and Rose did. She was not innocent and childlike, like Lucy and Poppy, and she never asked questions that Flynn could not answer. She was not critical of Flynn, and she fed him so well! Flynn loved his eldest sister, and at this moment, could only think of Eve's joy as his definite loss.

27

FISHY BUSINESS

It was April 15 and in some small, undistinguishable way things felt funny. Flynn sensed something suspicious, odd, maybe even fishy. Even so, no matter how hard he tried, he could not pinpoint what it was. Just as he was getting ready for bed, Rose barged into his room.

"Flynn!" she whispered, quite urgently.

"What?" Flynn nearly jumped out of his skin. He didn't get frightened often but Rose had found him deep in thought.

Rose must have been in distress, for she didn't even brag about how she had startled him.

"Henry has secret plans for Eve's trip to London," Rose blurted at once.

Eve was hopping on a train the next day, unaccompanied, and she was headed for London to visit Henry and meet his family.

"Rose! Do tell!" Flynn shoved his sister, eager for an explanation.

"Henry is going to propose to Eve tomorrow! I just know it," her voice trailing off. There wasn't as much joy in her voice as there should've been. If Henry was indeed planning to propose to Eve, this would be the perfect opportunity.

"Really? Who told you?" Flynn sat down on his bed. He wasn't shocked; it was bound to happen. But it would be a lie to say the word "tomorrow" didn't throw him for a loop.

"No one. I just know," Rose stated in full confidence.

"Oh, honestly, Rose. How can you be sure?" Flynn didn't think her hunch was sufficient evidence to rely on.

"You've noticed how strange Dad has been acting all week, haven't you?" Rose asked as if it was obvious.

"Course I have!" Flynn fibbed, for he would never admit to anyone that Rose was sharper than him, no matter how true it was.

Rose clearly caught his lie and made sure to point it out. "You didn't notice anything, did you?" She raised an eyebrow.

"Moving on," Flynn motioned.

Rose laughed under her breath. She'd won again and continued to elaborate.

"Dad has been on edge all week! I can just tell. He's excited and anxious about something. Something he cannot tell us. Something private."

"Well, what else can it be?" Flynn inquired, hoping for anything else.

"What else can it be?" Rose said, believing it couldn't be anything else.

"Do you think Eve knows?" Flynn wondered aloud.

"I'm sure she suspects something. As I do."

"And you think Henry must have asked Dad's permission already?" Flynn was full of questions.

"Yes," Rose nodded. "I'm guessing he asked last week when he was here."

"Well . . .," Flynn whispered.

"Well, what should we do?" Rose wondered.

"Nothing."

"Nothing?" Rose asked, alarmed. Flynn was many things but a quitter was not one of them.

"Eve is going to marry a good man. What's so bad about that?"

Rose did not appreciate how rational her brother was being. He was supposed to be upset.

"Marriage? Since when is that a good thing?" Rose laughed.

"Rose, if it weren't for marriage you wouldn't be alive. It's always been a good thing, we've just been good at ignoring it," Flynn stated in an abnormally wise tone.

"Flynn, what are you saying? Don't tell me you've got your head turned too." Rose couldn't fathom Flynn relenting.

"Course not, sister," he slapped her back.

"Are you sure I'm speaking to Flynn Bean?" She rested her hand on his forehead to ensure he didn't have a temperature.

"Stop it, Rose!" He swatted her hand away. "I'll quit saying insightful things."

"Good," she laughed. "Because it's concerning," she added as she left his room.

As she walked to her own room, she thought about the things Flynn had said. Maybe just this once he was right. But she would've been forced to abandon the alarm and distrust of change that she felt. So she kept it to herself.

28

BUTTERFLY FOREST

What a precious thing time is. Unpredictable, sometimes kind, sometimes wrapped in loneliness. Always in motion, no matter how slowly or rapidly it moves. Bea stood at the window thinking about the future. It seemed one moment ago when they were chasing sunsets and playing dress-up, and now the sky's colour had changed. Eve was engaged to be married and a new chapter was looming in the distance. Whether Bea was ready for a page turn she did not know.

"What colours will you choose, Evie?" Lucy asked, her voice dipped in excitement.

"And what kind of dresses will we wear?" Rose asked, hoping for something elegant.

"Will we be able to dance in them?" Bea badgered, for the dancing was all she really cared about when it came to wedding fuss.

"Bea, I don't think a potato sack could survive your dancing," Rose retorted with a scowl.

"Ouch!" Bea and Oliver said in unison.

All the Bean girls were gathered around Dad's oak table, peppering Eve with wedding questions. Oliver and Flynn stood in the background, eavesdropping.

"Can my pets come?" Poppy piped up.

"I don't know, Poppy," Eve scratched her chin. "I'll think about it."

Since "maybe" was an upgrade from no, Poppy left the table at once to tell Danny and the pets. Bea glanced at the kitchen clock. They'd been discussing the wedding for over an hour and Bea wanted badly to escape into the spring breeze.

Just as she was dreaming of plunging into the outdoors, she looked down on her lap to see a paper airplane sitting there. Someone must have put it there, but there was nobody in sight. She unfolded the airplane under the table to hide it from her sisters.

On the white parchment a note was scribbled, "Meet me by John Appleseed in five with your notebook and your bicycle."

Bea looked at the note, then glanced at her sisters to ensure she wasn't being watched. Escaping from wedding talk, she skillfully slipped away and started off toward Dr John Appleseed. Oliver stood against the tree's trunk with a mysterious grin on his face and a twinkle in his eyes, which meant only one thing—adventure.

"You're up to something, aren't you?" Bea knew that look in Oliver's eye.

"Maybe," he teased.

"Oh, really?" Bea put her hands on her hips. "Well, I'm very intrigued."

"Hop on your bike and quit your blabbering."

"Who gave you the right to order me around?" Bea asked, pretending to be bothered, though grateful for a call to adventure.

Oliver laughed under his breath, finding Bea's retort barely sufficient.

"Bea, we better scurry before they notice you've gone," he snapped and then pedalled off.

Oliver took the lead down the gravel path behind Lavender Lane that crossed through the open meadows. They wound through the moors and into the back side of the Yellow Woods, a Bean family sanctuary. The April sun danced in the birches as they rode along. They passed a hollow and mossy log that housed a family of squirrels, and they laughed as they saw two of them quarrelling over an acorn. They spied the stump where Bea loved to write and the nearby bush that was covered in bluebirds.

Just as Bea started to fall behind, Oliver parked his bicycle behind the trunk of an exceptionally colossal tree. It seemed equivalent to the width of a bus, and the branches above seemed to climb halfway to the stratosphere. Beyond the tree was a bed of soft grass and a view so magnificent it made Bea want to dance. She'd been here once before. Once long ago, when she was about ten years old. She'd stumbled upon it and she hadn't been able to find it since. It seemed to Bea that the beautiful place was hiding from her, and as she stood in its company once again, she realized how little it had changed in her absence. She could still see the town from atop the hill, the tree was just as large as she remembered, and the air surrounding it was still a refuge for hundreds of butterflies. She didn't blame them for hiding here because if she too had wings she would fly to the Butterfly Forest.

"Beautiful, isn't it?" Oliver moved toward the vantage point where Bea stood with her arms outstretched and her eyes closed. This is the kind of thing Bea did when she felt understood by things that weren't quite human. She couldn't help it, but then again, it would've been a mistake to try and help it.

"Beyond beautiful," Bea whispered in awe.

When she opened her eyes, Oliver was standing beside her with his hand reaching out. He tugged her toward the stratosphere tree. The two of them climbed to the same sturdy branch, where they sat with their legs swinging in the breeze.

"How did you find . . . ?" Bea gazed up at him.

"Instinct," was all Oliver could say.

"Life has changed so much since I came here last. Six years ago . . ." Bea hung her head. "But yet . . . it feels—"

"Like yesterday," Oliver completed her sentence with a sideways glance.

"Yes."

"Everything is changing so quickly," she added after long, silent seconds of thoughtfulness.

"Does it excite you?"

"That's what I try to tell myself," Bea paused. "That it's exciting and happy, but I can't help but cleave to what once was."

"Which is?" Oliver inquired.

"Childhood," Bea's voice softened at the thought of it. "We suspected it was endless, eternal even, but we were wrong. And growing up makes you realize how few things are forever, childhood isn't one of them. I'm just not ready to let go of everything."

"What will you miss most?" Oliver gently asked.

"The chaos," Bea said without hesitation. "Some crave peace and quiet, but not me. Eve chasing us around, acting like Mum. Flynn going on about something stupid. Rose hitting everyone with jabs and sparks. Lucy's cute comments, and Poppy's wild hair and messes. Now Eve's engaged to a great man, but engaged? Flynn is tall and rugged. Rose is smarter than me, and it is only a matter of time before she is taller than me," Bea groaned. "And Lucy is growing more rational and mature. Which is grand, but I can't stand it," Bea's voice cracked. "Why can't everyone just be young and imaginative like Poppy?" Bea's eyes welled with sorrow. "And soon we'll all be grown, and she'll be left all alone with just Dad and her pets. And it'll be so lonesome for her. I can't bear the thought of it!"

"Bea," Oliver scooted closer toward her side of the branch, "it hasn't begun yet . . ."

"What hasn't?" She wiped her eye with her sleeve.

"Our big adventure." He spread his hand out to the sky. "And I believe it takes an act of growing older for such an adventure to begin."

"What do you mean?"

"Adult freedoms, childlike heart. The necessities for an adventurous life. You must let go of some things to find new things. But that doesn't mean they have to be gone forever. They live inside you, and if you nourish them, they will thrive forever." Oliver brushed a strand of Bea's hair from her face.

"When did you grow so wise, Oliver?"

"Watching you, Bea."

Bea didn't ask what he meant. It sounded too complicated to explain and yet too comprehendible to question.

"Children don't have much freedom, do they?" she thought aloud as she and Oliver jumped from the tree to the meadow grass.

"No, they don't," was Oliver's reply.

"They can't explore on their own or-or talk to strangers," was Bea's interruption.

"They can't do wild things without parents," he laughed. "At least without their consent."

"Like when we took Dad's pickup without asking and went to find Vern," Bea laughed.

"Ha!" Oliver laughed, remembering the trouble they were in at first.

"Children aren't taken seriously even when matters are dire," Bea listed.

"Like falling in love. No adult would ever believe it to be real, even if it is."

"Love?" Bea didn't understand why Oliver would've taken such a sharp detour. "Do children even care about that?" Bea laughed.

"No," Oliver shook his head, "but I do."

Bea looked from the brilliant moors to the butterflies and then to Oliver. *"This would be a lovely place to discover love,"* Bea heard a voice in the back of her head whisper.

"Bea," Oliver stepped in toward her, "you're extraordinary." He gazed into her hazel eyes. He'd always loved Bea's eyes but never had they looked so endearing in the afternoon light. How they shone. How they seemed alive, imaginative, and yet a bit sad all at the same time.

Bea stood there letting Oliver gaze at her.

"Oliver," she said his name to hear the way it sounded in the spring air.

Thinking it sounded good, she let him lean in closer, believing that it would all be okay. But she'd misjudged herself. Oliver nearly kissed her. And right before his lips locked with hers, she fell to the earth as a whirlwind of emotions rushed through her so rapidly that she couldn't keep up with them. Dizzy with the noises in her head, the unfamiliarity of love, and the fear of losing it, she lay there quaking along with her patronizing thoughts.

Oliver knelt beside her, looking helpless as if he knew exactly what buzzed through her brain as he mourned the tragic reality.

In the pain-filled silence, Bea muttered two piercing words, "I can't."

"Why?" Oliver's asked, his voice beginning to break.

"I don't know." Bea looked at him as if she was cascading down a cliff in a rapid descent and knew she couldn't be saved.

"Yes, you do. Just tell me," he persisted.

"NO, I DON'T!" Bea roared as she jumped to her feet. She was just as confused as she was angry at herself.

Oliver recoiled in response to her outburst. But then, in an act of sheer courage, he stepped toward her again. "Don't stand there and tell me that you don't feel it. I feel this fire burning inside of me that I can't quiet, and I know that you feel it too. Tell me that you do," Oliver commanded her.

"I do," she forced the words from her lips. She knew them to be true, so why was it so hard to acknowledge them? "I feel it."

"So what is there to hide?" Oliver clasped her hands in hopes she would hold on.

"Because it can't be, Oliver. I see what love does to people."

Oliver didn't understand.

"I don't want to wax old and boring, Oliver."

"Bea, love won't make you bor—" Oliver uttered.

"Oliver, I'm afraid."

"Of what?" Oliver whispered, a look of defeat and heartbreak written on his face.

"I'm afraid of losing you," she wept and started away from Oliver, sure it was best to face her emotions alone.

"Bea," Oliver tried to stop her.

"You're not listening!" She ripped out of his grasp. "You're my best friend." She reached out to touch Oliver's face. "And if I were to lose you . . ."

Oliver interrupted her, "You won't." He too reached for her face to assure her, and she turned away.

"Oliver, if all failed, I would lose you. And even if I let myself love you, I might lose you still." She breathed helplessly.

"All this talk of losing is irrational," Oliver tried to tell her.

"I don't think it is." Bea's eyes were now streaming with silent tears.

"And . . .," Oliver said, beyond heartbreak.

"I'm so sick of losing. It has become my life, Oliver. And I'm SO sick of it! And I try to be brave, but I just can't afford to lose anything more! Especially you," she said much softer, almost inaudibly. "I just can't take that risk."

"Bea," Oliver's whole body was trembling. He felt feeble, frail, and even helpless, and what was he supposed to do with that?

"Oliver," Bea whispered through her sobs. She glanced at him like it hurt her eyes and then turned away, bearing her body that heaved in sadness like it weighed two tons.

29

NEW TERRITORY

Love can be natural and kind, as it was for Eve and Henry. As for Oliver and Bea, love inflicted wounds. After their conversation in the Butterfly Forest, Bea absconded, in her misery, to a small lake not far from Lavender Lane, where she sat on the dock in a trance.

The lake usually fuelled her imagination, but this time she didn't feel like writing as she ached far too sorely to move her pen. She knew, however, that it was vital for her to write in order to process her feelings.

So in solitude and sorrow she began writing. She wrote for hours on end until the sun went to sleep.

It must have been the early moonlight reflecting on the dark waters that invoked her inner voice. It whispered, "Go home."

Listening, she stood up and carried her stiff body down the lane.

As she entered the front door, her entire family stood in the sitting room looking stressed and borderline angry. Dad was fed up with her lack of communication, but when he saw that sad, broken look, his fury melted into sympathy.

The children peppered Bea with questions, all of which Bea shrugged off. Dad, who saw through her forced smile and shrugs, silenced the children and let Bea walk away without confrontation. She dragged herself to her bunk. Neatly atop her pillow was a handwritten note. It read:

If I can't love you, then I'll have to lose you. I can't stand to look into your eyes and know that they are not mine.

There was no signature but there was no doubt who wrote it. She clutched the note to her chest and cried again. She tried to cry silently so her family wouldn't hear it, but she found it impossible. Big swollen tears splattered Oliver's note, blurring and smearing the ink. Her sobs grew louder by the minute. It was her fault she'd ruined their friendship. It was she who ran from love, not him.

Eve, who knew a little something of love, sat with her back against the door and listened to Bea weep, waiting for the right time to go in and comfort her. The "right time" never came, and Eve simply couldn't take it anymore. She quietly snuck into the girls' room and tiptoed to Bea.

"You alright?" she asked in her sweet and understanding tone.

Bea knew that her sister's intentions were good but she couldn't decipher whether she wanted help or not. After all, asking for help was her biggest kryptonite. Half of her wanted Eve to hold her and understand, and the other half didn't want Eve to see her so weak. So in response to her noisy internal conundrum Bea shouted, "No!" and pointed to the door.

Eve looked at Bea, poor Bea, with an expression that was Mum's. This familiar glance encouraged Bea's trust. "It hurts." She opened the flood gates.

"I know." Eve rushed to her uncharacteristically frail sister's side. She held her and let her tremble, examining the blurred note in Bea's hand. Seeing its brutal words, she pulled Bea in tighter. She didn't tell her that it would be fine or that it would all go away, because she didn't know if it would be. She simply sat there and listened to her cry, and hoped that one day Bea would return to her spritely self, because seeing her in pain was unbearable.

30

BROTHERS AND BUNNIES

The next morning, Bea awoke from the kind of restless sleep that left more fatigue than renewal. Her face was tear-stained, her eyes puffy, and her heart seemed to weigh down her entire body. She tried to massage the place where it sat but it didn't soothe her.

She put on a brave face and made her way to the kitchen. Her family was all there, exchanging nervous looks. "What?" Bea forced laughter as she caught Flynn studying her. Each of the Beans turned their heads promptly, returning to their milk.

"Bea," Eve hesitated. "After chores the girls and I are going to Keswick for wedding shopping. Would you fancy joining us?"

"I'd love to!" Bea pretended to smile, but her family could sense her insincerity.

"Please stop acting strange, will you?" Bea requested. "Everything is quite all right!"

Everyone nodded except Poppy, who was swinging Dotty in the air. "You are the one acting strange!" she accused.

"You're right, Poppy," Bea said softly. "I will stop, all right?"

"Right." Poppy hugged Dotty.

When afternoon came, Eve rounded up the girls, other than Poppy, who wanted to stay home with Flynn and the pets.

Once they left, Poppy loudly announced that she was, "Off to the playhouse!" She sprinted through the meadow as fast as she could, for she had crucial matters to discuss with the pets.

"Attention, pets of all breeds! Attention," she boisterously demanded, flailing arms and all as she burst into the little coop. "The Bean family is in distress!"

Poppy dropped to the hay-covered floor and her head fell into her hands. It was official, she too was in distress.

Just as she was about to cry or yell or say a mean word she'd only heard Mr Petosa use, a cherished furry friend climbed into her lap. Poppy peeked at the creature through the cracks between her fingers. It was Petey who'd come to comfort her.

"Oh, Petey!" she exclaimed as she brought him to her cheek. "My lovely bunny friend."

Petey gazed up at Poppy with watery eyes. The kind of watery bunny eyes that secured her trust.

"They think I don't understand, Petey. That I don't sense sadness. But I'm almost seven, and I know more than they think!" she argued. "Do people ever think you aren't as smart as you are because you are a bunny?"

Petey blinked back at her.

"It's not like I didn't notice Ollie disappearing. I always notice when a friend goes missing! And Ollie Wollie is a good friend! I noticed right away, Petey, I did!"

"They don't think I'm very smart, do they, Petey? But I'm six and three-quarters. I can train animals to dance, count the flowers in the meadow, and I know bigger words than some eight-year-olds. I am smart!"

Petey didn't doubt it.

"Petey, why won't they tell me why Ollie left? He is my friend too, isn't he?"

Poppy could've sworn she saw Petey nod and offer words of wisdom. Whether it was her imagination or not, it was of no consequence.

"You really are a brilliant bunny, Petey." Poppy leapt to her feet. "What a lovely idea you've got!" She congratulated the little creature with a gentle pat on the head and flower bud from the meadow.

Poppy raced back to the cottage, where she'd use Petey's "advice" to take action. She burst in through the backdoor and ran squarely into Flynn, who was carrying a deck of playing cards. The cards flew into the air, and both Flynn and Poppy landed flat on their backs. Poppy scrambled to her feet and began blabbering at twice the speed her tongue was meant to go.

"Whoa, slow down, Pops. I can't hear myself think," Flynn demanded as he rubbed his bruised head.

"Where did Ollie go?" Poppy whined. "No one will tell me anything."

"I don't know, Pops," Flynn shrugged. "I wish I did."

"Yes, you do!" Poppy accused her brother with a pointed finger. "Grown-up people are always saying they don't know to avoid tricky questions."

"I really don't know, Poppy." Flynn put his hands in the air to confirm his innocence. "I don't think anyone really knows, except maybe Bea."

"Then I'll ask her!"

"It's not quite that simple."

"Grown-up people are always making things more diffi-cu-lt," Poppy struggled to pronounce such a big word, "than they really are."

"Grown-up people are idiots," Flynn thought aloud. "Sorry," he apologized, "don't tell Dad."

"Well, maybe there is a way we could find out." Flynn scratched his head.

"How?" Poppy bounced.

"Maybe we could get a hold of Oliver, call him," Flynn suggested. "He had his uncle's tele number written somewhere." Flynn rushed to his room and Poppy followed.

The two searched through the nightstand and the bookshelf until Flynn found a piece of white parchment wedged between the pages of a book with Uncle Vern's number scribbled on it.

"Here it is!" Flynn cheered as he ran to the telephone on the coffee table. Just as he was about to dial the number, Tommy barged into the cottage with urgent news.

"FLYNN!" he yelled. "Come here now! You've got to see this."

This was bad timing, but Flynn had to go to stay true to the "best mate honour code." And Poppy wouldn't be alone for long. "Poppy, can you wait right here until I get back?" Flynn asked. Poppy nodded and Flynn raced after Tommy, feeling much appreciation for Poppy's cooperation.

After what felt like ten minutes, Poppy couldn't wait any longer. She ran out of patience and dialed the number written on the parchment. After a while, a croaky voice bellowed back, "Hullo?"

"Hi," Poppy replied.

"If this is the Interpol, I'm hanging up," the voice warned Poppy.

"I'm not the Interpol, silly!" Poppy giggled.

"I guess the authorities don't sound this cute," Vern stated, thinking it safe to continue conversing with the little voice.

"What's your name, little girl?"

"Poppy."

"How lovely."

"What's yours?" Poppy asked.

"Vern."

"Vern?"

"Yes," Vern bellowed, "like a fern, but with a V."

"That's a nice name," she decided after much thought.

"I'm glad you think so, Poppy. It's short for Vernon." Vern secretly wished he got calls like this one more often.

"Vern is much better," Poppy blurted.

"Much!" Vern agreed. "Vernon makes me want to throw up."

"Me too!" Poppy laughed hysterically.

"Well, Poppy, why have yer called?"

"I wanted to know why Ollie Wollie has gone away," she said in a much more sombre tone.

"Ah yes, Poppy, would you like to speak to this Ollie Wollie?" Vern found the nickname to be quite humorous.

"Hmm-mm," Poppy replied.

"Right then, let me get him." Vern hollered out to Oliver, who was in the yard. He hollered so loudly that Poppy could clearly hear it on the phone. "Ollie Wollie!" Vern shouted. "You've got a call!"

Oliver dropped the hoe and bolted inside. There was only one person who called him Ollie Wollie.

"Ollie Wollie," Vern roared in laughter as he passed on the phone. Oliver shook his head at his uncle.

"Poppy," he whispered, "is that you?"

"Ollie, why have you gone away?" Poppy outright asked.

"Oh, Poppy! I wish it didn't have to be like this, but I can't change it." Oliver felt a new weight added to his shoulders, for he hadn't yet thought about how he had to leave Poppy too.

"But I miss you!" Poppy felt sadness burn in her eyes.

"I miss you too, Pops!"

"Then come back, Ollie," Poppy begged.

"I can't."

"Why not?" A tear dripped down her face.

"Oh, Poppy, I want to tell you, I do. But you must ask Bea. She wouldn't want you to hear it from me."

"Okay," Poppy said, almost silently.

"Oh, Poppy, don't sound so glum. Tell me about your pets," Oliver asked, hoping for something cheerful. "Ramsey, Petey, Daisy, Duron, and Pip. How are they?"

This was a question Poppy could answer, and answer it she did. For several minutes, she blabbed on about them. This made Oliver smile more than he had in days. Talking to Poppy was just what the broken boy needed to feel like he was home again.

That night, long after Dad had tucked Poppy into bed, the girls came home from their exhausting day of fun and wedding shopping. When Bea climbed in bed, she expected a long, restful sleep, but instead she lay awake half past the stroke of midnight, trying not to think of "the conversation." She thought a day with sisters would cure her, but it only heightened her stress. To be frank, she couldn't stop thinking about Oliver. He was like a best friend, a boyfriend, and a brother all mixed into one. "Brother!" she yelped in the dark. Suddenly she knew what would help her.

Bea crept out of bed and down the hall where Flynn's door was ajar. She peeked through the crack, and there was Flynn, half asleep. The bed next to Flynn's was deserted, with the blankets folded neatly at the foot of it.

"Bea," Flynn's eyes fluttered open, "is that you?"

"Yes."

Bea didn't expect him to be awake.

"What are you doing?" Flynn sat up.

"Couldn't sleep," Bea stepped inside, "but I didn't mean to wake you."

"You didn't," Flynn shrugged. "Turns out it's sort of nice listening to Oliver sleep talk."

Bea laughed. "You miss him too?"

"So he's not coming back then?" Flynn ignored her question.

"Not sure." Bea looked at the floor and then at her brother. "Flynn?"

"Yeah?" Flynn expected some big life-altering question, but instead Bea asked, "What did you and Tommy do today?"

"You won't tell?" Flynn questioned, relieved that Bea was in the mood to ask easy questions.

"I wouldn't dare," Bea swore herself to secrecy.

"We hid some booby traps in Mr Petosa's yard," Flynn whispered.

"Course you did," Bea burst into laughter. "Did he catch you?"

"No, we timed it right. Mr Petosa went to town to take that awful Ziggy to the vet. So we went mental," Flynn explained.

"Rightfully so," Bea laughed, and then the two of them laughed till nearly dawn, when they fell asleep at last.

TOP SECRET   ssayer

31

MEN AND MAIDS OF MISCHIEF

With Oliver gone, Eve's wedding approaching fast, Flynn felt it his duty to call a "TOP-SECRET" treehouse gathering. The meeting was communicated via pillow post, and when Bea found her invitation crumpled under her pillow the night before, her broken spirits seemed to lift, even if only slightly.

That evening, when Eve left for her date with Henry, Flynn and Tommy snuck to the treehouse. The others arrived minutes later to find Flynn with a clipboard in hand.

"Bea?" Flynn looked up from his clipboard as Bea entered.

"Yes?" Bea raised an eyebrow.

"Will you be our scribe?" Flynn thrust the clipboard into Bea's hands; writing was one of the things he loathed most.

"Most assuredly." Bea straightened up to give off a professional air. She took her seat on a stump in the front row.

She watched as Lucy, Poppy, and Rose filed in.

Flynn approached the makeshift pulpit with lots to say. "All right," he nodded, ensuring that everyone he invited made it. "I'm sure you are all wondering why I've called a meeting today."

They nodded in his direction.

"Well, with Eve getting married and our days full of obnoxious wedding details," he rolled his eyes, "I thought it would be grand for us to plan something of our own," Flynn scrambled for the right words.

"Like what?" Lucy was curious.

"A prank of sorts," Flynn elucidated.

Lucy turned the thought over in her mind, like a pig roasting over the fire. "A prank?"

"On Eve?" Rose perked up.

"Yes, and yes."

"I LOVE IT!" Bea shot up from her stump.

Flynn flashed Bea a malicious smile. "You do?"

Bea nodded enthusiastically.

"I knew you would." Flynn continued to grin.

"Wouldn't she be furious?" Lucy wasn't quite sure.

"How could she be?" Rose negotiated. "It will be her wedding day you know. She'll be in such a good mood that it will be the perfect time to get her good without much of a looming consequence," she added.

"I'm in," Lucy decided on a whim.

"Me too." Rose dropped her shoulders and smiled subtly.

"Poppy?" Flynn eyed his little sister with a nervous look.

"I fancy a good trick," Poppy answered, swinging her feet upon her perch.

"Well then," Flynn beamed. "Shall we brainstorm? Any ideas?"

"I know!" Tommy fluttered his hand anxiously in the air.

"And . . ."

"We could tell Mr Brown to make a special cake that is really wheels of cheese stacked atop each other with frosting slapped on top." Tommy cackled at his own evil idea.

"Now that could be funny," Flynn laughed along with his friend.

"Wouldn't that be a bit too mean?" Lucy could see Eve's expression when she took the first bite of the cake, and it wasn't pretty.

"It would only be a 'cheese' cake," Bea chuckled, for she was always the first to find a pun embedded in everything.

"Oh gosh." Rose shook her head at Bea. "Tommy, how long did it take you to think that one up?"

"Not long, just a week or so," he said, as if it was only a few minutes.

"Alright, alright! Order in the court, lads!" Flynn thumped the gavel on the podium as he impersonated Grandad Bean perfectly. The congregation roared in laughter at Flynn's brilliance, especially Bea, who couldn't contain herself when Flynn impersonated Grandad.

"Order, I say!" Flynn squawked, once again fuelled by the amusement of others.

After taking several minutes to recollect themselves, Rose piped up, "I've got something!"

"What if when they share their first kiss we hold up chalkboard slates and rate the kiss on a scale of one to ten?" Rose giggled at her own idea.

"How romantic," Bea snorted, but the others didn't rate the plan brilliantly.

"Eve won't like that," Lucy was certain of this.

"She'll think we have no respect for the merits of true love," Flynn mocked.

"How 'bout fake bugs in the drinks? Or whoopee cushions?" Poppy suggested.

"Can't go wrong with whoopee cushions," Lucy pointed out.

"No, Eve has always had zero appreciation for fart humour," Rose moaned.

"Why is that?" Bea asked, who'd found fart jokes to be obviously superior.

"What about fake bugs?" Poppy hadn't given up.

"Or stink bombs?" Tommy suggested.

"No!" Rose and Flynn shouted in unison, who'd had unspeakable experiences with stink bombs.

"It was worth a shot!" Tommy shrugged.

"Ooh! I've got one!" Bea's eyes lit up. "What if we made confetti and slid it in the vents of the car so it couldn't be seen? Then when Henry starts the car, the confetti will shoot everywhere!"

The whole treehouse shook with enthusiasm.

"Brilliant!"

"That's the one!"

There was nothing like mischief to set things right.

32

MISSING IN ACTION

Two weeks had passed since Oliver left and Bea had ceased faking happiness and was beginning to really feel it. Even though things were improving, a piece of her still wasn't there. Missing in action, lost. Thankfully, no one at the Bean home was trying to stick their noses in her business. If they had, she doubted she would have listened. So lying in bed she focused on what still made sense and hoped that it would be enough.

Suddenly her thoughts were interrupted by a tiny yet urgent gasp and a series of desperate whimpers. Bea shot out of bed like a rocket and fled to Lucy's bedside. Lucy's sheets were damp with sweat and her face was wet with tears.

"Hey," Bea whispered softly as she brushed Lucy's hair from her face.

Lucy cried a bit harder at her sister's kind touch.

"Did you have a nightmare?"

Lucy feebly nodded.

"It's over now," Bea said.

These words seemed to pull an explanation out of Lucy, "It was Poppy—" She shivered. "And the day at the swimming hole. When I couldn't save her, no one else could."

"Come here." Bea grabbed her from her bed and held her. She held her as she shook, but Bea didn't silence her trembling. For she knew exactly what it felt like to tremble in the familiar way that Lucy did, and somehow being with her was not just for Lucy's comfort but also Bea's as well.

"Lucy," Bea whispered, "you know the feeling you felt when Poppy was drowning and you couldn't help her?"

Lucy let out a high-pitched whimper that turned into a series of cries.

"I know that feeling."

"You do?"

"Yes, I felt it the strongest when I was six years old. When you were born."

Lucy's whimpers became a little more controlled.

"I don't remember anything about the twins being born except how funny they smelled. But I remember nearly everything about you being born. I remember realizing that our family wasn't complete without you, and I remember how excited I was. I remember being notoriously impatient when Mum left for the hospital. I didn't sleep a wink that night. For several days, I only saw you through glass and I couldn't hold you because of your complications. I remember crying in Dad's arms, not sleeping much, and feeling powerless because I couldn't help you. You were five days old and had already suffered more than I had in my whole life, and I wanted to take that from you. But I couldn't." Lucy had stopped crying and was now listening. "When Mum let me hold you for the first time after the doctor's stitched you back up, I remember believing that you were the most beautiful baby in the whole wide world and that I loved you so much. That was the first time that I felt real love. The kind that cannot be contained."

A single tear glistened on Lucy's cheek.

"And I've always loved my siblings very much but not so much as I love you. And however cruel it sounds, almost losing you made me love you differently."

"Really?" Lucy had never heard this before.

"Hmm-mmm." Bea smiled.

Lucy gazed up at her sister.

"So next time you are taken back to that day when Poppy almost drowned, remember that she didn't, that she is still here for you to love."

"You're right," Lucy said.

"And, Lucy, I know you don't always like it, but it's not a bad thing to be worried about the people you love. It shows how big your heart is," Bea breathed.

"Thanks, Bea," Lucy cried. "But . . ."

"But what?"

"How are you?" Lucy sincerely asked. She had wanted to comfort Bea since Oliver left, but Bea had a knack for escaping situations that made her feel vulnerable.

Bea fumbled with her hands. "Many people suffer more than I do," she quietly commented.

"But yet you still suffer," Lucy replied.

Bea stared at Lucy. "It would be ungrateful to say that I suffer. Not with everyone I have to love," Bea pronounced.

"Not everyone."

"Oh, Luce, Mum is still with us."

"I'm not talking about Mum."

"Then who?" Bea hesitated.

"Bea, we all miss him terribly, and I know you do too." Lucy confidently but serenely said the words that Bea most needed to hear but she ran from.

"Lucy, no."

"Bea, you don't have to hide that you love him! That is not what love is supposed to be." Lucy eyed her sister.

"Get some sleep," Bea smiled as she headed for the door.

"Where are you going?"

"I don't know."

33

THE GOOSE CHASE

Bea did not know where she was going, but who did when they were headed somewhere they'd never been? After speaking with Lucy, her perception changed entirely. With new thoughts consuming her, she had to go somewhere peaceful where she could sort through them. So she ran to the wood behind the meadow to listen to the babbling brook and to finally understand what she was meant to do. It was five a.m. when she got there, and eight a.m. when she left.

At eight a.m. she ran inside to retrieve her things and crashed into Lucy, who was the only one up.

"What's going on?" Lucy followed Bea as she hastily rummaged through the dresser.

"I've come to my senses thanks to you, Luce." Bea bent over and kissed the top of her head, and in a flash, she fled out the door with a satchel slung across her shoulder and a reminiscent sparkle in her eye. She said nothing else, but Lucy knew exactly where she was going, and she couldn't help but grow anxious with excitement. Bea started off on her blue bicycle down Lavender Lane with a buzzing mind, heading in the direction she imagined Oliver went.

. . .

At eleven a.m., Rose heard a familiar knock at the front door. She was alone in the house and engrossed in a book titled *History's Most Influential Dancers*, and though the rest of her family would have called the novel "boring," she couldn't pull her eyes from the page. The knock persisted, and against her will she tore herself from her book and went to the door.

"You!" she blurted as she saw the beggar at her door. She did not want to see him. Not after he'd abandoned her sister.

"Rose!" Oliver gasped, clearly excited to see her.

"You snake," Rose pointed her finger at Oliver. "You slithering, selfish, dubious snake!" Clearly, Bea hadn't told Rose the whole story, for Oliver had neither been dubious nor selfish.

A bit frightened and surprised, Oliver hesitated, "May I come in?"

"No, you may NOT!" Rose put her hand on her hip. "You put my sister into a blubbering depression, and you expect me to just embrace you! Huh? Is that it?"

Oliver tried to speak but he couldn't. He had no idea he had hurt Bea so much, and that was the sharpest dagger of all.

"She doesn't need any more hardship, especially from you," Rose explained loudly. "So why don't you just do what you do best and RUN AWAY!" she howled, though she wouldn't have said such things to a friend she loved so dearly if she knew the full story. But assuming she was right to be enraged, Rose spoke harshly.

Without another word, Oliver turned away. Heavy with the pain he had involuntarily bestowed upon Bea, and distraught with the worry that he could never make it right, Oliver skulked away, the passion he had brought with him to Lavender Lane suctioned from his soul.

. . .

At nine a.m., Bea and her bicycle boarded the morning bus to the little town where Vern lived in hiding. At eleven a.m., she hopped off the bus and rode her bicycle the fifteen minutes to Vern's doorstep. She wanted to stop and admire the remarkable progress Vern had made with his yard, but her mind was far from the spruced-up shrubberies.

Quickly, she knocked, and when the door swung open, she blabbered on at twice her normal speed to get all her questions out. Not understanding half of what Bea said, Vern interrupted, "This is bad," he stated bluntly.

"Bad?" Bea's heart dropped.

"Sort of funny actually," Vern chuckled, as if stuck in his own head.

"What?" Bea shot at him; she didn't have time for a funny story.

"Well, Oliver may or may not have caught a bus to go find you," Vern laughed nervously.

"Find me?" Bea's eyes widened to the size of bowling balls.

"Funny, innit?" Vern flashed a hopeful half smile.

"Funny?" Bea did not agree. "I'd hardly call it that. Can I use your tele?"

Vern let Bea in and she ran to the telephone to dial the home number.

"Hello?" Rose blurted on the other end of the line. "Who is this?"

"Rose, it's Bea," Bea urgently greeted her sister.

"Bea, you wouldn't believe what just happened!"

"Lemme guess, Oliver came looking for me?"

"Now, that's just freaky," Rose muttered slowly, as if processing the whole situation. "Speaking of, where are you, Bea? Lucy was very vague when I asked."

"You'll never guess," Bea shouted.

"Try me," Rose snapped back.

"I'm at Vern's house. You know, Oliver's uncle," Bea laughed, though she really didn't find it funny.

"Oh no," Rose's voice dropped in realization.

"Oh no what?" Bea harassed Rose.

"Are you there to fetch Oliver?"

"Yeah," Bea was feeling extra suspicious.

"Well . . .," Rose hesitated.

"Oh, Rosie. What did you say?" Bea was beyond worry. This couldn't be good.

"Well, if you weren't always bottling things up like gin and hiding from your own sister, none of this would've ever happened!" Rose tried to defend herself.

"I am deeply sorry, Rose, I really am," Bea spoke softly. "But, Rose, I must know, there isn't exactly an abundance of time."

"Alright, I sent him away! Sulking, in fact. My apologies."

"Well, can you catch him?"

"It might be a lost cause, but I'll try," Rose admitted.

"Thank you, Rose. You can catch him, I know you can," Bea assured. "And I'll be there as soon as possible—tell Oliver I'm coming." And then, without another word, the two sisters hung up and went to their separate tasks. Bea turned to Vern in urgency. "Vern, I'm terribly sorry, but do you have any spare change?"

"Of course, I do, Bea! I may seem mad and poor but I'm actually quite rich!" Vern raided his dresser drawers and returned with a handful of coins.

"Come on now! What are we waiting for?"

Bea laughed and followed Vern in a jolt out the backdoor to the corner of the yard where a sizable rusty lump sat concealed beneath oil-stained clothes. Vern tossed the filthy sheet into the thorn bushes and climbed into the old wide car. Bea stowed her bicycle in the ample backseat and climbed in beside him as Vern turned the key into ignition. The car, called Mags, whined beneath them.

"Come on, ole girl," Vern encouraged as he attempted to start the car for the third time, "Come on!"

"It's okay, Vern," Bea softly whispered, but Vern shooed her whispers away.

"Mags, girl, this is important, we need you," Vern whispered to the car as he caressed the dashboard. In reply to Vern's plea, Mags

235

rumbled beneath them, barely alive yet thankfully determined to get Bea to the bus stop. Vern began rolling cautiously down the drive until he gained more confidence in the car, then he slammed his foot on the accelerator and Mags shot down the dirt road like a bullet flying through rain.

"Woah!" Bea held on to her head as if to keep it from flying through the fragile windshield.

"We've got a bus to catch." Vern tried to conceal the thrill he got from the whole situation and a drag race in Mags.

Vern slammed on the brakes just moments before he collided into the little blue sign that read "Bus." Bea and her bicycle carefully climbed out of the car, relieved that they'd both made it out of Vern's vehicle alive.

"Thanks for everything, Vern," she beamed. "I owe it all to you and Mags."

"No time for appreciation, Bea. You've got a nephew of mine to catch." Vern motioned for her to board the open bus.

"Right." Bea pivoted on her heel with a smile and hopped onto the crowded bus. She took a seat near the back and thought about what she might say to Oliver when she saw him. Bea couldn't contain her anxieties and anticipations on that bus, much to the other passengers' annoyance.

"Will you quit shaking that ruddy leg of yours," an elderly man ordered from in front of her.

"I can't hear myself think!" his knitting wife added.

"Oh, sorry," Bea absentmindedly apologized, her mind was indebted to other matters.

. . .

At noon, Oliver was headed not to the Grasmere bus stop but to the Windermere train station, ready to blindly hop on a train and see how far away it could take him. All he knew was that he wanted to go far from here, away from Bea and even the thought of her. He had completely changed course after speaking with Rose and he set his mind on leaving. For good. There wasn't a bus to Windermere for three hours, so unable to sit still, Oliver began to walk.

It was twelve-thirty when the rain started. Oliver didn't have wellies or even an umbrella. All he had was a silly old raincoat that kept his hair dry, but with his heart so heavy, the rain made him feel right at home. Confused thoughts slow-danced through his mind, "Why?" "Is it all over?" "Why did I ever leave the orphanage in the first place?" His thoughts drowned out the outside world, and he had little awareness of his surroundings.

. . .

It was one o'clock when Bea stepped off the bus and into the pelting rain. Her heart raced as her eyes shot in every direction in search for Oliver. "Oliver, Oliver, Oliver," she whispered through her teeth.

"Excuse me, miss," a sweet old lady tugged Bea's arm.

Bea jumped in surprise and spun around to see a little lady sitting politely under the covering of a pink umbrella.

"Sorry, did I frighten you?" the woman chuckled, clearly apologetic.

"No need to fret," Bea smiled. "Can I help you?"

"I was just wondering, are you looking for someone? I couldn't help but notice you seem a bit disoriented."

"You could see all that?" Bea joined the woman on the bench. It felt wonderful to be understood. "He must have just passed through here, I hope I didn't miss him." Bea shrugged and then lit up quite suddenly. "Say, ma'am, how long have you been here?"

"About an hour," the lady beamed. "I'm on the next bust to Brighton to visit my grandies!"

"That's lovely," Bea tried to be polite but time was stripping away. "Have you seen a boy of about seventeen pass through here of late?"

"What does he look like, dear?" The woman rested her plump hand on Bea's nervous one.

"Tall, thin, dark hair, probably looked a bit sad," Bea described.

The woman chuckled heartily at Bea's description. "I know just the one, dear," the observant woman sparkled. "He went that way." And she pointed toward Windermere.

"Much thanks, ma'am!" Bea flung her arms around the little old lady, and the woman accepted the embrace, though she was a bit surprised by it.

"Go." The woman motioned down the road. "Go get him!"

Bea laughed and mounted her bike like a warrior flying through the rain. She rode with an unstoppable fire. No longer was she afraid or conflicted but fuelled by passion and courage. She rode and rode, trusting the woman had led her in the right direction, until abruptly she halted. All she saw was a blur of a boy in the distance. It was not just any boy, but a boy she knew, loved, and missed. "Oliver," she mouthed his name. And that is where she lost her sense. She thrust her bicycle into the underbrush and did the only thing her buzzing head could think to do: hit the ground and run. Run to him.

"Oliver! OLIVER!" she screamed as she sprinted toward him.

Oliver turned in what seemed to be slow motion to see a yellow blur racing toward him. *"Is it?"* he thought. *"It couldn't be . . ."*

But before he could know for certain, Bea leapt into his arms, alarming him out of his sad trance. She flung her arms around his neck, and he held her.

"It's you," was all Bea could say. And all Oliver could do was stare, wonder, and say, "Bea?" in a tone of utter bewilderment.

"I'm assuming Rose didn't catch you in time to tell you," Bea laughed, seeing the befuddled look on his face.

"Tell me . . .," Oliver questioned.

"This," Bea whispered and smiled as she reached for his face.

Oliver blinked twice to ensure he wasn't watching himself dream.

Bea inched closer to him. Her eyes glowing, she kissed him and he kissed her, and for one moment everything sped up and slowed down at the same time. Fireworks exploded inside of them, the rain still descending upon their heads. It was then that everything made sense to Oliver. No more explanations. No more questions or nervous looks, just sound understanding. Just love. Just Bea.

"I had no idea Rose was so smitten with me," Oliver teased.

"Rose? Smitten?" Bea chuckled. "I don't see it."

All at once, the shattered pieces seemed to fall into place, and when Bea and Oliver finally broke apart, they fell into laughter, bursts of it. The kind of laughter that welcomes a new chapter. The kind of laughter that you never grow weary of.

34

HOME AGAIN

Lucy looked up from her book and glanced at the clock. She'd been reading for twenty minutes and yet it felt like an hour had dragged on. Lucy was supposed to be reading a chapter book to Poppy, but her eyes kept wandering from the page.

"What are you looking at?" Even Poppy could tell Lucy was a bit distracted.

"Oh, nothing," Lucy lied and returned to the book.

Lucy and Poppy were home alone for an hour or two while the others were out and Dad was at work. Lucy never liked being alone in the cottage. Even the tight quarters felt big when it was just her and Poppy.

"Did you hear that, Poppy?" Lucy cocked her head in the direction of the kitchen.

She wasn't usually this apprehensive when she was home alone, but ever since Bea had left that morning Lucy couldn't relax.

"Hear what?" Poppy didn't hear anything.

"Nothing," Lucy shook it off and began again.

"Did you hear THAT?" Lucy jumped for the third time.

"No," Poppy shook her head. Lucy was supposed to be reading to her, not pointing out every creak that came from the floorboards.

"You heard that one, right?" Lucy questioned yet again.

This time Poppy heard it loud and clear. The girls turned toward the direction of the noise. Lucy tiptoed to the edge of the room that turned sharply into the foyer. Poppy hid behind Lucy. Tentatively they peeked around the corner to see the lock on the door turning slowly with a small click. As the knob twisted, Lucy's heart pounded in suspense, she gasped, and the door swung open. Her imagination caused her to expect a burglar or a kidnapper, but instead a bright face popped through the crack in the door.

"Anybody home?" the voice echoed through the entryway.

"BEA!" Lucy squealed, running to her, and Poppy followed. "I thought you were a burglar!"

"It's just me," Bea laughed, but as Lucy peered over her sister's shoulder, she discovered that it was not JUST Bea at the door. Behind Bea stood an equally bright faced individual who had been greatly missed.

"OLIVER!" Lucy jumped out of Bea's arms and into his, and Poppy followed.

Oliver snickered as he hugged the two girls with all his might.

"You came back!" Poppy observed with enthusiasm.

Oliver looked from the girls to Bea and said, with his eyes locked with Bea's, "I didn't get very far."

Bea smiled at this in a warm and gentle way that confirmed her gratitude that Oliver was safely home.

"And you'll stay?" Lucy hoped.

"For good," Oliver said, and he was confident in his forthright assurance.

An hour passed and an additional Bean seemed to burst into the cottage every fifteen minutes. Just as Oliver was getting resituated in Flynn's room, Flynn and Tommy came storming into the kitchen, blabbering on about all sorts of topics.

"I cannot believe that game last night," Flynn went on as he searched the biscuit cupboard.

"Unbelievable," Tommy agreed.

"Do you really think Jane likes me?" Flynn changed the subject.

"Flynn! Enough about Jane!" Tommy roared from behind the icebox door.

"Alright, alright, she's just so fascinating," Flynn confessed with a dazed look.

"Oi, Flynn! Tommy!" Oliver slid into the kitchen to show himself.

"Oliver?" Tommy blinked twice to ensure he was truly there.

"OLIVER!" Flynn shrieked in surprise. He was so surprised that the jar of jam he was holding dropped from his hand and shattered into a million pieces. Ignoring the shards of glass and spilt jam, Flynn launched at Oliver with no warning.

"I missed you too," Oliver laughed as Flynn squeezed him. He'd never realized how much he meant to the boy.

Flynn's tight grip took Oliver's breath away, literally, and Flynn had to be pried off him by Bea.

"Flynn, you nearly killed him," Bea teased with a playful push.

Tommy, who found Flynn's reaction hilarious, fell to the ground in laughter.

"Flynn loves Oliver! Flynn loves Oliver," he jeered.

"Oh, shut up," Flynn smacked his friend. "It's been a while." He flushed pink.

Rose was the next to come through the door a few minutes later, and she did not do it quietly.

"Bea? BEA! Are you back?" Rose shouted between gasps. She was fully dressed in her ballet uniform but she was in total disarray. Her hair was undone and wild, and she was at her knees, gasping for air.

Bea and Oliver ran to greet her, and relieved to see Oliver back, Rose embraced them both.

"I didn't spoil everything!" she cheered.

"Not this time, Rosie," Oliver bantered, but she didn't even tackle him for it. She was too glad to have him home.

Eve came in third with an armful of dresses practically burying her. She kicked the door shut behind her and announced to the house, "I've got the bridesmaid dresses."

"Eve!" Oliver ran to help her.

"Oliver! You're back?" Eve dropped the dresses, confounded.

"Yes!"

"Oh, I'm so glad!" Eve embraced him at once.

Dad was the last to shuffle through the front door. The day at the wood shop had been a long one and his head hung low as he approached the cottage. Nothing could better soothe his aching head than a hot meal shared with his children. When he slid through the door, the lads in the living room didn't even turn. He didn't holler his usual, "I'm home," for he didn't dare interrupt the magic happening around the fireplace. He simply stood in the doorway smiling at them. Poppy was telling a boisterous story of her latest adventure. Eve had completely forgotten supper; she'd been swept up in her family. Bea sat next to Oliver, looking much too pleased to claim anything other than love—a face Dad did not miss. Lucy impersonated Donald Duck perfectly, sending everyone else into a laughing fit, and the twins were right in the mix. Everything seemed to settle into its rightful place.

35

CHAOS

Summer came quickly that year. By late May, the moors were swept with a lush kind of green that demanded adventure. The many storms of the winter and spring were replaced by bright days and pleasant nights. June 23 was the day that always danced in the back of Eve's mind, and when the day finally approached, Eve held her breath as she watched her new beginning unfold.

"Tomorrow's the day, Evie," Bea reminded her sister as Eve walked to her bedroom.

"Indeed it is, Bea. I don't think I'll be able to sleep tonight," she exclaimed.

"Don't expect to," Bea patted her sister on the back, bidding her goodnight.

To Eve's surprise, and Bea's too, each of the Beans slept soundly that night. The sun had been awake for hours when Henry peered into the front window of the cottage to see a quiet house. In distress, he pounded on the front door like his fist was made of thunder. At the alarming knock, Eve shot up in her bed. Blurry-eyed, she studied her alarm clock. It was eight o'clock and she was supposed to be up hours ago.

"Oh no!" In a panic, she leapt out of bed and pulled on her robe. She rushed to the door and invited Henry in.

"Eve! Have you seen the time?" Henry asked, nervous to break the news to her.

"Eight o'clock, Henry!" Eve dropped her head into her hands. "I should've been up hours ago!"

"It's alright, Evie. We can make this work," Henry soothingly assured her.

"You are not even supposed to see me yet." Eve was starting to spiral. "It's bad luck!" Eve looked down at her sweaty robe and bunny slippers thinking nothing could be a more foreboding sign of poor luck than being seen like this on their wedding day.

"That's just an old wives' tale." Henry invited himself in. "And you are NOT bad luck, Eve Marie." Henry kissed her head. "Come on, let's go wake the others!"

In thirty minutes the tables had turned and the quiet house was exploding with noise, bodies, and anxiety.

Henry's father, Juliette (the woman who'd practically raised him), and Juliette's two-year-old son Jack were the first to offer their help.

"Ah, Juliette, Dad," Henry invited them in. "Come in, come in! We need all the hands we can get!"

Poppy rushed to Jack, whom she had befriended the night before, and picked him up.

"Poppy?" Where are you going?" Rose yelled as Poppy bolted out the backdoor with little Jack bouncing on her back.

"To make sure the pets are ready," Poppy loudly explained over her shoulder as she ran. After much consideration, Eve agreed to allow the animals to be a part of the ceremony, and Poppy couldn't be more thrilled about it.

Aunt Kit was the next to come through the front door. She stormed in with a bowl of pudding in her arm. Flynn was running in the opposite direction, following Eve's orders, and did not see his aunt coming. The two collided in the foyer and pudding splattered everywhere.

"Hello there, Flying Flynn." Aunt Kit had been calling him "Flying Flynn" ever since he could walk, and never had the name been so fitting. "Where did you come from?" she snorted as she smeared the pudding that splattered on her vest across his face.

"Aunt Kit!" Flynn hugged his aunt, getting more pudding on her sleeve.

"How's my favourite nephew? Staying sane with all this wedding fuss?"

"Barely." Flynn sampled the pudding on his face. "It's very good, Aunt Kit."

She playfully pushed him down the hall, laughing, and joined the girls in the kitchen.

"Lucy! Set the biscuits on the farthest table," Eve ordered as Lucy picked up the plate of biscuits.

Lucy nodded and started out the door.

"Aunt Kit!" Bea exclaimed. "What happened to you?"

"Ah, nothing." Aunt Kit tied an apron around her waist. "How can I help?"

May and Arli were the next two to join the preparations.

"Eve 'almost' Eddington!" May squealed. "Why aren't you dressed? You are getting married in an hour!"

Eve looked at her feet, she was still wearing her bunny slippers.

"Oh, May!" Eve laughed. "This is a disaster."

"Come on, Eve, let me fix you!" May gripped her wrist and yanked her down the hall.

"Has anyone seen Ramsey?" Poppy flew into the kitchen with Jack nearly falling off her back. She was out of breath.

"Is he not by the playhouse?" Lucy asked.

"No!" Poppy shouted, clearly worried.

"Well, why didn't you tie him up?" Rose interrogated.

"I'm sure he'll come back, Pops," Bea assured, her eyes locked on the recipe she was studying.

"I can't find him anywhere!" Poppy's eyes welled with fear. This made each of the women in the kitchen look up from their tasks.

"Oh, Poppy," Aunt Kit knelt at Poppy's level, "we'll find him, okay?"

Poppy nodded at Aunt Kit's promise.

"Boys," Aunt Kit addressed Oliver, Flynn, Tommy, and Danny, who were in the sitting room, "go find Ramsey this instant. It won't be a proper wedding without Poppy's pets there."

The boys stood up and marched out the door, happy for a job away from the chaotic kitchen full of women.

Oliver stepped into the unassigned position of "captain" and directed each boy to an area to search.

"Flynn, you look near Petosa's yard and cross the fence if you have to," Oliver commanded. "Tommy, you look in the meadow."

In unison they said, "Aye, aye, captain," and went their separate ways.

"Danny, you search the garden. Ramsey cannot resist butternut squash."

Danny nodded and departed at once.

"And I . . . will search the wood," Oliver confidently said aloud.

Twenty minutes later, Ramsey was found whining in the wood with his paw caught up in a thorny shrub that was badly in need of pruning.

Oliver called for Danny and the two heroes gallantly pried the clumsy dog free. Oliver caught him before he could get too far and fastened a leash around him.

"Do you want to take him to Poppy?" Oliver asked Danny. "She'll be over the moon to see him." Oliver laughed as he handed Danny the reigns.

Inside the house, Bea was pressing her dress when she started to smell something burning. She picked up the iron to see that it had burnt right through the fabric! Bea screamed and Aunt Kit ran to help her patch it up. Rose rushed to aid May, and Lucy, who was the only one with spare hands, was ordered to take over the prank project. Since

Henry's suit was in the attic, Lucy assumed his things would be too. She raced up the attic steps two at a time and searched for his car keys.

"Looking for something, Lucy?" an intense looking man asked. His hair was stone grey and his eyes were just as grey.

"Ahh!" Lucy jumped, throwing the keys into the air.

When she turned to see him there it made her heart drop. Mr Eddington (Henry's father) was quite a rigid-looking man and his voice was just as stern.

"Sorry, dear, did I frighten you?" He held out his hand to help Lucy up.

Lucy had not yet discovered his gentle heart. "No, I'm fine." Lucy scrambled to the floor.

"So tell me, what are you looking for?" he asked in a stern yet gentle way that called for honesty.

"I'm feeling guilty now," she confessed, "but my siblings and I were planning a wedding prank. I was sent to fetch the keys."

"You know what, Lucy?" Mr Eddington paced the room, the floorboards creaking beneath him.

"What?" Lucy asked, terrified as to what he'd say next.

"I like you," Mr Eddington stated grimly.

"You do?" Lucy's voice was soaked in surprise.

"Why so surprised, dear?" Mr Eddington chuckled.

Lucy shrugged.

"Is it my grimace?" Mr Eddington asked, clearly self-conscious about the matter.

"Grimace?" Lucy didn't quite know how to answer his question.

"I've been told that I have a permanent grimace etched on my face. People say it's quite frightening. Have you noticed?"

Lucy laughed, but her giggles quickly drowned out as Mr Eddington did not find it funny.

In a serious tone, he analysed the matter. "I think I was born with it. It's always been with me. And no matter how satisfied I am on the inside, it never really shows."

"I don't think it's such a bad thing, sir."

"And why is that, Lucy?" Mr Eddington was very curious.

"Because you can surprise people with how kind you really are," Lucy observed.

"Hmm . . ." Mr Eddington scratched his chin in consideration. "How very insightful that is, Lucy."

"Thanks!"

"Yes, your father must have taught you very well," Mr Eddington thought aloud. "Now, tell me about this prank of yours."

Pleased with the friend Mr Eddington was proving to be, Lucy motioned for him to follow. "Come this way! I could use some help."

Mr Eddington followed and the unlikely pair raced out the door to complete the mischievous mission.

ADVENTURE BOUND

36

A NEW CHAPTER

"Woah, Eve!" Rose clasped her hand to her mouth.

Eve stepped out into the light wearing her mother's wedding gown.

"You look amazing!" Rose admired the grace of both the gown and her sister. Both were equally magnificent in Rose's eyes.

"I feel like I'm taking her with me." Eve blinked back at her reflection in the mirror.

"One day it will be you in this dress." May nudged Rose.

"I can assure you it will NOT," Rose said decidedly.

"Perhaps she'll marry for the mere idea of a wedding," Eve suggested, laughing.

"How cruel yet so awesome." May dropped her head in amusement.

In the following half hour guests filed into the meadow, taking their seats amid the brilliant colours of summer.

The children (minus Eve and Poppy) tread down the aisle, taking their places on either side of the archway that crawled with pink roses, where Henry and his father were already waiting. The boys were dressed in grey and the girls in pink. Gathering the pets, Poppy and Danny made their way to the back of the meadow.

"Danny! We've never had a crowd quite like this!" Poppy yelped. "Isn't it exciting?"

Danny, however, did not look as elated as Poppy.

"I've never seen so many people in my life." Danny's face took on a tint of green.

"Me either!" Poppy bounced. "Big day, isn't it? One I cannot, will not, ruin with mischief," Poppy crossed her heart.

"Roger that, Poppy." Danny looked as if he might throw up, but he didn't.

"Need any help, Poppy?" Dad asked his daughter as she, Danny, and the pets prepared to walk down the aisle.

"No, Daddy," Poppy smiled confidentially.

"That's my girl," Dad winked. "Break a leg!"

"Break a leg?" Danny urgently whispered to Poppy. "I don't want to, Poppy!"

"Relax, silly! It's a thea-tri-cal term," Poppy stuttered on the big word.

Poppy climbed onto Bess' back and the music began. Danny led the animals bravely down the aisle as Poppy waved directions with her baton. They'd made it successfully down the aisle with no hiccups! Phew! Poppy took her place next to her sisters and Danny joined his mother in the second row. Now it was Eve's turn!

At once, the backdoor swung open and Eve, beautiful Eve, came toward them. The sunlight found her and made her shine. The congregation turned with mouths agape. Dad's eyes lit at the sight of her. Watching as she approached, he was taken back to the day he married Marie in this same meadow. How proud Marie must be of her namesake.

"I thought you were your mother." Dad took his daughter's arm. "I wish she were here."

"She is, Dad. Can't you feel it?"

Dad took a deep breath in and exhaled. "Yes, I feel it."

Dad stopped under the canopy of roses, embraced her one last time as Eve Bean, and the next time he embraced her she was Eve Eddington.

Once the words "I pronounce you man and wife" were proclaimed, loud celebratory chants rang through the meadow. Amidst hugs and well-wishes the music started and the Beans rushed to the dance floor. Soon the rest of the guests followed the music and Lavender Lane was full of dancers.

Eve scanned the meadow; she couldn't seem to catch her breath. Though the day had been chaotic and imperfect, she did not care like she thought she would. All her careful planning and checklists and perfect tartlets seemed completely insignificant. She was surrounded by the delightful people that built her life. Those who raised her, taught her, drove her mad, made her laugh, smile, and those who stood so loyally beside her. Now that was all that mattered.

A slow song came on and Henry grabbed her arm and pulled her in close.

Rose demanded that Flynn dance with her to save her from Henry's creepy French cousin that kept following her.

"But I can't dance," Flynn said.

"It doesn't matter, blockhead, I'm your sister!"

"Oh yeah!" Flynn laughed. "I don't care what you think!"

Rose rolled her eyes.

Tommy asked Lucy to dance, and he did it in the *most* gentlemanly manner.

"You are a girl. I am a boy." He tapped her shoulder. "I have no one to dance with, you have no one to dance with."

Perhaps Lucy only danced with Tommy to shut him up, and who would've blamed her?

Bea, however, was nudged by an apple thief who had ideas of his own. "Say, should we add some spunk to this party?"

"How much spunk do you have? Cause we are going to need a LOT of it," Bea replied.

Oliver jumped into the air and spun around, revealing just how much spunk he had to offer.

"That'll do," Bea laughed, and the two pranced around, adding more than enough personality to the party.

Danny danced with Ramsey, and Poppy deserted all other options and skipped to her *one* daddy.

"Ahh, Poppy. Are you the only one who hasn't been snatched up by boys?" Dad mounted her on his toes.

Poppy giggled and promised, "I won't ever get snatched up by any boy, Daddy."

"Good."

A few songs later and ready for a breather, Flynn caught Bea's eyes. Without any need for words, they headed for the treehouse and the others followed. Although Eve had more than enough to keep her attention, she noticed almost immediately and ran to Dad, leaving Henry to listen to his great-aunt's boring story.

"Where'd the others go?"

Dad replied at once, "To the treehouse I saw. You should join them." He winked.

Eve did exactly this. She pulled up her dress and ran to the top of the hill. She climbed the familiar rope ladder, only to find Bea, Oliver, Rose, Flynn, Lucy, and Poppy sitting on the bare floor with a plate of stolen biscuits as the centrepiece.

"Eve!" Lucy shot up.

"Hello, family," Eve smiled, joining them on the dusty floor.

Though her siblings had never seen her so happy, a look of longingness was evident in her eyes.

"You happy?" Rose asked.

"Exceedingly."

"This is a big moment, Evie. A new beginning," Bea observed.

"Indeed it is." Eve's face lit up. "I cannot wait to start my life with Henry."

"Why do you have to go?" Poppy was tired of saying goodbye.

"Goodbyes aren't easy are they, Poppy?" Lucy understood.

"This isn't goodbye," Eve spoke up.

"It isn't?" Flynn asked, hopeful this meant she would stay.

"I'm not going anywhere," Eve assured.

"Except London, of course," Rose shot back.

Eve laughed aloud, *got to love Rose.*

"I'll still visit and call and love you, even if it is from a distance."

"You sound so much like Mum," Flynn smiled happily.

"You all don't realize it, do you?" Eve eyed her brother.

"Realize what?" Lucy inquired.

"How capable you are. How strong you are," Eve paused. "A year ago I didn't believe you could ever survive without me. Selfish, I know, but true. But you have grown into brilliant, bright, and fearless people who can thrive in their own soil."

Each listened to Eve like it was their own mum speaking to them again. Although they wished to cling to their sister who had made them feel like their Mum had never left, they knew Eve was right. So they hugged her until they laughed.

"Come on," Eve motioned. "The dance floor is suffering without us."

The children danced for an hour more until it was time for Eve and Henry to begin their life and the guests had gone. Henry helped Eve into the passenger seat and turned the key into ignition. To their great surprise, confetti shot everywhere, turning their beginning into a fiesta.

Eve rolled down the window to see Oliver, Bea, Rose, Flynn, Lucy, and Poppy all at their knees in laughter, along with her suspicious-looking father-in-law not far behind.

"Good one, lads," Eve and Henry sneered.

The pranksters stood beaming at their sister as she blew them kisses and waves. Eve's eyes welled with tears of joy as her siblings chased the car down the lane. When they turned, a new view was waiting for them.

As Dad stood at the door watching his daughter turn out of sight, he couldn't be more excited for her. Interrupting his quiet thoughts, his children ran at him yelling, "Come on, Dad! Come on!"

Dad couldn't combat their plea to follow. So he placed Poppy on his shoulders and followed, practically sprinting to keep up. Oliver and Bea led the way down the gravel path that crossed through the open meadow to the backside of the Yellow Woods. They skipped through the birch trees, giggling as they went.

After what felt like ten minutes, Bea and Oliver halted at the edge of the hillside. Hundreds of butterflies still lived happily in this little sanctuary. The "stratosphere" tree caused Dad to marvel; he'd never been here before. He joined his children at the edge of the hillside. They stood against the warm wind with their chins held to the sky. Grasmere looked so lovely in the evening summer light, but nothing was more brilliant than the view of his brave children standing against the wind.

"Isn't life sensational?" Bea spoke up, a surge of passion rushing through her veins. "I could chase it forever."

For a moment no one spoke. Each Bean felt too overwhelmed by the electricity in the air that night.

"Cheers," Oliver called into the distance, "to a life of chasing skies!"

"Cheers!" the Beans echoed Oliver's call just as loudly, truly believing that many of life's wondrous mysteries were yet to unfold in front of their marveling eyes. And simply stated, the Beans couldn't wait.

Shelby Eve Sayer began writing at age 6. At 16, she found herself in a worldwide pandemic that fueled creativity, resulting in her first full-length novel.

Buckle up for a fresh voice that has a knack for expressing joy in both an insightful and colorful way. You do not want to miss being a part of this author's beginnings. When she is not writing she can be found on an adventure or surrounded by her spirited family.

Aggressive investor

These are proactive investors who are ready to lose 50% or more of their portfolio value in exchange for the hope that they could gain so much more. We're talking about doubling their money or tripling their money. They're okay with losing half or even all of their money.

Your age, believe or not, plays a very big factor in how you should invest. If you're below 40, knock yourself out with growth stocks. You can afford an aggressive investment strategy if you're in this age range

Too aggressive

When investing in stocks, your profit will be a percentage of your investment. Now, the amount or the percentage that you can earn may vary from investment to investment. Hence, it is logical to say that the more money you place in an investment, the more money that you can make. Take note, however, that the more money that you place in an investment, the higher will also be your risk. The truth is that no matter how much you know about a particular stock or how much information you have regarding a specific investment, there is still a risk that you can lose it. This is one of the reasons why people want to diversify their investment — and which is a good thing to do. Although being aggressive can make you earn more money, it is also an effective way to make you lose a big part of your investment or even your whole investment in one go. Instead of being too aggressive, you should focus on increasing your rate of success. This means that you should focus on making the right investments over the wrong ones.

Suddenly getting too aggressive is also bad for your bankroll or portfolio. It is an effective way to ruin your strategy. For example, let us say that your strategy involves investing 5% of your total funds per trade. However, you suddenly take an aggressive approach and invest 40% per trade. Instead of having 20 trades, you can now only make 2 trades. Now, considering that there is no assurance of making a profit or getting the right investment all the time, those two trades can fail you. When that happens, you will end up with lots of losses that would be hard for you to recover. Hence, be careful with using an aggressive strategy.

If you are an aggressive investor, the majority of your investment money is placed on short-term and intermediate investments. A lesser percentage is on long-term investment.

CHAPTER 8:

INTRODUCTION TO STOP LOSS

When entering a position, you must have a predefined exit point, in order to limit your risk. This ensures that you don't stick with your losers if a trade doesn't work out as planned. You acknowledge your losers and sell them, taking your losses humbly, and moving on. That's a long-term win, despite feeling like a loss.

Stop Loss Percentage

You will hear the term stop-loss percentage frequently when you trade. This percentage is a value that you set to determine to what extent you can take a loss. If you set the percentage to 10%, and the value of the stock that you invested in begins to fall by 10%, you should let go of that stock so you can maintain your capital and accept the loss. This is an extremely important percentage that you should bear in mind when it comes to trading in the stock market, and this is especially true for stock traders. Many traders worry that they will incur a loss if they sell a stock without waiting for the price to increase. This is the wrong way to approach the situation. If you wait for the price to increase, you may lose out on an opportunity to make a profit. You may also risk getting your capital stuck in that stock alone. You should instead choose to assume a position from the same place or invest in a better stock. If you use this method, you can ensure that your capital is not locked in a bad investment. Consider the following example: if you buy 100 stocks from a company at $1 each, you will have invested $100 of your capital in that stock. You hope that the price of the stock will increase to $1.05 by the end of the day. You should place a stop-loss percentage of 10$ on that stock if the price drops to lower than what you expected. So, you should set your stop loss amount at $0.90. If the price of the stock falls to that number, you know that you should let go of the stock.

CHAPTER 9:

HOW TO READ STOCK CHARTS

This chapter is going to take some time to show you the different parts of these stock charts and teach you how to read them for your own trades.

Identify the Trend Line

When you look at a stock chart, you will notice a line that goes up and down for the stock. This is going to show where the stock is and where it has been over a certain period of time that you are looking like. While this one is pretty simple, we need to point out a few things to help you see what this line is about.

First, understand that all stocks, even ones that are strong and doing well, take huge dives and huge climbs throughout their lifespan. It is important to realize that this is normal and you shouldn't work on your emotions because this could lead you away from some great stocks that are only having a temporary downturn for a little time. You shouldn't react to huge gains or large drops. The trend line should lead you to dig a bit further into the stock.

Realize that, sometimes, a downturn in the stock isn't always a bad thing. For example, Apple had really great stock growth from 2009 to 2012, but from 2012 to 2013, there was a big decrease. Does this mean that the company was failing? No, there was just some different things going on in the company that led to a lower perception of them and made it harder for them to make as big of profits. Steve Jobs retired during that time, and Apple Inc. tried to expand into other markets where it was just too expensive to compete.

These things were easy for the company to overcome as they made some changes afterward. Good investors who dug a little bit deeper and saw these temporary issues may have jumped on the stock during that time when it was at a low price and then saw it grow and give them a lot of profit as time went on and Apple was able to recover.

Look for the Resistance and Support Lines

Once you have had some time to take a look at the trend line, it is time to look for the lines of resistance and support. These are the levels where a stock is going to stay between within a given period of time.

The level of support is a price that the stock is unlikely to drop below unless some big news happens to come out and causes the sock to go even lower. Then, there is the level of resistance, which is the level that the stock is unlikely to go above, at least for a little period of time.

Knowing these two points can help you to make some important decisions when it comes to your trades. It can also help you determine your risk to reward ratio when you are deciding whether to enter into a trade or not. Even if the stock or security ends up staying within that range, these levels can make it easier for you to get profits from your trades.

If you are watching the news or paying attention to the market, you will learn how to spot when a breakout is going to occur. This is when the price of that security will go either below the support line or above the resistance line. You want to watch out for those and pay attention to them to help you make the right decisions for your trade.

Of course, there can be some times when these numbers are going to change and the lines won't' stay the same. If a major change occurs or a big news announcement is made with the company, then these two lines can change. In addition, the resistance and support levels are not going to stay the same forever. If you want the stock for a longer period of time, you will see that these two lines are going to move as the stock prices change as well.

Since you are working with swing trading, you are only looking at a small area of time, so the resistance and support lines are probably going to be a good thing to watch out for. You should be able to see that the stock stays within that range for at least a few days, and you can certainly purchase when the stock price gets to the support level and then sell when the stock gets close to, at, or above the resistance levels.

Know When the Dividend and Stock Splits Occur

When you are looking at the charts for these stocks, you will be able to see if, as well as when, the company was able to issue a dividend. You can also check if there was ever a stock split.

A dividend is going to occur when the company or the board of directors more likely decide to hand out some of its earnings to the shareholders. This is only going to happen if the company earned enough profits to cover all its debts and obligations and then still has some leftover. If you own these stocks, you will earn a bit of the profit. Some companies are going to issue dividends, and some don't. Some people want to earn dividends on the investment and will search out these kinds of companies. But, as a swing trader, you won't hold the position long enough for it to really matter, so you don't need to look for these.

There is also a time when there may be a stock split. This is a move that is done strategically by the board of directors of the company where they decide to issue out more shares of stock to the public. For example, one year, Apple did a seven to one stock split. This means that, for every share of stock that you owned before the split, you now have seven of them. If you owned 100 shares before the split, you would now own 700.

When this happens, the value of the company isn't going to change, but the price of the share might. Companies will often do this if they find that their price isn't in line with competitors so that they are able to attract some of the smaller investors to come into the company since the share of the price is going to decrease.

When this kind of split occurs, you will find that it shows in the stock chart as well. Many times, when this kind of split happens, there are going to be more people who are willing to invest. It is usually going to be a good company that does a stock split, and more people are willing to come on board because the share price goes down. This increases the demand and can help increase the overall share price that is there. Knowing this can be important when you take a look at the stocks that you want to invest in.

Understanding the Trading Volumes Historically for a Security

When you look at the very bottom of a chart, you may see that there are a lot of small, vertical lines. These are going to be the trend of the volumes at which the stock is traded. These volumes are good to know, but they definitely shouldn't be the only determining factor when you are trying to decide whether to purchase a stock or not. Usually, these volumes are going to increase when there is any major news, whether good or bad, about a company.

When you notice that the volumes are increasing, you will also notice that this can cause a shift in the price of the stock, and this shift is going to happen quickly. It is important to remember, though, that it is not a good idea to assume that there is a correlation between the stock price and its trading volume. However, it is good to know what the volumes have been in the past and what they are doing now before you make any decisions.

Knowing the history of a particular stock can be a great way to figure out whether it is going to in the same way as it did in the past and whether it is a good idea for you to enter into the market or stay away from it for now. In some cases, the stock may go against its historical values because there is some big news released about the company at that time. This means that historical data isn't the only thing that you should take a look at when working on your trades. You need to spend some time digging deeper to figure out what is the best trade, but the historical data can certainly give you a good starting point and can add to your research as well.

These are some of the basics to help you out when reading your own stock charts. Each industry and each stock and security will have their own charts, so learning how to read them early on can be a great asset. Once you have taken the time to master these techniques, you should be able to analyze the historical activity of a stock at a high level.

CHAPTER 10:

WHEN TO BUY A STOCK AND WHEN TO SELL IT

The Best Time to Buy Stocks

There is, fortunately, an even easier method to time your purchases of stock.

In 2008, Coke had earnings per share (EPS) of $1.51. In 2009, Coke traded as low as 18.70, on a split-adjusted basis. At that price, Coke had a trailing P/E of just 12.38, an earnings yield of 8.08%, and a dividend yield of 4.39%.

By comparison, today Coke has a P/E of 23.52, an earnings yield of 4.25%, and a dividend yield of 3.05%. The stock has more than doubled from the lows, all while paying a healthy dividend every year.

Anyone could have bought Coke below $20 in 2009, but very few did. It did not require inside information, or stock tips. All that it required was nerves of steel to buy when it appeared that the financial world was ending.

How long into a bear market should one wait to buy a great business?

One method is just to wait for the dividend yield to get to 4%, or the trailing P/E (calculated using the company's last 12 months of earnings) to get to 15 or lower on a stock like Coke. That is the "valuation method."

The second method is the "market timing" method. It involves waiting a fixed period of time into a bear market before buying- – or waiting for a large peak to trough draw down in price.

For example, Coke peaked at 44.47 (split-adjusted) in July 1998. It fell until March 2003, trading as low as 18.50. In other words, it fell roughly 58% from peak to trough.

Again, Coke peaked at 32.79 in January 2008, before the financial crisis really got started. It fell until March 2009, trading as low as 18.72. In other words, it fell roughly 43% from peak to trough.

Using this "market timing" method, you would wait for Coke to sell off 40-50% from its last highest price, and then buy your position.

Since Coke is a blue-chip stock that is included in indices like the Dow Jones Industrial Average and the S&P 500, it tends to bottom at the same time that the general stock market bottoms.

The 2000-2002 bear market lasted roughly 2 years and 7 months. The 2008-2009 bear market lasted roughly 1 year and 4 months.

Let's say that the stock market peaks and then falls for more than 1 year. Further, there is plenty of pessimism on TV, in the newspapers and on the internet, and all of your friends are selling their stocks.

That is the time you want to be loading up on businesses like Coke, especially if it has fallen over 40% from its peak, has a P/E of 15 or less, and has a dividend yield approaching or exceeding 4%.

A time like this will come again. I do not know if it will happen in 2016, 2017, or later, but it is certain to come. Not even the Fed can stop it from happening.

So you want to be ready when this opportunity arrives.

It is July 2016 as I write this. The stock market has gone straight up since March 2009. We have had more than 7 years of a strong bull market, leaving stock valuations (P/E's) high and investors complacent.

Now is the time, in Buffett's words, to be fearful while others are being greedy.

If you raise your cash levels now, you will be ready.

You will have the cash available to buy great businesses like Coke during the next bear market.

When to Sell a Stock

The last step for an investor to claim his gains is to sell his stock. Assuming that the investor followed the previous steps correctly, the investor will almost be guaranteed a large gain. However, the investor needs to decide when to sell the stock in order to maximize his profit. An investor wants to avoid selling a stock too early or too late because it will not allow him to maximize his gains. For long-term investors who look at business fundamentals, there are only a few cases in which they should sell their shares: the business model changes, the business becomes financially unstable, or if the market price is above the fair price.

The first reason to sell one's shares is if the business model changes. The business model is the way the business operates: the customer the firm targets, the way the firm makes money, the products the firm sells. When the firm changes a significant portion of its business model, an investor should consider whether the business is still worthy to invest in because the changes may make it less profitable. For example, in 2014, Amazon was an online store and that is about it. However, in 2017 and 2018, it made significant changes to its business model. The firm added many new services and business segments: Kindle Direct Publishing, Amazon Web Services, Whole Foods, and smart stores. Anyone who owned Amazon's stock before these additions and changes must consider whether the company is still worth owning because the changes could make the firm weaker. For example, when Amazon decided to buy Whole Foods, some investors were concerned that Amazon made a poor decision by investing in physical stores because many people believe that they were dying out. Considering that Whole Foods represents a significant portion of Amazon's expenses, some investors might have sold their shares. Thus, an investor might want to sell his shares of stock if the firm makes significant, adverse changes to the business model.

Investors should also look for adverse business trends when deciding to sell a stock. This means, if a company starts to show signs of failure, the investor should sell his shares because it is likely that the share price will fall along with the business. There are multiple indicators when looking for unfavorable trends.

One of the most important trends to look for is the slow death of an industry. The best example of a company that is experiencing a slow death is Barnes and Noble (BKS)- a major player in the book industry. In the early 2000s, ebook started to become popular among everyday readers. Consequently, readers read less from physical books, leading to less sales for Barnes and Noble. The decline of the physical book industry was paralleled with a decline in Barnes and Noble stock price. On April 1, 2010, the firm's stock price was at $14.46. At this time, some investors realized that ebooks are going to take over, and they sold their shares. However, some did not pay attention to the macro-industry trend, and they decided to hold their shares. Due to their lack of awareness of the industry trends, they had to take major losses. During April of 2019, the stock price was around $5.10; negligent investors lost over 60% of their investment because they did not realize that ebooks were trending. Thus, it is important for investors to look at industry trends.

Investors should also look at financial trends when determining when to sell a business. Unlike when one looks to purchase a stock, investors want to look for declining revenues and profits on the income statement as signals to sell the stock. Investors want to sell the stock if the profits are falling because it could signal the decline of the company. Assuming that an investor purchased his shares in a company while its net income and revenue were increasing, he has most likely made a sufficient return on investment. As long as the company is still growing, the investor should not sell his shares because the value of those shares would most likely rise in value. On the other hand, if the firm starts to see their profits fall, it could signal that the company will start to decline. Then, the investor should sell his or her shares because, over time, the company will become less valuable. The best example of a large firm that started to fail is General Electric (GE), a conglomerate.Throughout 2016, General Electric made about six billion dollars in net income. Although this statistic might make the company seem like a good investment, it was on a downward trend. In 2017, the company lost eight billion dollars and in 2018, it lost twenty billion dollars. If an investor recognized that the firm's profits were declining, he could have avoided large losses; from 2016 to 2018, the stock price collapsed by over 65%. Thus, an investor should look at financial trends in order to look for warning signs when deciding to sell a stock.

The last reason an investor should sell his shares occurs when the market price of a stock is above the stock's fair value. Remember, the fair value of a stock is equal to its future value divided by four (review the end of the chapter called **Cash is King: When to Buy a Stock** for a more in-depth review on the calculation). If an investor owns a stock when the market price is above its fair value and continues to hold it, he will not achieve his annual goal of an average 15% gain because the stock price is likely overvalued, which would cause it to fall. Moreover, if the investor owns the stock when it is trading above its fair value, he would have a severe opportunity cost because he could be invested in stocks that are deeply discounted instead of overpriced; by investing in discounted stocks, he would have a larger long-term gain. Thus, an investor should sell his shares if the market price is above its fair value.

If none of the three selling situations- the business is no longer stable, the business model significantly changes, the market price exceeds the fair price- occur, then the intelligent investor should hold his shares because the stock would be trading below its intrinsic value, assuming the investment was not made in a speculative company and the research was thoroughly completed by the intelligent investor. When a stock is trading below its intrinsic value, it is discounted, allowing investors to make a near-guaranteed profit. Therefore, unless one of the conditions occur, the beginner investor should not sell his shares because it will most certainly increase in value because it is trading below its intrinsic value.

CHAPTER 11:

DOLLAR COST AVERAGING

What is Dollar-Cost Averaging?

The term dollar-cost averaging is a strategy used by both traders and investors in purchasing similar dollar amount investments across specific periods of time. This strategy enables traders to regularly buy investments of a particular cost in order to grow their investments. Under this strategy, assets are purchased regardless of price.

When you start investing, you will probably come across this term. Dollar averaging is a strategy that has been around for quite a while now. There is a general acceptance by experts that investors who implement this strategy regardless of different conditions like the markets and at set intervals tend to perform much better than individuals who invest based on emotions.

Emotional investors tend to be overconfident one minute and in full panic mode the next. Because of this, they tend to expose themselves to numerous risks especially where they do not have a proper investment plant but are simply guided by their emotions.

The best part regarding this strategy is that it eliminates the emotions from investing. You are able to invest regardless of how you feel. This is highly advisable because emotions tend to mess up investing and cause immense losses to investors.

Dollar cost averaging is when an investor uses a set amount of money every month to purchase shares of stock no matter how the market is doing. It allows the investor to avoid investing a lump sum in the market at a bad time. If an investor purchases shares of Johnson and Johnson (JNJ) but, the next day the stock falls 10% due to an unforeseen problem with the company, the investor starts off with a 10% loss. That means the stock price has to rise by about 11% for the shareholder to break even. However, if the investor dollar cost averaged, and bought half of the shares initially and the half after the 10% decline, he would not need to recover 11% to break even. Since some of his shares were purchased at a lower price while some at the higher price, the shares that he purchased after the decline do not need to break even. Rather, the stock price needs to only rise by roughly 5% because the shares purchased after the decline would not be starting at a loss. Thus, dollar-cost averaging allows investors to diversify each of his holdings across a range of prices, mitigating the effects of entering a position at a bad time. Overall dollar-cost averaging is an excellent strategy for an investor to diversify his investments across time.

However, dollar-cost averaging is not perfect. First off, dollar cost averaging requires an investment on a periodic basis. Most investors dollar cost average on a monthly basis but, it can be done on almost any interval. The investor only needs to be comfortable with it and, he must be consistent with it.

However, whenever the investor dollar cost averages, he must always pay a commission; usually, it is $5. A small fee of $5 can be destructive to many beginner investors. If an average investor has $800 per month to invest in stocks and he currently has 4 positions, he can only devote $200 per stock. Assuming the commission is $4.95, the investor must receive a 2.5% gain just to break even. Over time, 2.5% will make a big difference in the return on investment. One way an investor can mitigate the effects of a commission is by investing in one stock each interval. This will allow the investor to invest the same amount of money and pay the commission only once; if he invests in 4 stocks in one interval, he will have to pay the commission 4 times. However, this will reduce the effect of dollar cost averaging. If an investor prolongs the interval, too much money might be invested at the wrong time. On the other hand, if an investor reduces the interval, he will be able to have a position at many different prices, instead of just a few, spreading the risk of a bad entry. Another way to lower the effect of a commission is by investing more money at a time. If a person invests more money, he needs a smaller gain per share in order to break even. However, this is not realistic in the short term for many beginner investors since it can take a long time to build up one's income. Nonetheless, there is a solution; reduce the commission. Although investors do not have control over the commission, they do have control over the brokerage firm they invest with. One brokerage firm, Robinhood, allows investors to purchase shares without commission. Only a few brokerages allow people to invest in stocks commission free, and Robinhood is the most prominent of them. The catch is that the stock researching capabilities are quite limited; however, this should not be an issue for the beginner investor because the information about corporations can be found on websites like yahoo finance. For a beginner investor, it is the best option to set up a Robinhood account so he can take advantage of not having to pay commissions in order to dollar cost average. Even though he will be invested with an "inferior" brokerage, it will allow him to make more money, which is really what matters at the end of the day. Therefore, beginner investors should open an account with Robinhood in order to create diversity in their portfolio.

However, when an investor dollar cost averages, it is important to remember the fundamentals of investing. As explained in the chapters called "The Logic of Value Investing" and "Cash is King: When to Buy a Stock," an investor should never purchase a stock while the price is high and expensive. Rather, he should purchase the stock at a discounted price that can be calculated. If an investor is dollar cost averaging, he never wants to buy it at a price above the Black Friday price. If he does, he will not be able to obtain a solid gain. Even if the investor already owns the stock, he does not want to purchase more shares above the sale price because that money could be used to buy shares in a company that is trading at its sale price. Also, a beginner investor should only use dollar cost averaging to decrease his cost basis. For example, if a dollar-cost-averaging investor bought a stock that was at its sale price of $30, but, one month later, it is trading at a price of $25, he should buy more shares in order to lower the average cost of his investment. If he invested in a good company that is protected with a moat and has been increasing its profitability, the beginner investor will most definitely make his money in the long run, assuming he does not sell his shares early. By lowering his average total cost, his percent gain will increase because there would be a larger difference between the future stock price and average total cost. However, if the investor bought the stock when its price went from $30 to $40, which is no longer at the sale price, the investor would not be using his money efficiently because he could be buying stocks that are on sale. Also, by dollar cost averaging when the stock price is higher, he is increasing his cost basis, which will reduce his percent gain because there would be a small difference between the future stock price and the average total cost. Thus, an investor should only dollar cost average if the stock is still at or below its sale price and if it will lower the investor's cost basis.

Understanding Dollar Cost Averaging

Instead of an investor putting a lump sum amount of money in assets, this approach requires a different approach. An investor will generally put in small but regular amounts on a number of investments and then grow these amounts periodically.

This allows you to spread out the cost basis and gives the investor an opportunity to slowly invest their funds in smaller amounts over a couple of months or years. This ensures that the investment portfolio is protected and insulated from different situations especially in an ever-changing marketplace.

For instance, when prices are rapidly rising at the stocks market, the investor will end up paying a lot more compared to other times. However, the reverse is true when the markets are slow. The investor will be able to grow their investment at low prices and hence insulate themselves. This is the benefit of using this specific investment strategy.

How Dollar Costing Averaging Works

Dollar-costing, as has been defined earlier, is an investment tool used by fund managers, investors, and other stock market participants to build wealth or savings over an extended period of time. This strategy provides a way to manage and possibly neutralize and possible volatility at least in the short term across the markets. The application of this is clear in 401(K) accounts.

Holders of 401(K) accounts are able to choose a pre-agreed amount of their pay to be invested in index or mutual funds of their choosing. This amount will be deducted from their pay as a fixed but regular amount remitted on a monthly basis towards their 401(K) account. It is possible to apply this investment strategy beyond 401(K) accounts and into other investment opportunities like index or mutual funds. Investors can also use the same strategy to invest in dividend investment plans through regular contributions.

Therefore, instead of putting large sums of money into an

investment, an investor will slowly but surely work their way into an investment through small but regular contributions spread out over set periods of time. There are certain benefits associated with this investment approach.

One of the outstanding benefits of using this investment strategy is that the cost basis is spread out over a number of years and at varying prices. This helps to ensure there is sufficient insulation against any market price changes in the future. Also, it implies that investors will experience a higher cost basis during moments of fast rising share prices than during normal stock price movements. Setting up an Investment Plan

There is a way that an investor can plan their life so they can invest using the dollar-cost averaging strategy. To achieve this, the investor will need to accomplish three major things. These are listed below.

1. Determine the amount of money you wish to set aside each month or each pay period for purposes of investing. As an investor, you should ensure that this is an amount that you can set aside comfortably and without pressuring your lifestyle. This amount also needs to be prudent because if it is too little then it will not be of much use.

2. The next step is to establish an investment such as a 401(K) where the funds will be directed. Keep in mind that these funds will very likely be held for a long time

so it is crucial to ensure that any money set aside will not be needed to cover any essentials such as rent or paying bills and so on. Funds are often invested for five to ten years. It is advisable to think about this time period before choosing this investment strategy.

3. Remember that the payment intervals can be of any length but standard. These intervals can be monthly, weekly, or quarterly depending on various factors such as pay frequency and so on. This money is invested in a security or fund that the client wants. Most of the time an investor will set up an automated payment system that deducts funds automatically and then makes these available to the fund and so on. Sometimes investors work with brokers but it is very possible to invest without necessary using the services of a broker.

Example on How to Setup an Investment

Jayden is employed by XYZ firm and has signed up to a 401(K) plan. His employer pays him a net salary of $ 2,000 a fortnight. Jayden makes the conscious decision to set aside 10% of his fortnightly payment towards investments. He chooses to commit 50% of this 10% towards a retirement plan proposed by the employer. He then decides to remit the remainder towards an S& P based Index Fund. In summary, he will be remitting $ 100 towards his employer's plan and another $ 100 towards the Index Fund.

Implications

The dollar-cost averaging strategy has been extremely visible and popular in the 401(K) accounts. Individuals and organizations that invest in these accounts do so regardless of market conditions. In the long run, this approach turns out to be beneficial in many ways least of all is the overall low cost of investment.

There is only one significant drawback relating to this strategy. Should a stock market bubble take place, or you enter a position in the market where there is significant value increase, then the costs relating to the investment will be much higher than would have been the case.

CHAPTER 12:

TOP 10 STOCKS IN UNITED STATES

The New York Stock Exchange (NYSE)

The NYSE (www.nyse.com) is located on the corner of Wall and Broad Streets. It is the largest in the world as far as the market value of the companies traded on it.

Prior to the terror attacks of September 11, 2001, it used to be possible to stand at the stock exchange's gallery window and watch it in action. Now, to enter the gallery, you need to get a special entrance license, or become a photographer for CNBC, Bloomberg or others, or know someone with a key function who can request a permit for you. But once in the gallery, you'll see something amazing that is part of a disappearing world. Traders scurry among dozens of work stations, broadcasting commands with odd hand signals, and navigating their way through mountains of notes transferred from buyer to seller and carelessly let to fall on the trading floor.

Because I was acquainted with the well-known television commentator who goes by the name "Dr. J," I was lucky enough to receive the amazing chance to join a CNBC photo shoot of S&P 500 options traders in the Chicago Stock Exchange. I stood, fascinated, surrounded by dozens of traders shouting and pushing as though in a football game. Later I learned from Dr. J, a former pro-football player, that one of the conditions of acceptance for work on the trading floor known as "pit" is the height, weight, and physical ability to push aside competing traders!

The AMEX Stock Exchange

The American Stock Exchange (www.amex.com) was established in New York in 1842. AMEX is the third-largest stock exchange in the US, after the NYSE and NASDAQ. Trade there focuses mainly on stocks of small to mid-size companies and a range of ETFs, Exchange Traded Funds, about which we will learn more later. AMEX operates similarly to the NYSE, using the tender method of their market makers (we'll learn more about them later, too). AMEX belongs to NASDAQ and its volume of activities is relatively low. AMEX, like NYSE, has also moved most of its processes to quick, effective computerized execution.

Founding NASDAQ

1971 saw an important change take place. The NASDAQ stock exchange was established, and unlike the NYSE, NASDAQ computerized all its trade processes. The NASDAQ computers are in Connecticut and link to more than 500 market makers' computers, allowing electronic trade in one click. Within two decades, and with the proliferation of the Internet, NASDAQ was accessible in the home of every trader. For the first time, the road to private trading was opened. We can, in fact, say that the profession of day trading as we know it now was born with NASDAQ's founding.

London Stock Exchange

Some few years later in London, 1693, the first bonds began to be traded. Immediately afterwards, several British public companies began trading. London's first stock traders operated in coffee shops on Change Street, adjacent to the Royal Exchange, the trading center they were not allowed to enter because of their known "bad habits."

Growth Stocks

These are stocks whose historical record indicates that they are growing and will grow faster than the economy now and in the near future. Obviously, this is subject to a lot of change and variation. What is a growth stock today could stagnate next week, depending on the health of the company and multiple other factors. Brokers are always keeping an eye out for these stocks, so they tend to be priced at the highest point the market will bear. Their risk assessment is usually in the average to higher-than-average range.

Blue Chip (or Bellwether) Stocks

Blue Chip stocks are the reliable bets of the stock market. These are stocks that are usually old companies that have been performing steadily, paying off respectable dividends for years or even decades. Their risk profile is low to moderately low, and brokers tend to hold them long-term.

Income Stocks

The main point of differentiation between these and other

stocks is the amount of dividends that are paid out each quarter. This is where they get their name; 50-80% is typically sent to the stock holder regularly and that acts just like any other income. These shares are typically in companies that are older, mature, and moderately paced growers. The risk is low to moderately low because they aren't expected to rise drastically in share price. That might sound bad, but it isn't the point of owning these stocks, the dividend is.

Value Stocks

A somewhat subjective term, a "value stock" is one that is considered underpriced in relation to its potential. This potential is determined by looking at the company's earnings and other measures that we'll discuss when talking about how to choose a stock in a later chapter. Once you have those skills down, you'll be proficient at finding stocks that are a good value for money.

Cyclical Stocks

When share prices historically track with the economy overall, we refer to them as "cyclical." This means that when times are booming, these companies boom along with them, and when times are tougher, their fortunes tend to fall as well. Companies in industries like airlines, automobiles, and construction tend to fall in this category. The important thing to recognize about this type of stock is that in the short term, their risk level is relatively high, but because they almost always rebound, that risk is lowered significantly when held over a long period of time. Defensive Stocks

Companies that fall in this category can be thought of as the opposite of Cyclical Stocks. They are less vulnerable to economic shake-ups because they're in industries that people buy from in any economic climate. Things like utilities, food, and drug companies are in this category. They are on the lower end of the risk spectrum, and usually modest but steady earners. This can change though depending on new products and other factors, so don't discount them in a risk-tolerant portfolio.

Speculative Stocks

These are stocks that do not have a strong recent earnings history but for other reasons show promise. Some dot-com startups fall into this category as do established companies that have taken a downturn but are under new and exciting management, or introducing a promising product. These are very high-risk investments but the reward can be enormous.

Share Class

Typically, each share comes with a percentage of ownership in the company and one vote in the control of the company (usually for the board of directors who make decisions about the way stock is used.) In some cases, a company will split the stock into two classes and one will carry more voting weight. This allows the company to ensure that a small number of people make the decisions. It also prevents an outside investor from being able to buy up enough stock to effect a hostile takeover. In a company like this, the shares would be labeled Class A and Class B and displayed with their company name on the ticker with a lowercase letter that signifies this. For example, if the company's abbreviation was ABC the ticker would read ABCa and ABCb. Class B stocks are usually the common stock of the company, with each share entitling the owner to one vote. Class A stocks still represent the same percentage of the company in terms of ownership but would confer say, 10 votes per share. The final key difference is that if the company goes bankrupt and its assets must be liquidated, Class A shareholders will be paid before Class B shareholders. Note: all debts must first be repaid before any of the shareholders are paid.

CHAPTER 13:

SHOULD YOU HIRE A STOCK BROKER

Most people who want to invest in the stock market cannot put in too much effort. They do not have the time to study the market and make the right investment. This is when they will turn to a broker. A broker is someone who will help you trade your stocks. When you want to trade in the stock market, you need to be a member of the stock exchange. Otherwise, you are not allowed to trade in the market. To become a member, you will need to know the steps to follow, and a broker can help you understand the same.

Brokers are always a part of companies that are members of the stock exchange. Some brokers also choose to go out on their own, but they will be members of the stock exchange. Since the broker only follows the market, they know exactly what stock you should look at. They can advise you about the investments you need to make based on the analysis they perform and your risk tolerance. The final decision, however, is yours. If you do not want to trust your broker fully, you can perform some analysis to assess whether the stock is indeed good to invest in.

Depending on how much money you have, you can choose to hire a part-time or full-time broker. A full-time broker is someone who will constantly work on your investment profile. The broker will invest in the right stocks to ensure that you will make a profit. This broker will look at the trends of the market and alert you if there is a good deal that they come across. A part-time broker is someone who will only buy and sell your stocks. He will not give you advice or spend time to help to maximize your profits. The former will charge you more since he spends all his time on investing for you.

We will look at the different types of brokers later in the book. Always perform research and hire a broker who is both trustworthy and reliable. Ask people you know about a broker they will recommend. You can also read the testimonials to see which broker you should approach. These testimonials are proof of who you can and cannot trust.

The role of a stock broker is to take investors' money and put it to work in the stock market. Now, you generally hear the term "stock market" commonly used as an umbrella term to refer to financial markets in general. As you will see in this chapter, the more appropriate term to be used in this case should be "financial markets" as there are several different types of markets.

In that regard, the stock market is where shares of a publicly traded company are bought and sold on a daily basis. When I say, "daily basis" I mean Monday through Friday as all markets break for the weekend. As a day trader, this is something that you need to keep in mind as Friday afternoon should be the time in which you are powering down. Later on, we will discuss why this is a fundamental tenet of day trading.

Since the United States, and virtually all nations that have mature stock markets, have regulations in place which limit the amount of participation an average investor can have in the stock market, virtually all trading is done through brokerage firms.

I am sure that you have the seen the ads on television for these firms (I will not name names in order to avoid it appearing that I am endorsing anyone). These firms offer a myriad of products and funds in which they can place their money. These funds are managed by individual stock brokers, or money managers, who are duly licensed.

These brokers are the ones who actually place the trades and make the deals happen on a daily basis. It should be noted that a licensed broker has something which is known as a "fiduciary responsibility". This means that their responsibility is to make money for their clients and not for themselves.

You might be scoffing at that last point, but that is what's on the book. Whether they actually do that, is up to the financial institution and the brokers themselves. However, if a rogue broker goes out and does their own thing, the chances of this stock broker landing in jail are almost assured.

Choosing a Stockbroker

You cannot trade or invest in the stock market if you can't buy or sell shares in the stock market. To do so, you would have to set-up an account with a stockbroker that will facilitate these transactions for you. Like any service provider, not all stockbrokers are equal. You would want a broker that can provide you the best service without charging you over-the-top fees. Here are the considerations you must take when choosing your broker:

Suitability to your needs

You know your objectives in regards to buying and selling shares in the stock market. Therefore, you have an idea of how you would be doing your transactions in regard to trying to achieve these objectives. Brokers would have different features, and it is important that your choice can provide what you require. Important features to consider include charts, financial data, analyst support, educational resources, broker assistance, and customer service channels.

You have to consider if the broker would let your trade in the stock exchanges that you are planning to enter. If you intend to invest in investments other than stock, you might also want to consider brokers that offer the securities you want. Some brokers can provide access to cash equivalents, bonds, and funds for those seeking a one-stop venue for investments. On the other hand, there are those providing access to commodities, options, forex, and other high-risk and specialty asset classes for more advanced investors. Lastly, you would have to consider your knowledge and experience. Some brokers are beginner-friendly by providing a simple platform for executing stock trades. But, some users prefer a broader range of investment that might confuse those that are just starting out.

Client protection and insurance

You have to make sure that the broker you choose follows the law and provides protection for its clients. It should have a relevant regulatory body (such as FINRA in the United States) to authorize its operations to ensure that it provides a fair and honest service to investors. The broker should also provide investor protection insurance for customer cash claims, and deposit insurance for deposit products in the event that the company fails. They should also protect your personal information in their systems, and offer two-factor log-in authentication. Lastly, the broker should have a form of guarantee protection that will reimburse losses caused by fraudulent activities.

Consider Minimum deposit amounts and fees

Most stockbrokers require a minimum deposit to open an account. A basic stock trading account will typically require a minimum balance of $ 500 to $ 1,000. But, if you want to open a margin account, you would have to prepare a relatively higher amount and must consider their interest rate for making a trade on margin.

As for fees, you must be careful of brokers that advertise fees that seem too good to be true. Check the fine print in the agreement and see if there are any hidden and additional fees.

Lastly, brokers generate revenue from the commission fees

charged on your trades. These are often charged in two ways – on the volume of your trade or on the frequency of your trades. You would have to choose the broker that works best with how you would choose to buy and sell shares.

Trading platform

If you can, test the platform before you start using the broker to buy and sell shares. It does not matter if it's a web-based or app-based. What you are looking for is a platform that lets you place an order smoothly. It should let you trade the securities that you need to trade and create orders that you require for your goals and schedule.

The trading platform should also provide real-time data. You should be able to set-up watchlists and alerts so you can get notifications, preferably via text. You should also consider if you would require trading in extended hours and if the broker would charge extra for it.

Take a look at the charting features available on the platform. See if it plots the data that you want to see and if you find it easy to do so. Do not settle for a broker that lack any of the basic indicators - volume, simple moving averages, RSI, Bollinger bands, stochastics, and MACD.

Lastly, you should find it easy to use the brokerage's platform. It should only take you more than 30 minutes to get used to browsing the different menus and pages and grasp how to create and execute trade orders. At the very least, the broker should provide a short video tutorial on using the platform.

Client education

Even if you can find the generic and basic information in this book and other sources online, brokers are a valuable source of information for stock trading. Market updates and fundamental data can provide great insight from experts that will equip you to create better decisions. Of course, this depends on the quality and capability of their sources and staff.

Ease of transaction with the broker

It is important that you can easily add or withdraw money from your brokerage account. Delays and long turnaround times can make you miss sudden opportunities even if you schedule your deposits regularly. Moreover, you should choose a broker that will let you add or withdraw funds with the methods available to you – bank or wire transfer, debit or ATM card, or linked bank accounts.

Customer service

Choose a broker that provides access to customer service quickly and easily. This is even more important when you are just starting out and require additional assistance in the beginning. Check if they provide the customer service channel that you prefer.

CHAPTER 14:

A QUICK INTRO TO MUTUAL FUNDS

Before you buy into a mutual fund, you should be fully aware of what it really is and how it works. Most people are not familiar with what a mutual fund tries to achieve and how it goes about it. Even more importantly, you should be familiar with how mutual funds have performed in the past. After all, asset management is a highly measurable business and it's quite easy to compare and analyze how investment products actually performed.

While the idea of collective investment schemes is quite old, the mutual fund industry as we know it has only been around since the 80's. The overall idea is to allow for anyone to participate in the general stock market, even with smaller amounts in the simplest possible way. Of course you could participate in the markets by simply buying a basket of stocks, but you'd quickly realize a few practical problems with that. If you're looking at an index such as the S&P 500, like the return and would like to replicate it, you'd have to buy into 500 stock positions. Well, some have such small weights in the index that you could probably get a close enough replication by just buying half of the 500 member stocks. But you'd have to keep track of the weights and the membership changes and actively manage your portfolio to match the index. If you don't, you wouldn't get the same return as the index. Perhaps more, perhaps less, but not the same.

And what if you would like to invest $ 100 a month for long term saving? It wouldn't be possible as you can't buy fractions of a share. Even if you want to follow the Dow Jones Industrial Average with only 30 stocks, you can't buy them with for such small amounts. Even if you could, you'd have to handle weight rebalances and all the other hassle that most people simple don't want to do, and would not be able to do.

Enter mutual funds, the savior of the poor people and the democratizer of financial markets. Each fund aims to follow a specific and predefined index, and as a small investor you can simply place your $ 100 with the fund and it will be pooled with everyone else's money and invested to replicate the index. Almost.

As the mutual fund is measured against a specific index, they are relative investments. This means that their job is not to make money for their investors. Go on, read that last sentence one more time. A mutual fund is tasked with attempting to beat a specific index. If that index loses money, the job of the mutual fund manager is to lose slightly less money than the index. In a bull market, his job is to make slightly more than the index. So far fair enough, as long as you're aware of this.

A core concept in mutual fund world is tracking error budget. It's not like a mutual fund manager can do whatever he likes to beat the index. Far from it. Tracking error is a measurement of how much the returns of a fund is deviating from the index.

The daily returns for the fund are measured against the daily returns of the index. The allowed tracking error, or tracking error budget, is normally very small. The fund simply is not allowed to deviate much from the index.

Mutually Assured Destruction

What a mutual fund actually does is to take almost all the money in the fund and allocate it in-line with the index. If a stock has a weight of 5.2% in the index, you buy somewhere between 5% and 5.4%. There's very little leeway for the mutual fund manager to impose his or his bank's investment views. They can at times make slightly larger deviations from the index, but bear in mind that this can be very dangerous.

There's an old expression in the business that governs much institutional investment behavior. "No one ever got fired for buying IBM." What this means is, that if you do what everyone else did, you don't risk anything personally. If you lose, everyone lost and you won't get blamed. On the other hand, if you made your own independent decision and bought what you thought was best, ending up losing the same amount, you might very well get fired or at least receive blame. The safest course of action, in particular if you have a comfortable job, is to do as everyone else does.

The result is that we have a giant mutual fund business where everyone does the same thing.

Perhaps it doesn't sound so bad. After all, if they invest in-line with the index, you should get what you wanted, right? No, not so fast. There are bills to be paid too. A decent mutual fund manager makes seven figures a year. The bank will take a management fee, custodian fee, administration fee etc. A mutual fund will of course do all trading with the investment banking department of the same bank that issues the fund, and there's no incentive to get those fees down. There are many different ways to siphon money out of mutual funds and that's a reason why banks love them. They are very profitable.

High fees aren't necessarily a problem, as long as the performance is there. For this to happen, the fund needs to do much better than the index, so that fees can be paid and the investor still receives better than index performance. Given the enormous success of the mutual fund industry, surely they provide strong long term returns and show clear value to their customers, right?

It's a good thing there are people whose job it is to keep track of these things. Let's consult the S& P Indices Versus Active Funds Scorecard (SPIVA).

Exchange Traded Fund

The idea of exchange traded funds is brilliant. In its original shape they were simply a logical extension of the idea behind mutual funds. With the mutual funds, the general public gained access to the broad markets. They could suddenly achieve a broad diversification and participate in the equity indexes without having large investment amounts. They also didn't need to care about the individual investment decisions as this was handled by the mutual fund manager. But as we've seen, mutual fund managers don't perform as advertised. ETFs offer a simple solution. The idea is to have a computer manage the fund with the mission to replicate the index exactly. The money in the ETF is distributed to all the stocks in the index it's supposed to track at the exact weightings of the index itself. No deviation, no delays, very low fees, very low costs all around. The result is a vehicle which tracks the index extremely closely. If you really want to buy the index, buy a passive ETF. That's how you get the index. A key point that I want to raise in this book however, is that buying the index might not be very attractive. It's certainly more attractive to buy a passive S& P 500 ETF than to buy an active mutual fund with that index as benchmark of course.

The original ETFs were all passive index trackers. This is a great concept. What you need to be careful with though is the growing number of structured products that are being packaged as ETFs.

Just as a simple example, take something like a short ETF. If you buy a short ETF on the S& P 500, you'd expect to get the inverse performance. If you'd buy a double short ETF on the same index, you'd expect a double inverse performance.

That's true, but only for a single day. See, in order for these funds to be able to offer the exact inverse performance in a single day, they need to be rebalanced daily. If you've got a background in options, you already know where this is heading.

Compare the long term price development of a regular S& P 500 ETF, a short ETF and a double short ETF on the same index. Figure 2-1 shows how the short ETFs tend to fall all the time, except in times of very extreme, short term negative moves in the index.

What you need to understand with short ETFs is that you're trading gamma, not delta. Option traders should have already seen this coming. What this means is that the short and double short ETFs are much more sensitive to change in volatility than to directional change in price. When you buy these short ETFs, you're really putting on a short volatility position.

In all fairness, it has to work like this. If you want to match the inverse performance on a single day, this will be the effect. The problem is that it's not exactly explained to people who trade these things, thinking that they can get inverse performance over a week, a month or a year.

INVESTMENT IN MUTUAL FUNDS

We have analyzed the rudiments of fundamental analysis and technical analysis. The greatest difficulty that will have been noticed is the need to constantly monitor the performance of equities. In fact, it must not have been overlooked that, in the first phase, that of the investment, it is necessary to be equipped with analysis tools deriving from constant monitoring: time series, financial statements, information that allow the extraction of data and the processing of the same, in order to arrive to the selection of the short list of shares to bet on.

In the case of technical analysis, it will certainly be necessary to start from historical data, from the last x stock market sessions, in order to identify the patterns and to be able to spot the shares on which it is possible to activate a growing trend.

Once the investment has been made, monitoring must continue, especially in the case of an investment activity of the "trading" type. In fact, it is necessary to proceed constantly with the continuous processing of data, the analysis of the answers provided by the algorithms and the constant decision on what to do. Buy, sell, overweight or underweight? These are the questions that plague traders day by day. Without time interruptions, continuously.

For the same long term stockholders, who hold substantial portfolios, life is no less hard. In the text, we have probably taken the concept of the duration of the investment to the extreme, stating that once the stock picking has been carried out, the long term stockholder operator basically waits for the target date to draw conclusions. It is useless to observe that in reality the dressers monitor, at regular intervals, the progress of their investments.

Certainly, an infra-daily update of the portfolio is not carried out, however with constant periodicity, monthly or weekly, a trend analysis is certainly carried out. And a rebalancing of the portfolio with respect to the benchmark becomes a natural activity. As can be seen, investing in equity securities requires, in order to increase risk immunization, the application of the diversification principle, but as the number of securities in the portfolio increases, the complexity of monitoring also increases.

However, we have not talked about a very important investment factor: timing. The timing of the investment, or the time when the investment is made, is very important, since the price at which you buy can determine the result in terms of profits and losses of the investment itself.

The choice of the wrong moment in which a security is purchased, therefore becomes a prerogative for the loss of capital or for a lower profit for the investor.

Since nobody has a crystal ball, it will be clear that an investment made entirely in a given instant has a very low probability of "hitting" the peaks of minimum or maximum, absolute or relative, in the trend of the share price. Yet most non-professional investors persist in pursuing the right timing. Let's take an example that will clarify the problem in a very simple way.

An investor has 10,000 euros and is, we assume, completely unaware of the issue of diversification. He wants to invest in stocks because he has "heard" around that the stock market makes a lot.

What will the investor do? He will invest in the action that is "on the shields", or in the action that, on the day or days prior to his investment, seems to have performed better and has been "mentioned" by all the financial newspapers. The investor therefore typically enters a positive trend in the action itself.

What if the trend is in its terminal phase? The investor sees his investment grow for a short period, even if, unbeknownst to him, the "peak" is close ... Once the maximum is reached, the price of the security will begin to fall ...

What will the investor do now? He will think that it is a phase of settling, that the stock will go back up and will wait for a later moment to sell ... But maybe this will not happen and the stock will continue to go down ... In the best case, the inexperienced investor at this point sells, accumulating the loss.

In the worst ... The investor will adopt the fateful thought "It won't be worse than this." And it will try to obtain other savings to invest on the same security. Unfortunately, in these cases the stories are not with a happy ending and soon the investor will find himself with a handful of flies in his hand.

We specifically exaggerated in the narrative to explain one of the typical non-professional investor behaviors that follow the "timing". That is, they tend to never sell when the stock grows, as they "fear" not to benefit from further appreciation.

Likewise, they do not sell when the accumulated loss exceeds significant percentages, in the hope that the stock itself will rise. In summary, these investors tend to "fall in love faithfully" with the security they invested on.

From what has been said, it can therefore be easily concluded that "professional" monitoring and the choice of timing represent a serious problem for those who want to face the world of investment in stocks. How to overcome these limits?

A first "professional" investment tool capable of allowing investment in "shares", overcoming the problems of monitoring and choosing the timing, is represented by mutual investment funds.

A Mutual Fund is an investment instrument, managed by a professional operator called "Asset Management Company (AM)", consisting of a set of financial assets managed according to predefined rules. Mutual funds collect the assets of a set of investors who decide to invest in the fund's holdings.

What is one of the fundamental characteristics of the Fund? Having to comply with the "predefined investment rules". The regulations of each fund contain, in particular, the rules in terms of the presence or absence of the "Benchmark" to be followed, the risk limits to be respected, the reference time horizon.

Why then can investing in a mutual fund be a valid alternative to direct investment in shares? The answer is most rational.

It is possible to choose, based on one's own attitudes and appetite for risk, the "equity" fund, basically 100% made up of shares, which "replicates" the investor's will, respecting his will and allowing, however, to increase the probability of obtaining optimal results in terms of diversification, selection of the most profitable titles and with the best timing.

For what reason does this happen? Because mutual funds are managed by managers who operate professionally, day by day, working towards the best result of investments in shares. The asset management companies evidently adopt the best performing software aimed at the most profitable manager of the collected assets.

It is in everyone's interest, Managers and AM, to perform at their best. The asset management companies earn from the investment in the funds. Indeed, customers and investors pay commissions for managing the investment made. But it is clear that the commission is typically commensurate with the very important work done.

The monitoring, it will be evident, is carried out constantly. On the investments made, on the market potential and on the respective threats. The invested portfolio is subject to continuous processing for compliance with the "underwritten" constraints in the regulatory environment and for the search for the best profit.

At the same time, the software favors such monitoring. But there is an additional aspect to consider. Timing. By investing, even on the same security, as investors subscribe for units, the fund accumulates capital on securities at "different" prices.

The timing problem is therefore overcome by subscribing at different prices, as subscriptions and investments take place continuously.

As a result, the funds obtain "average" or "average" prices over time, thus reducing, in fact, the risk of price volatility and the choice of a timing, so to speak, wrong.

Although therefore each investor who makes a single investment will see the investment take place on a certain date, what will count for the evaluation of his investment will be the fund's NAV, or the Net Asset Value of the fund itself. This is given by the averaged values of the fund's investments in securities. This is not the place to go into detail about these concepts and how NAV is calculated.

The message that should however be passed is that the mutual fund allows you to "mediate" the prices, in the face of continuous investments of your collected assets, reducing the possibility that "all" the assets are invested in a given moment and eliminating, in fact , the possibility that the Fund invests at the maximum (or even minimum) price of a security.

There is therefore a valid alternative to direct investment in a portfolio of shares:the purchase of units of mutual funds that "approach" the investor's desire, removing the latter from the hindrance of becoming a trader or a stock exchange player. In fact, the investor has only to express his "constraints" and manifest his characteristics as an investor.

The investor will then be able to choose from a "range" of different Funds, of different investment houses and with different Benchmarks. Furthermore, the investment in Funds has an additional advantage: for each fund and, in an almost equivalent way, for each manager, it is possible to identify the track record of the results obtained and measure the ability to "beat" the benchmark.

In fact, there are finance sites specialized in funds that allow the definition of a ranking, a ranking, of funds by category. Those who want to invest in shares, through the funds, can therefore inquire by "reading" the rankings and analyzing the results obtained by each fund.

Once you have chosen the Fund and made your investment in it (through Home Banking or in a Bank Branch, with the support of your trusted Financial Advisor),the Fund Manager will take care of allocating the best of the capital in shares, to monitor the trend with respect to the benchmark and to make purchases, sales and any other operation aimed at making the portfolio result more efficient, in compliance with the previously stated constraints.

A particularly important site in this area is Morningstar. The Morningstar company publishes on-line a very detailed analysis of the Funds present on the market, of the classifications of the same (for example Geographical Funds exist, such as Global Equity Funds, European Equity Funds, etc ..., Sector Funds, such as Technological Equity Funds , Pharmaceutical Equity Funds, etc ...) and, more importantly, comparison sheets are published, which report performance and risk data.

Without, even in this case, wanting to go into detail, it is sufficient to note that there is a very useful screening tool on the site, in order to be able to orientate oneself within the universe of the offer existing on the market. It can be really useful to learn how to use the information offered by the site, getting deeply into the metrics used.

Compared to the Funds, an investment instrument that follows a similar logic is represented by ETFs, i.e. exchange-traded funds. These tools aim to replicate "Benchmarks", carrying out minimal interventions in the purchase and sale policies of the underlying the fund itself.

Although they have the advantage of having much lower costs (commissions), at the same time, by replicating indices, they have the disadvantage of being "unmanaged" or "passively managed" investment instruments. The manager, where present (in some cases "software" manages the investment policy), is limited to carrying out operations that bring the invested assets as close as possible to the asset allocation of the Benchmark.

On the contrary, the managers of the Funds, in compliance with constraints and also with a benchmark, still have degrees of freedom within which to move, consequently trying to do the best interest of the investor.

For those who want to make equity investments indirectly, it is therefore preferable to rely on the action of the Managers, who exercise the picking on the shares based on their potential and not with the ultimate goal of replicating a basket of a Benchmark.

Why Sell ETFs and Mutual Funds?

If you've decided, for whatever reason (they're all good) to invest through ETFs and mutual funds -- especially those funds that mirror major indices -- the next question becomes: is there ever a case to be made for selling these?

The Case For Never Selling

Dalbar, Inc. is the nation's leading financial services market research firm. One of the industry components they measure is investor behavior. Over a recent 30-year period, the annualized rate of return for the average investor in an equity mutual fund has been +3.66%. That, according to the latest 2016 release of Dalbar's Quantitative Analysis of Investor Behavior (QAIB).

To give that some perspective, the U.S. inflation rate for the same period of time was an annualized 2.65% per year. [Inflation Calculator] Meaning, for the 30 years ending December 31, 2015, the average equities mutual fund investor was getting ahead by a paltry 1% a year.

It gets worse for investors trying to protect themselves from downside risk by spreading their investments among equity and bond ETFs. Over the same 30-year period, the annualized rate of return for the average investor in a blend of equities and fixed-income mutual funds has been just 1.65%. Factor in inflation, and those investors have actually lost ground.

What makes this so troubling is that the S&P 500 index produced an average annual return of +10.35% during that 30-year period. But that's not what investors got, even investors who bought the funds that mirrored the S&P 500.

What's wrong with this picture? Why such a gap (of almost 7 percentage points) between the returns of actual fund investors and the returns that could be expected from holding representative indices? According to Dalbar, there are a number of factors including: the periodic need for cash (planned and unplanned), fund expenses (i.e. management fees), and voluntary investor behavior.

The latter is by far the largest contributor to investor underperformance. So what is this bad investor behavior that so drives down investment returns? Three things: panic selling, excessively exuberant buying, and attempts at market timing.

You might call this Investor Psychology 101. Investors (you, me, professional money managers) are constantly tempted to chase returns. With the chase on, excessively exuberant buying drives up prices beyond the rationale of the company fundamentals. Before long, we're looking at a correction waiting for a catalyst.

When a fund or stock begins going down in price, the average investor can handle it for a while. But if that downward action is accompanied by increasingly negative economic news, political turmoil, or any of the other known catalysts of crashes, the odds are there will come a point when the pain of the paper loss crosses a threshold and becomes too much. The investor hits the sell button. This is panic selling. The fear, of course, is that the fund will continue to plummet and drag your portfolio down to the center of the earth.

Sadly, the average investor typically reaches that pain threshold at or near the bottom of the trough. The behavior is so predictable they've got a name for it: capitulation. It's the kind of panic selling that builds momentum, exacerbates volatility, floods the market with securities that are being sold at lower and lower prices causing yet more selling. It all spirals down dramatically toward a cyclical bottom.

But the average investor doesn't know the bottom is in sight and doesn't understand that psychology. Getting out at any cost becomes paramount because he sees no bottom.

There is one thing all market corrections have in common: they eventually stop correcting.

But there is one thing all market corrections have in common: they eventually stop correcting. And now begins the second of the two-part humiliation: the average fund investor, burned and spooked by a market correction, is now reluctant to get back in.

With individual stocks, there may be good reasons to get out and stay out. But with the market as a whole, and funds that reflect that market (or some portion thereof), every correction has been followed by rally back to breakeven and then up from there. That rally may be head-spinningly quick or long and hesitant to fulfill. But the average fund investor, spooked and burned, will miss some or all of that recovery.

Multiply that behavior a few times? Welcome to the 1.6% average annual return.

Now admittedly, +1.65% annually (or +3.66% for equity-only fund investors) is better than nothing. Holding cash during that time would have generated nothing, putting cash holders at an even greater disadvantage to the ravages of inflation.

But 1.65%? Really?

Really.

One obvious solution is to buy those equity funds, or that mix of equity and fixed-asset funds, and hold on for dear life. And I do mean dear life. Shrug at marketplace euphoria knowing a correction is around the corner. And steel yourself during those inevitable crashes.

Statistically, a market correction of -10% will happen once a year on average. Every couple of years, you can expect a -15%

correction. And every 3.5 years: -20% or more. Recognize that market corrections are a healthy part of a normal marketplace expansion. It helps knowing that after a drop of -10% to -20%, it typically takes just 4 months for the market to get back to breakeven. Bear markets (greater than -20%) require longer, 2.7 years on average by some estimates.

By never selling (in a panic or otherwise), the buy-and-hold crowd never miss the boat once market corrections and crashes begin their recoveries.

Buy and hold, and if you have a 30-year-plus time frame, you should come close to matching the indices your funds are mirroring, less management fees. In the grand scheme of things, those are pretty good returns.

If I lose you now, I'll understand. No need to keep reading. After all, an 8% to 10% average annual return is awfully hard to beat. And easy to achieve! Just buy the market, hold what you buy, ignore the periodic sound of train wrecks.

Best of luck, and it's been nice having you as a reader.

The Case For Selling

What? Are you still here? I thought--

OK, if the argument for buy-and-hold didn't take, I can only think of 4 reasons an investor might be prompted to sell the likes of ETFs and mutual funds.

1. You bought the wrong fund.

2. You need to raise cash.

3. You don't have a 30-year time horizon for holding investments. A 5 or 10-year horizon, for example, makes buy-and-hold considerably more dicey. If that's the case, it makes perfect sense not to want to follow a crashing economy down into the depths of a recession knowing your portfolio may not have time to recover before you'll need that money.

4. You want to make more than the 8% market average afforded the buy-and-holders who can wait for the payout.

This book can't help you with 1 and 2. But 3 and 4? Well, we'll see what we can do.

Earlier, we touched on a set of red flags that might signal to an investor it's time to sell an individual stock, signals that have nothing to do with macro-market trends. And of course, there may be a reason or two to want/need to sell an ETF or mutual fund.

But assuming we're happy with our fund selections, or happy with our stock picks (no red flags), how do we go about protecting those assets in the event of overall market downturns?

That, of course, is the crux of this book.

179

On a side note, there are whole training courses devoted to hedging one's trades with the likes of swaps and derivatives, but such "insurance" can be complicated, can get expensive, and effectiveness can be elusive. And because of that, beyond the scope of this book.

For investors holding stocks, mutual funds, or ETFs who are looking to protect those assets simply and effectively from market crashes and the like, we're going to focus on a more elementary solution.

That would be GETTING THE HELL OUT OF DODGE. Preferably, before being carried out of Dodge in a pine box. Translation: selling those risk assets in times of peril and moving into cash.

If that sounds an awful lot like trying to time the market, yes, we're talking about trying to time the market. The same dreaded market timing that makes up one-third of the trifecta of voluntary investor behaviors that consistently shaves almost 7 percentage points off average annual returns.

Admittedly, the idea of market timing has gotten a bad reputation -- and deservedly so. Numerous studies (including those by Dalbar) confirm that the vast majority of actively managed portfolios that move in and out of the market underperform those that are passively managed.

But why? Two reasons: 1) it's really hard to predict the market, and 2) the average investor is constantly embroiled in a pitched battle with fear and greed. Yes, there are some technical indicators that can foreshadow potential calamitous events. But even for the investors who understand those technical indicators, there is a difference between watching them unfold on a paper chart and acting on them in a live trading scenario.

An all-too-common example. A stock or fund you're holding begins slipping and finally hits some technical indicator on a chart, and you dutifully sell because that's what you do when you're a technician following a timing scheme like a simple moving average (we'll be seeing more of this in a moment). Boom, sold.

But then, no sooner than you've sold, sentiment changes; the stock or fund reverses course and starts heading back up. Panic sets in! People you don't know know something you don't know! And you're about to miss the boat! So you buy back the stock/fund, only at a higher price than you had sold moments (or days/weeks) ago.

Whew, that was a close call. You didn't lose too much money, you rationalize, and now you stand to gain what people you don't know are about to gain. And then, guess what? The stock/fund makes another u-turn and proceeds back down. Realizing that your first call was the correct call, you sell once again, this time exacerbating your losses.

Whew, that was a close call. Maybe now is the time to move away from the computer screen and-- wait! What's that thing doing? It's going back up? What the--

You can imagine what happens next.

It pains me to admit, but that was me in any number of trades throughout the years. It might seem comical, but I suspect at least some of you can relate. The point is, I know how hard it is to implement a timing strategy. Even without the clownish back and forth on the buy/sell button, many investors fool themselves into thinking they are perfectly rational investors when in fact they are slaves to the gods of fear and greed.

So, how do we make market timing work? And make it work with individual stocks as well as ETFs? How do we turn a loser's game into a winner's game?

Here's how. We're going to take emotion and guesswork out of the equation and replace it with a cold mechanical strategy. And then we're going to test that strategy to demonstrate that it works.

CHAPTER 15:

POWERFUL TESTED STRATEGIES YOU CAN TRADE ON TODAY!

All advance investors apply various strategies to their portfolio. Like magician, most investors won't share their secret tricks of the trait, until of course it's not a secret anymore. I can't say I have a magic formula or a secret sauce. However, I've been trading for 30 years, and along with my mistakes, I also learned some strategies through just trial and error.

In my sincere attempt to take you from novice to advance investor in one book, I like to introduce some of the basic, yet powerful strategies that can make huge difference in your investments. We will keep most of these strategies straight forward and basics, but powerful (I also have more advance strategies that are overly complicated and may write its own book, sometime in the future).

Back Test Every Strategy Before Implementation

Back-test simply means go back in the past (1yr, 2yrs, 5yrs, 10yrs, how back in the past depends on how long in the future you would like to hold this security. Is it a quick in/out or are you planning on holding this for a while?) and to see how often you would have made/loss money applying this strategy. Some strategies work great on some stock but not on others, so back-test it.

If you went back 1 year, invested $1,000 and implemented a strategy (discussed below) and realized you would have been right 3 times and wrong 1 time and you would have made $200. Then you can go back 2yrs, 5yrs, 10yrs and see how you would have done. If you back tested and the results are positive, then you can attempt to introduce that strategy into that security. Remember not all strategies work on all security & there are no guarantees; the minute you apply a strategy and it doesn't work, back-test again to make sure its still the best strategy available. Therefore, its pertinent that you back-test with enough data, to ensure that the odds are definitely in your favor!

Strategy 1

Time Frame

Today many television programs, magazines, newspapers and online articles sensationalize the news. They are in the market of selling their product, not necessarily informing you of the truth. This is obvious in today's political culture; exaggerated one sided story broadcasted to create emotional anguish. This is also true of the stock market news, to lesser extent. Every small move in the market, is presented to you as doomsday! This creates panic that makes you want to tune in and worst has you go in/out of market, when you shouldn't be. The following strategy will help you rules out lots of noise and volatility that may happen every day and instead focus on larger, more significant movements of the security or the market. Of course, if you are day trader or very short-term trader, you probably won't want to use this method.

Some stocks have a trend but it's hard to see and when you apply an indicator is so hard make sense of it on the chart. The security seems to go all over the chart. It is too erratic to fit any MAVG or a good indicator. GOOG is one such example.

This is a daily chart of GOOG from June 2015-Dec. 2018 with 50-day MAVG. You can see the crossing of the MAVG frequent. If you are using MAVG as your indicator in this example, you will be going in and out unnecessarily and frequently.

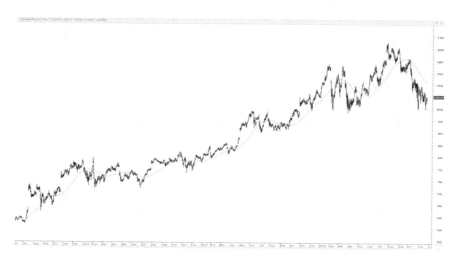

Most all charts are defaulted as a daily chart. You will find that you can modify charts setting to weekly, monthly or even custom days. In some cases, when you change these settings, it may seem like you are looking at brand new security. You may get a lot clearer view of the behavior of the stock. It may allow all indicator to fall in place.

This is GOOG on weekly chart with the same 50-day MAVG.

You can see this will yield a lot better predictor of a trend, it will cut out daily noise. This will prevent you from going in and out of the security unnecessary. You will also be better able to predict larger trend and not panic on every move the stock is making.

All securities are different, but if the charts aren't making good trendy sense, try adjusting the frequency to 3-day, weekly, bi-weekly and on occasion monthly (long term 401k funds).

Some of these strategies are contradictory to other strategies. For example, RSI > 80 will tell you to sell but what if at the same time price has just crossed above MAVG then which in one of the strategies should you follow? That's why it's pertinent that you back-test your performance for each strategy you are implementing, to see historically how many times has the RSI>80 and MAVG crossed the price and which strategy prevailed most of the time. If this happened 50-50% of the time, none of those strategies are reliable. This is critical because some stocks exhibit certain behavior. Not all these strategies may work for you, and not all strategies work on all securities. You really do have to spend some time applying the right strategies, right settings to right security. This will take some time. You may have to tweak some of the strategies. As you get more confidant, you will start to add your own nuance to these strategies or create your own that works for you. But what if you tried several strategies and none of them fit that security? MOVE ON! There are approx. 4,000 stocks you can invest in.

As you get better and understand different indicators and what they mean, you can add multiple strategies to form one strategy. For example, you may only get into the position at crossing of 2 MAVG and RSI is just coming over 30 on a weekly chart but you may sell when RSI > 80. I can write almanac on all different scenarios, I hope this has opened your eyes on various possibilities.

Strategy 2

Stop Buy Order

In earlier strategy, we discussed the stop loss order, if you are in a position and the market starts to go down, you enter a stop loss order, a price at which you will get out of the position. But what is a stop buy order?

In a stop buy order you are purchasing security when it hits a strike price that is higher than the current price. Once the price hits specific price outlined on the trade, the stop buy becomes a market order. The buy-on-stop price always is set above the existing market price.

For example, stock XYZ is at $95, I place a stop buy order at $100, when the stock goes from $95 to $100, I will purchase the stock at $100! Uhm mm...why should I wait for the stock to go up to $100, when I can buy the stock at $95 (for cheaper) today?

This all depends on your overall plan. We know that many stocks move in trends/consolidate/trends.

For example, this stock is at $45, rises and remains between $60-$65, then rises and remains between $75-$80 and then drops and stays between $65-$70 then rises to $95-$100. At this time, you don't know if the stock is due for a drop or rise, however based on its pattern you assume that if it breaks $100, its due for a climb up. Therefore, you only want to purchase this stock if it breaks the $100 marker!

Another reason could be, that at $100 it is going break a MAVG, and you noticed that once it breaks a MAVG it continues to climb up but if it doesn't then it drops!

Stop buy traders believe this prevents them from buying early in uncertainty, and they are ok with less profit, because they believe it gives them higher assurance.

Strategy 3

Reversal Catch

Nobody has a crystal ball, you will even find brainiest guys/gals arguing on CNBC in a language you don't even understand. Surely, they must know more than you know. They are throwing out terms that are in a foreign language. Follow them, see their picks and you will realize they are wrong half of the times. Hell, you can be right 50% of the time too. When a lot of money is on the line and your emotions are high, you will react more to stock market fluctuation than sticking to your own strategy! You will sell when you are supposed to buy and buy when you are supposed to sell. I advise you to stick to your strategy, with clear buy/sell signals before you enter the position. Let's say you are still wrong, or the volatility of the market, gets you out of the market/into the market and then takes off in the opposite direction! This has happened to me several times. I would own a security, let's say XYZ-$55 and it starts to go down on me, I had clear direction to sell, so I put a stop loss at $50, the price comes down to $49.96, I'm sold out of the position. I stop following it for a while and after 6 mos. I look at the price and it's $150! When this happened few times, I started to develop a strategy called "Reversal Catch". In this strategy, once I get stopped out, let's say at $49.96, I continue to follow the stock more vigilantly than before!!! To make sure execution of my trade was not just due to stock volatility but a long-term downtrend, and all my other reason to sell this stock were valid.

If the price is turning on me and headed in opposite direction I will get back into this position! Yes, I will lose some money since most likely I will now get sold out at $49.96 and will probably buy based on certain other parameters at higher price, possibly like $55. I also won't just randomly get back into the position. One it has to be that I just got stopped out on the volatility of the market and all other conditions are the same. Secondly, I must have clear reason to enter the position again. At times I will have reevaluate the condition before rebuying the stock, sometimes I will anticipate reversal catch buy price before even selling the stock. I may need to have reversal entry price points to be defined, for example crossing of MAVG, or breaking previous resistance or another indicator that I was following before I got sold out. It's hard for me to have the exact entry points here, but just know it's ok to lose some money and get back in/out of position than to have the wrong trade executed. Now, you most likely will lose money doing this trade, since you will probably have purchased/sold at the wrong time and you are buying/selling this at higher/lower price than you wanted to. This is ok, especially if this is a long-term position. Even in semi short term position (1-6 months), this could be ok. Don't be stubborn, if the market turns on you, or you just got sold out at the bottom, don't be afraid to re-evaluate and hop back on even for some short-term loss! Don't sit on the sideline, hoping the market continues in one direction because you are in/out of the position, market doesn't know when you bought/sold the stock, and frankly the market doesn't care!

Strategy 4

Buy on Dips!

This is a risky strategy! In this strategy, you want to be careful to own ETF or solid stocks, you plan to own. We are going to look at the same "MA" stock as we did in strategy 4. In this strategy, we are going to add to our position every time the stock dips below MAVG. We will be incorporating 40-day MAVG into this chart. Every time stock dips below 40day-MAVG will we be buying or adding to our position. In another words we will be buying on dips when the stock comes down and will accumulate much more at this price. You can see the potential return, following this strategy!

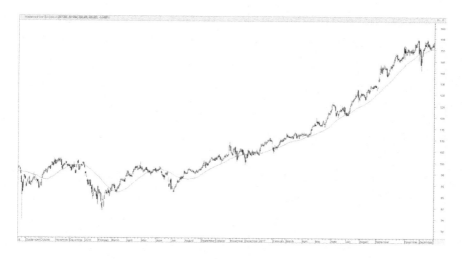

Reason this is a risky strategy, is because if you are buying on dips, what happens when a dip turns into a long-term bear market? This is the reason you want to own ETF or great companies that around for a long time, because you want to be certain that these companies are going to bounce back! Secondly, you want to purchase these great companies at a lower price is because they are a bargain! If you did valuation calculation from prior chapter, you would know if they are a bargain or not!

Another cons to this strategy is if the market is going to dip for a while, you must have enough capital to continue to purchase on down market and be able to hold a long time!

Despite above reasons, you still may not want your capital tied up for extensive amount of time in down market. In that case you need to have an exit strategy, which will alert you to buy on dips but get out during bear market! We are going to do this by introducing a 2nd MAVG to the same chart. This MAVG is going to be 100-day MAVG. In this example we will be buying on dip below 40-day MAVG but will be selling it all at 100-day MAVG. You need to make sure that touches at 40-day MAVG are a lot more than at 100-day MAVG, as you don't want to sell all frequently. Of course, you can modify/adjust MAVG to fit the right stock.

There is also a third indicator, however in my opinion not that reliable, "Death Cross". It is basically when 50-day MAVG crosses below the 200-day MAVG. You can back test it to see if this is a profitable indicator for a particular security.

Strategy 5

Trailing Stop Strategy-Prevent your losses and lock in your profits!

This strategy works well with stocks that are momentum/trendy stocks. Stocks that tend to show you a diagonal line up are ideally the best ones. Once you have made some money in the stock, this strategy will secure your profit and ensure you won't lose but gaining all upside potential if the stock goes up. Here is how the strategy works.

This strategy involves placing a stop loss order. A stop loss is an order to sell stock, once it reaches a certain price. A stop-loss is designed to limit an investor's loss on a security position.

Once you are in the position (you own the stock). And the stock has risen, you will place stop loss below the fluctuation of the stock and/or below the previous support. The stock naturally fluctuates, it doesn't go straight up or straight down, it moves in zig zag (fluctuation). You want to put stop loss order below the fluctuation and below the previous support, this will give stock some chance to fluctuate without you being sold out! If the stock changes trend and begins to dive on you, your stop loss order gets activated and your stock is sold (making whatever profit you have made thus far on the stock or if you just bought it, you may have some loss based on risk you were willing to take). If the stock goes up, you are still in the position and now you will cancel the old order and move the stop loss order up, locking in your profit!

Let's say 1st you did your homework and found a momentum stock with diagonal chart, of course there are no guarantee the charts will continue its trend up, but we are going to assume it's going to continue what it has done in the past. You see chart for 'MA' appears to fit that model. So, you buy 'MA" for around $100 in September 2016. You will then place your stop loss below the last support, which is around $94 (where the horizontal line is placed). If the stock goes below $94, your trade will get executed and you will sell the stock for $6 loss! Therefore, that is your risk, you will never lose more than $6 per share in this example and you must be willing to take that risk. However, if the stock goes up (as we predict based on prior historical chart) you will be raising the stop loss, locking in the profit until stock goes below your stop loss order. As the stock is rising, I'm raising in my stop loss, as you can see with horizontal lines. On December 1st, 2016, my stop los order is executed at approx. $145. I did not get the high price of $155 just few days ago, however $100 to $145 in approximately 2 years is a good return.

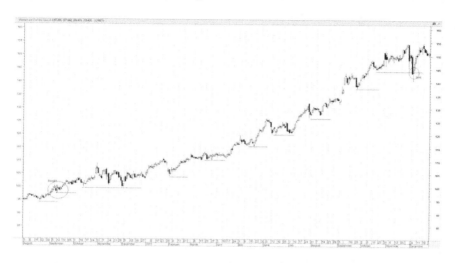

Strategy 6

RSI-Relative Strength Index

RSI is usually plotted for 14 days, with a two horizontal lines at 20 and 80. A buy signal would be generated when RSI crosses the oversold line (20). Sell signal are generated when RSI crosses the overbought line (80).

In this indicator, you really do need to pick the right stock. Some stocks appear to stay above or below the line for quite a while. When stocks do this, they are either on a down or uptrend, in that case this is not the best indicator to use. Other stocks remain between 20-80, these stocks don't give clear overbought or oversold condition. Ideally you would want to see stocks with spikes above or below the lines and drop back down. This may be stated rather simplistic, and in my

195

experience, you can't rely on this unless you have back tested (as with any of the other strategies, but especially this one). This strategy does not work well with many stocks. This may be a good secondary strategy, if you are on the fence about getting in/out, and you need some additional reassurance, consider RSI and see if it's below 20 or above 80 and then back-test to see if it has been reliable.

In this example I'm using BRKb, with 35/70 RSI. I am putting an order to sell anytime RSI reaches above 70 and will buy when RSI reaches below 35. My buy orders are more accurate than my sell order. Many times, after I sold a stock it continues to rise. In this case I can possibly buy the stock when it reaches below 35 but use another indicator to sell. Red lines shows the RSI is less than 35 and will be buying and blue line indicates I will be selling. You may get multiple buy signals and multiple sell signals, therefore don't sell all your holdings at once, but sell them in batches. If you have 300 shares, sell 100 each time.

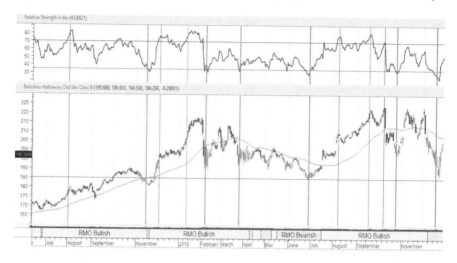

Strategy 7

Channeling Stocks

No matter how much research you do, some stocks just titter-totter! In previous example, if you had purchased "HALL" on Jan 1, 2016 around $11.75 and held on to it until to Dec. 31st, 2017, its worth at $10.25. There would be no major win or loss. If I bought and held this stock, I would not have made any money.

You can see within this timeframe, the stock reached $11.50 at least 7 times and it reached $10.25 at least 7 times. What if I bought it around $10.25 and sold it at $11.50 seven times?

197

In this strategy you would find stocks such as these and continue to buy and sell them at price interval. I've done this for last 2yrs on this stock. You would find the resistance and support and buy and sell them repeatedly.

You would probably not want to be too greedy by waiting for the stock to come all the way down or all the way up, you want most touches at resistance and support. To prevent further loss, you may want to have another deep support in case the stock turns on you and gets out of the channeling pattern.

There are some stocks that are just not buy and hold stocks. Don't fight them, just look at the chart, if you noticed these patterns, don't think that because you bought them, and you did your research they are going to shoot for the moon. For example, if you look at AT&T "T", Early 2000 the stock was worth approx. $40, and end of 2017 the stock is worth about $40. Last 18 years there has been so much news, so many rumors, etc., don't fight the chart, even if this stock rises to $100, there are many good performers out there, don't fight 20 years of history. In defense of "T", this may not be completely accurate since "T" is known to provide great dividends, but nonetheless dividend can be taken away at any time the company decides to.

Strategy 8

Moving Average Strategy

One of the most used and most effective strategy is the moving average (MAVG).

This strategy is used to gauge the direction of the trend. Moving average, averages out series of market close and plots them. For example, a 10-day MAVG will take last 10 closes and averages them out and plots them. Therefore, if the market is moving up, the average of closes will also rise.

Once you plot the MAVG, if the trend of the stock is moving up the MAVG will also be moving up but will be below the stock price rising steadily under the stock price. If the stock price is trending down, you will see the MAVG above the stock price falling with the stock price.

Go ahead, plot a moving average and look! This is the best way to learn!

Magic happens when the stock price and MAVG cross each other, this signifies change of a trend. Thus, in this strategy one would buy and hold a stock as long as MAVG is below the stock price, and when the stock price crosses MAVG and MAVG is now above the stock, one would sell as this signifies a downward trend!

Contrary when the stock crosses the MAVG and starts to climb above the MAVG, this would signify a buy signal.

In this strategy, you would look for cross of MAVG with stock price and buy/sell on this signal over and over. You would rinse/repeat.

Below is a chart of CMI from 3/2015 to 12/2017 with a 100-day MAVG. I would sell as price goes below MAVG and buy as price comes above MAVG.

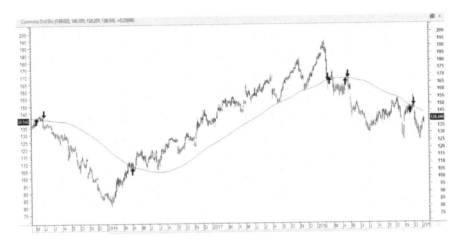

Most common MAVG plots are for 10-day, 20-day, 25-day, 50-day, 100-day and 200-day.

Which MAVG should you use?

You can try few of them and back-test to see if any fit the chart, sometimes it's trial and error.

Typically, you would use 10-day MAVG for short term investing and 200-day MAVG for long term investing i.e. retirement account. Also note that the nature of every stock is also different. Some stocks are more volatile (move up/down quickly) and if you use shorter MAVG it will give more buy/sell signal, you may not want to go in and out of position during market volatility. The best way to figure out which MAVG is right is to do back-testing. Look how many times you would have won/loss and how much you would have profited using a 10-day, 50-day MAVG.

CONCLUSION

If you wanted to learn how you could make money efficiently and make huge profits by investing only small amounts of money, we have shown you that you should choose to invest in the stock market. There are only some people who know how to invest in the stock market because they have learned how to do so. If you follow the information in this book, you can learn how to do this too. You will gather plenty of information about stocks and the different types of stocks you can invest in. This book also sheds some light on the different techniques you can use to invest in stocks.

As a beginner, you may make mistakes when you start investing in stocks. This is absolutely fine because you will start off with a small amount of money. But you cannot do this in the future because you will tend to invest larger amounts of money. It is important that you always learn from the mistakes that you make. Remember, every experienced trader also made mistakes at the start, but they always learned from their mistakes. It is this experience that will help you do well in the market.

All the best!